EXPLODING BUDDHA

EXPLODING BUDDHA

A Gideon Jones Novel

Paul Leonard Williams

EpiphanyMill Publishing

This is a work of fiction. Names, characters, places, and incidents either are the product of the author's imagination or are used fictiously. Any resemblance to actual persons, living or dead, events, or locales is entirely coincidental.

Text Copyright © 2017 Paul Leonard Williams
Cover Art Copyright © 2017 Whendell Souza

All rights reserved. No part of this book may be reproduced in any form or by any electronic means, including information storage and retrieval systems, without permission in writing from the publisher, except by reviewers, who may quote brief passages in review.

Published in the United States by EpiphanyMill Publishing, a division of EpiphanyMill LLC. Mesa, AZ

EpiphanyMill Publishing is a registered trademark and the balloon colophon is a trademark of EpiphanyMill LLC.

Visit us on the Web! EpiphanyMill.com

Library of Congress Cataloging-in-Publication Data
Williams, Paul Leonard
Exploding Buddha / Paul Leonard Williams. – First edition.

ISBN 978-1-947691-02-5 (intl. tr. pbk.) – ISBN 978-1-947691-03-2 (ebook)

[1. Detective-Fiction. 2. Supernatural-Fiction. 3. Martial Arts-Fiction.] I. Title.
Library of Congress Control Number 2017961379

The text of this book is set in 11.5 Apollo MT.
Book design by Rod R. Garcia
Edited by E. M. B.
Shuriken, Bullet, and Yin Yang designed by Jonathan Williams

Printed in the United States of America

10 9 8 7 6 5 4 3 2 1
First Edition

EpiphanyMill LLC. Supports the First Amendment and celebrates the right to read and write.

I dedicate this book to my father, who brought me up "old school", teaching me the importance of hard work, discipline, integrity, and honor.

I miss you dad.

You may not be interested in war, but war is interested in you.

 ~Leon Trotsky (1879-1940)

I knew it was time to leave town when the Buddha exploded…

 ~Gideon Jones

Foreword

This may be stating the obvious, but I must start by expressing how deeply honored I am to be writing this forward for my dear friend, Paul. I truly hope that you enjoy his breakout novel as much as I did (and still do).

If there is any one thing that I would like for you to keep in mind as you read this book, is something that you might find inspiring. Paul is a storyteller, through and through, but prior to Exploding Buddha, he'd never actually put pen to paper professionally. That said, his first draft was 'rough' in the truest of senses, and friends and family members alike were rather harsh in their collective critique of his writing. Simply put, Paul's mechanics were rusty, and the initial flow was difficult to follow. The mistake that his loved ones were making, was trying to read his masterpiece as a finished novel, and not as a first draft. Having worked in the industry for several years, I asked Paul to read it to me. I closed my eyes, opened my mind, and was immediately drawn into the magical world of Gideon Jones - hook, line, and sinker.

Needless to say, it took a few deep edits to get to the polished adventure that lays ahead of you, but the time and effort were well worth it. Just imagine, had Paul listened to his friends and family, he might have just given up writing before he even got started.

I envy you, dear reader, for getting to experience this book for the first time. I can only live vicariously through your enjoyment now, and eagerly look forward to the next thrilling book in the Gideon Jones series.

Cheers, Mazel Tov, and Live Long and Prosper!

~ Rod R. Garcia - Mesa, Arizona (October 8, 2017)

Special thanks to my best friend, Rod R. Garcia.

He not only believed in me, but took the time to teach, and help with so many things.

This book would not have been possible without him.

Love you bro.

Scroll I
The Horn Heist

Chapter 1

Time to Pay the Piper

"I knew it was time to leave town when the Buddha exploded. That is very rarely a good sign. I came to this realization as I went sailing through the air, courtesy of the second explosion I'd seen up close and personal in as many days. A bad week, even by my standards. It's odd, the things that go through your mind when the concussive force of a massive explosion knocks you off your feet and sends you flying."

"I noticed the peculiar flapping sound my trench coat made, and I enjoyed the sensation of weightlessness. I wondered if that was what it felt like for Superman when he took to the skies."

The reporter switched off the tape recorder, visibly annoyed.

"This is going to be a piece for the San Francisco Chronicle, not some dime store novel. Just start at the beginning Mr. Jones."

"Hey, this is my story, Mac."

"It's Mark, and it's not supposed to be your *story*. It's supposed to be an account of the incident at the Tin Hau Temple."

"Incident? Talk about an understatement. That's like saying World War Two was a little misunderstanding. Don't you worry though Mac, I'll tell you all about what went down at the temple."

"It's Mark."

"Right. Mark. Well Mark, you see there's some background, certain *events* that led up to the night of the *incident* that your readers will want to know about. So just sit back and relax, because you are in for one hell of a story. And if you don't write it down word for word, for it to fit some sort of newspaper format thingy, then *fine by me.* Just let me *tell it* like I want. Fair enough?"

There was a pause, and the reporter wrinkled his nose like I'd just told him to take a bite of a shit sandwich. But he eventually let out a sigh. "Fair enough." He relented. "But please start at the beginning, and progress chronologically. Don't jump back and forth," he added while switching the tape recorder back on.

"OK Mac," I said. I took a moment to enjoy the face he made at my intentional use of the wrong name, then I closed my eyes. I let my mind drift back to the day the whole mess had started.

"The day had kicked off for me like any other. I went for my morning run, then wolfed down some breakfast, and finally headed over to the office where I sat, and I sat, and just to mix things up a bit, I sat some more. Morning turned into afternoon and still, I sat, listening to music at my desk."

The DJ on the radio announced the song that had just played was "The Power of Love", the new chart-topper from *Huey Lewis and the News*, who would be stopping into their hometown of San Francisco the following week on their big 1985 tour.

I would have liked to have gone, but as always, I was short on funds. It was Thursday. The week was already half over, and still no new clients.

I'd long since abandoned all pretexts of trying to look busy. I sat behind my desk, shuffling cards mindlessly, doing my best to 'will' a client through the office door. Lately though, the only visitor I got at the office was the frickin' mailman.

Not that I have anything against mailmen per se. It's just that mine kept bringing me more damn bills!

Speak of the devil, or would that be 'think of the devil'? I heard him approaching the office door, but something about his approach wasn't right.

For starters, he was almost an hour early. My mailman usually didn't show up until a little after four-thirty.

I'd first assumed that it was the mailman because he's the only regular visitor I get at the office. Walk-ins are rare, paying clients usually call first. Plus, his footsteps were too heavy... too... *determined.*

The regular guy meandered. He took his time, and more often than not he was humming.

This guy, who was clearly not the mailman, paused outside my door, probably reading the plaque. I say *he* because if the resounding thuds of his footsteps were any indication, then this guy was pushing four hundred pounds. In my experience, most women just aren't that big. I imagined this massive bowling ball of a man, one who waddled more than walked.

Then he burst into the room! It was one of Mancuso's enforcers.

I'd gotten the massive part right.

The man-beast that stood before me looked like there must have been a rhinoceros in his family tree, only one generation removed. He had to have been at least six and a half feet tall.

His face was pitted with acne scars, he sported a unibrow that would have made a cave man proud, and his nose somehow managed to be both bulbous *and* crooked at the same time, like someone had beaten the snot out of a flesh-colored wad of silly putty with a baseball bat.

He wore an angry scowl like he knew he was ugly and was mad as hell about it.

In a failed attempt to compensate for his face, he wore a white 'wife beater' tank top that showed off his physique, and man, what a physique!

This guy wasn't just big, he was powerfully built. He must have lived at the gym. His muscles had muscles, and he had fists the size of babies.

The behemoth pointed a massive, sausage-like finger accusingly in my direction, and bellowed in a gravelly voice that sounded as if he'd been smoking two packs of cigarettes a day, since the tender age of three. "Time to pay the piper, Gideon!"

He was indeed an imposing figure, and the way he stood there, supremely confident, it was obvious that he was used to intimidating the hell out of people, and equally used to people rushing to comply with his orders.

I'd seen his type before: assholes who grew physically bigger, but never managed to outgrow the playground bully mentality. He was larger and more physically powerful than most, and he used that fact to control people with fear.

He probably got a perverse pleasure out of having that kind of power over others. Unfortunately for him, I don't scare easily, and I get an equally perverse pleasure out of tormenting assholes.

Especially bullies.

He just stood there, like he expected me to jump up and give him money, or beg for more time. I ignored him though and continued to focus on shuffling my cards.

I probably should have said something, but like I said, I never liked bullies, and damn it, I had always made my payments. *Always.* In fact, I made it a point to pay Mancuso first, a bit early as a matter of fact. Hell, I'd paid more in interest than I'd originally borrowed by that point. But did that earn me any slack? Nope. When the actual due-date came up, he sent a thug down to lean on me like I was habitually late.

Well, I wasn't about to drop everything just because Mancuso's goon showed up. Even if I didn't have anything to drop, it was the principle of the thing.

Rhino Man would just have to wait a bit.

Patience, however, was not Rhino Man's strong suit. As he stood there, his eyes narrowed to slits, and he started breathing faster; only not normal breaths. It was the kind of breathing one normally associates with great big grizzly bears or even dragons.

"You fucking deaf?!? I'm talking to you, asshole!"

I ignored the insult and remained seated, calmly shuffling the cards. "Now's a bad time. I'm busy."

Rhino Man was *not* happy with my answer. "The money Gideon! NOW!"

"I said, I'm busy. It can wait a bit."

"I said, NOW!!!!"

"How about 'No'?" I calmly replied as I continued to shuffle the cards.

My nonchalant attitude must have really riled him. There was outrage plastered across his face and a murderous look in his eyes. He was so mad. He was practically foaming at the mouth. "How's about I break your face, smart ass!?" He bellowed.

With that, the man-mountain charged forward.

I sprang out of my chair and darted out in front of my desk. I didn't rush out to meet him or try to scramble out of the way and make a break for the exit. I just stood there in his path, oozing belligerence, daring him to come at me.

And boy, did he ever come at me. He moved surprisingly fast for such a big man and built up enough momentum to smash me to a pulp. It was certainly too much momentum for him to stop at the last second. I suddenly dropped down on all fours at his feet, my shoulders level with his ankles.

He tripped over me and crashed spectacularly to the floor, face first. He broke his nose so badly that it practically exploded in a bloody gush.

"Hey," I smiled, "I thought you were supposed to break *MY* face?"

I don't care how much time you spend at the gym, you just can't toughen up your nose. If you've ever been socked in the nose, you'll understand: not only does it hurt, but your eyes water up, and you can't see so great. He was just lying on the floor, curled up in the fetal position, with his face buried in his hands.

It looked like he was trying hard not to cry, so I felt confident that I was in no immediate danger when I sidled up and leaned in close, to add insult to injury. The big jerk had it coming anyway. He could have waited a few more seconds. There was no need to attack me like that.

"Does that hurt? Cause it sure looks painful. Well, I wouldn't worry much, I seriously doubt it's fatal. Besides with that hideous face, I just did you a favor by rearranging your nose like that. Believe me when I tell you, it can only improve your looks."

That last bit was either too much, or he'd regained his bearings by that point, because he whipped a wild back-handed strike at me. A primal roar preceded it, so I had plenty of warning. I managed to leap backward and avoid the blow.

Jeez! This guy was an amateur.

He sprung to his feet and came at me with a wild haymaker. Rhino Man had obviously relied on his size his entire life and had never bothered to really learn how to fight. He hauled all the way back to Kansas with that baby, so I saw it coming from a mile away.

I easily ducked under the punch and came in close at an angle to deliver a vicious upper cut to his floating rib.

Some fancy footwork allowed me to slip in behind him, where I delivered two quick lefts and another right to his kidneys. I heard the air involuntarily expel from his lungs with the last blow, but I didn't let up. Instead, I lifted my right leg high, so that my knee was all the way up to my chest. Then I stomped down hard with my right foot, on the back of his leg, behind his knee.

He dropped down hard, right on his kneecaps.

By that time, he was kneeling with his back to me. I then cupped my hands and clapped them together as hard as I could on either side of his head, right over his ears. Once again, all the gym time in the world won't toughen up your eardrums.

Rhino Man was rolling around on the floor yowling. Apparently, he was in a great deal of pain.

The fight was over.

He was making a hell of a racket though, and I didn't want word of this little incident getting back to my landlord. So I leaned forward and positioned myself to deliver a nice, clean, right cross that would mean lights out for Rhino Man, and put him right to sleep.

At least that was my intention.

But Rhino Man was rolling around too much. Not to mention, he didn't have the glass jaw I was hoping for. It wound up taking several rights, and few lefts before he went nighty night.

Oh well. So, he was going to have a few nasty bruises to go along with his busted nose and bleeding ears.

Broke my heart.

What goes around comes around.

Karma's a bitch.

Chapter 2

The Summoning

Takeshi watched from the shadows as the guards patrolled the grounds of Councilor Nonomura's estate. He noted additional personnel had been added that night.

It will make little difference, he thought. *If the councilor fears our wrath so much, then he should have voted as he was told after accepting the money; not declare a change of heart after spending nearly half, and make empty promises to repay. The fool has sealed his own fate.*

It wasn't long before Takeshi had recognized a pattern in the patrols, and chosen the best time to make his move.

His black clothing made him nearly impossible to spot in the dark, and his training allowed him to move as silently as a specter. Like a black wisp of smoke in the dead of night, he slipped past the guards unnoticed.

Then, like a panther stalking its unsuspecting prey, Takeshi slowly and patiently made his way to the structure that housed the giant, industrial-sized air conditioning units which cooled the politician's massive estate. Their steady hum masked any sound Takeshi might have made as he removed a rope and grappling hook from his small pack, and prepared to ascend to the roof.

Just then, a guard rounded the corner, his eyes widening with surprise. Takeshi struck faster than a cobra. His hand was open with the thumb and index finger forming a V, as if he was reaching to pick up a glass of water; except his hand was rigid, and his fingers pressed together.

The blow struck the guard in the throat, crushed his windpipe, and rendered him unable to yell for help. He thrashed about on the ground in panic and pain, his lungs crying out for air he could no longer take in.

Takeshi quickly scanned the area, to ensure he had not been seen by any others. Then, he calmly strode to where the guard was thrashing on the ground and violently stomped on his head, like one might crush a bug. Takeshi's heel fractured the guard's skull like an eggshell.

A low wall surrounded the air-conditioning units. The enclosure stood only five feet high. It was only there to conceal the units for aesthetic purposes, but it left just enough room to allow a tech to squeeze in and service them. It was there that Takeshi unceremoniously dumped the body. Then, using the rope and grappling hook, he climbed up to the roof.

Once there, Takeshi used his tanto knife to cut a hole in the air duct and climbed in. He knew that taking that route would be cramped and slow, but it would also circumvent all the guards and security measures Nonomura had inside his mansion.

Takeshi used a small flashlight to reference a map of the duct system before making his way to Nonomura's room.

The deep, resonant sound of the sleeping statesman's snoring made it relatively simple for Takeshi to locate his private quarters.

Takeshi didn't remove the vent's grill. Rather, he snaked a tiny video camera, no larger around than a pen, at the end of a bendable stalk, and used it to survey the room. He studied the display on a small screen that was strapped to his wrist. The apparatus, which resembled a large digital watch, was one of the newest developments to come out the research and development branch of Kagami Corp. The multinational conglomerate was a convenient guise under which the Kagé Clan could safely operate.

Nonomura's bed was directly underneath the vent.

Takeshi took out a spool of waxed dental floss. He used the camera to guide his way, coiled the floss out, and lowered it further and further until it was just above Nonomura's open, snoring mouth.

Once the floss was in place, Takeshi uncorked a small vial of saxitoxin, a type of poison derived from the deadly puffer fish. Then, using an eye dropper, he applied several drops of the toxin to the dental floss. The lethal fluid trickled neatly down the length of the floss, and directly into Nonomura's mouth.

The poison would take approximately an hour to kill the old man, which would allow plenty of time for Takeshi to make his escape.

Just minutes later, the assassin was in the back of a limousine. He changed out of his field uniform, into an expensive tailored suit. Once he was done, he used the limousine's car phone to place a call.

The phone barely rang once before it was answered.

"It is finished?" a voice inquired.

"Yes," Takeshi replied.

"Good. Now go to the Yokohama tower to meet with Daraku. He wishes to speak with you."

Takeshi grimaced. He loathed meetings with Daraku, but he gave no indication by the tone of his voice.

"I am on my way."

Since headquarters was not terribly far from Nonomura's estate, and traffic was characteristically light for that time of night, Takeshi was soon standing somberly in a Kagami Corp. elevator, riding down to the bottom floor for his dreaded meeting with Daraku.

A chime sounded, signifying the elevator's arrival at the bottom floor. The sound struck Takeshi as ominous, rather than melodious, and he steeled himself in preparation.

He always had a strong aversion to Daraku.

The doors parted, and Takeshi boldly strode into the dimly lit parking garage, offering no visible indication of any apprehension.

He was Kagé after all.

There were only maintenance vehicles on this level, and at this time of night it should have been deserted. Nevertheless, he scanned the area to ensure that he was indeed alone.

Only after he was completely certain, did he produce a single, brass key from his jacket pocket. He made his way to an unobtrusive door marked 'supply locker', and unlatched the padlock.

Once inside the cramped, narrow room; Takeshi made his way past several rows of metal, industrial shelves, each filled with stacks of unmarked boxes. At the back of the room, behind the last row of shelves, was a thermostat. The assassin carefully adjusted the dial to forty-nine degrees. The numbers were the security trigger for a hidden door, which slid open quietly after a few seconds at the setting.

In Japan, four and nine are unlucky numbers. The number four in Japanese is pronounced shi, which is the same pronunciation for the word death. The number nine is pronounced ku, which is the same pronunciation for agony, or torture.

How fitting, Takeshi thought. *Just as frost is the harbinger of winter, Daraku is the harbinger of torture and death.*

Other than the rough-hewn stairwell carved into the earth ahead, winding downward into what might have been the cold pits of Hell itself, the dim light from the storeroom revealed little beyond the door.

Takeshi pressed a button within the stairwell, and the secret door slid shut, cutting off the already inadequate light, and leaving him in utter darkness.

He produced a small flashlight from his pants pocket and turned it on. The flashlight's beam cut a small swath through the darkness but did little more than illuminate the first few steps before him, so he would not stumble and fall. The true size of the mysterious chamber ahead was impossible to determine.

The assassin stepped forward. The darkness swallowed him and his little beam of light whole. It would have been unnerving to most, but Takeshi was no stranger to the shadows. He descended the stone steps into the darkness below without hesitation. His footsteps echoed off the stone walls, suggesting that he had entered a large cavern, but there wasn't enough light to confirm that.

As he proceeded downward, Takeshi began to sense something unnerving. He could tell by the sound of his footfalls that the walls of the chamber were growing steadily closer, but it was more than just that.

Panning left and right with the flashlight confirmed that he was no longer in a chamber at all, but rather a narrow passageway. The walls were damp and seeped a murky, dark-hued liquid. Takeshi couldn't be certain if it was water. Truthfully, he didn't want to know.

As he continued onward, he began to sense a presence. He paused and panned the flashlight back and forth again, but saw nothing. He switched off the light and listened, reaching out with his highly tuned senses, but still, nothing.

As he was about to switch the flashlight back on, the sensation returned, stronger than before.

The hair on his arms and the back of his neck stood up, and a chill ran down his spine.

Takeshi was by no means a skittish man who jumped at shadows. He had faced, and dealt out death countless times. He was the most feared assassin in all of Japan. The Yakuza spoke his name only in hushed, fearful tones, as if saying it too loudly would somehow conjure his spirit, instead referring to him as 'the angel of death'.

Why the reaction, if it isn't fear?

Then it dawned on him. He had indeed been in this presence before. It had always manifested itself in different ways, but in his line of work Takeshi had come to recognize it like an old friend.

He was in the presence of evil.

Daraku's laughter suddenly burst forth, echoing off the walls, seemingly coming from all directions at once. It was impossible to pinpoint the source of the laughter, or even tell how close, or far away he was.

In fact, it seemed to Takeshi that the laughter was somehow in his own head. He detested how easily the wizard misdirected his highly tuned senses.

"Are you going to just remain in the dark, Shinobi?"

Daraku had used an archaic term for ninja. He did that now and then with certain words, as if he had lived so long, and in so many places, that he occasionally forgot the vernacular of the time.

Takeshi turned the flashlight back on, and Daraku was standing directly before him. He was not draped in the flowing robes one usually associates with wizards but instead dressed in an expensive tailored suit, not unlike the one Takeshi wore.

The assassin bowed deeply.

Daraku stopped laughing, and offered a slight nod, acknowledging the gesture of respect.

Both men were lean but athletic, and tall for Japanese. Each stood five-foot-ten. It was there the similarities ended, however. Takeshi's jet-black hair was cropped short, and he was clean shaven, giving him the appearance of a businessman in his tailored suit. Daraku however, had long hair that he wore in a top knot, and he sported a mustache and full beard, which was remarkably well groomed. The beard was not bushy, as the wizard kept it well oiled.

Regardless of its neat appearance, the century's old style paired with modern-day attire made for an odd combination.

To Takeshi, Daraku's suit seemed more of a perfunctory courtesy, than a genuine attempt to blend in. The wizard's appearance was still eccentric.

As if to confirm Takeshi's assessment, Daraku turned away. He began waving his arms back and forth, gesturing in the air erratically.

To Takeshi, Daraku appeared drunk.

"What are you doing?" Takeshi asked.

"Hold your tongue, Shinobi. This requires great concentration. Besides, you should be grateful. I am disabling some newly added security measures." Daraku began mumbling unintelligibly under his breath. Slowly the mumbling increased in volume, and pale green light emanated from his hands.

Takeshi could not make out what Daraku was saying. Whatever language his ramblings were in, it was one which he'd never heard.

Daraku continued unabated, his incantations growing louder and louder. As the volume increased, the green light from his hands grew brighter, giving off far more light than Takeshi's flashlight.

The additional illumination revealed that they had reached the bottom of the stairs. The stairwell ended in an alcove with a single door on the opposite wall.

Daraku's voice grew impossibly loud, becoming much deeper and resounding than humanly possible. It grew so loud in fact, that it began to hurt Takeshi's ears. He could actually feel the bass reverberating within his chest. Just when he began to fear that his eardrums might burst, the din abruptly ceased.

Glowing green symbols materialized, forming a circle on the stone floor, and a vertical line on the door.

Daraku rushed to the circle and stood at its center.

The symbols on the door that had been glowing green a moment earlier suddenly turned red. "Come stand with me Shinobi. No matter what you see or hear, do not leave this circle."

Takeshi's eyes were fixed upon the door. The red symbols suddenly blurred and formed a single thin line. Then, to his amazement, the line started to expand like curtains, parting to reveal something beyond. "Hurry Shinobi!" Daraku warned. Takeshi did as he was told, and rushed to join Daraku at the center of the circle.

Daraku interlaced his fingers in an odd gesture and puffed up his cheeks. Then, while simultaneously shifting his hands and fingers into a new configuration, he exhaled with surprising force.

The glowing green symbols on the floor morphed into a single line and formed an unbroken circle around them. Meanwhile, something was beginning to push through the door, or rather through the glowing red curtain of light that formed a second portal; a doorway within the physical door. The wooden door itself remained shut.

What emerged was hideous, and frightful to behold.

At first the thing appeared crippled, but that was only because it had to stoop to fit through the doorway. When it passed through, and finally stood erect, the thing was over nine feet tall. It was bipedal, vaguely man shaped, but hairless with putrefying grey skin, covered with black splotches.

Its arms were heavily muscled, and reached all the way to the floor. Long fingers ended in wicked looking claws that seemed capable of tearing a man to pieces as easily as Takeshi could shred a piece of paper. It had a snout rather than a face, not unlike that of a hyena, except that its maw hung impossibly wide, revealing razor sharp teeth, several inches in length. The rest of the thing's face and head were covered with eyes of varying shape and size. The eyes were placed at odd angles, lidless and burning with accusation and hatred.

Upon seeing Takeshi and Daraku, the thing tilted its head back and howled unnervingly.

"Oni!" Takeshi cried, dropping into a defensive posture while simultaneously drawing his tanto knife.

"Yes, a demon. Very astute Shinobi." Daraku replied sarcastically. "Now put away your blade and stay inside the circle. You are outmatched."

The demon rushed forward and hurled itself at the pair, ready to tear them to bloody shreds. Instead, it collided with an invisible barrier and rebounded off from the force of impact.

Outraged, the demon attempted to rake them with its claws, but again the barrier protected them. Dazzling, green sparks erupted from where its claws met the barrier, making a loud crackling sound, like a giant beetle caught in a bug-zapper.

"Enough!" Daraku bellowed, his voice so supernaturally loud that even the Oni appeared stunned. "You are here to attack intruders, not your master!"

The demon gave pause and tilted its head, regarding the pair curiously. After a few moments of unsettling silence, it spoke. An eerily perverse voice came from a mouth not designed for speech. "Yooouuu are not my massster, wizzzard."

Daraku stretched out his hands, as if to choke the demon, but stopped short of leaving the circle. He stayed there with his arms outstretched, his fingers flexing. Takeshi heard him hiss, "den", the Japanese word for lightning. Suddenly, green bolts of electricity lanced out from his fingers and struck the demon.

The creature yowled in pain as the bolts struck him. It collapsed to the floor, writhing in agony. Daraku kept up a continuous barrage, his arms outstretched, repeating "den", over and over, chanting it, like a mantra. The fetid tang of the demon's burning flesh wafted over them, assaulting Takeshi's sinuses, and burning his eyes.

Finally, Daraku relented.

The demon immediately sprang back up, incensed, and ready to attack again.

"Would you like more? Or shall I send you back to the fiery pit from whence you came?" Daraku bellowed.

The demon froze. "Nooooooo… I shall ceeeassse".

Daraku nodded, pleased. "Do not try my patience again demon. The next time I will not be so lenient. You can easily be replaced."

Defeated, the demon retreated through the portal. Daraku waved his arms and chanted once more. The portal sealed shut, and the glowing symbols winked out of existence.

Daraku boldly strode out of the circle, walked directly to the door, and turned the knob. Takeshi hesitated, not eager to face the demon again. Daraku noticed Takeshi's apprehension and laughed as he flung the door wide open. "This is my study, Shinobi. The oni was sent to another dimension. It can only return if I summon it, or an intruder tries to gain access to my study without my consent."

The wizard Daraku arrogantly paraded into his chambers.

Takeshi remained outside, still none too eager to follow. He always did have an aversion to Daraku.

The assassin's thoughts flashed back to the elevator ride, seemingly ages ago, and Takeshi steeled himself in preparation. It would be unwise to show any sort of weakness in front of Daraku. Takeshi fearlessly strode into the dimly lit study, offering no further hint of unease.

He was Kagé after all.

Chapter 3

The Mancuso Malady

Now I may have made short work of Rhino Man, but I don't want you to get the wrong idea here.

Being bigger and stronger than the other guy is usually pretty damned important in a fight. I'm obviously no runt. I stand six-foot-one and weigh in at two hundred and five pounds. And it's not two hundred and five pounds of flab either.

I work out.

In fact, I hit the weights five days a week, and I go for a run almost every morning. I take Sundays off. I'm not talking about a leisurely jog here. When I say run, I mean run. I push myself. Same thing with the weights. I don't just go through the motions. That, combined with healthy eating, and being the ripe, old age of twenty-nine, pretty much puts me close to peak physical condition in my prime.

All that being said, I was physically no match for Rhino Man. What enabled me to eat him for breakfast was my training. I'm a serious student of the martial arts. I've been training for nearly fourteen years, and I have a fourth-degree black belt in both Judo and Karate.

Martial arts is my one true love.

Not only do I have years of training under my belt, but I've also had the incredible good fortune of having top-notch instructors. So I'm far better equipped than most when it comes to a fist fight.

In my line of work, it's a good idea to be able to take care of yourself in a fight. Trust me, it's come in handy more than a couple of times. My point is, I know what I'm talking about when it comes to physical altercations. Don't go believing that crap you hear about size doesn't matter in a fight, 'cause it does. It matters! It matters a whole lot. It can be overcome. I mean, I just proved that with Rhino Man, but I'm the exception, not the rule. They don't give out fourth-degree black belts in Cracker Jacks boxes! It takes training; years and years of hard training. So don't go running off half-cocked, and start picking any fights.

I've learned the hard way, that there are consequences for your actions in this life. For instance, Rhino Man was a bleeder. I had to hurry up and grab some paper towels and water from the cooler to clean up the mess he'd made, before all the blood stained my hardwood floor! On top of that, I had to drag Rhino Man's heavy ass out of my office, and down the hall to the stairs. My office is on the second floor, so it was no easy task. He really was heavy. Like I said, it's a good thing I work out.

Those weren't the primary consequences I had to worry about though. As good as it felt to kick Rhino Man's ass, Mancuso wasn't someone you wanted angry with you, if possible. I was going to have to figure out a way to smooth things over with him.

You see, from day one, I was behind the eight ball. I do what I can to bring in business. My name's in the Yellow Pages, but the jobs just don't ever seem to be big enough or come in often enough for me to get ahead. Thus far I've managed to pay rent and keep the lights on, but I'm no stranger to the occasional late notice. What really gets me though, is that I'd be doing just fine, if it wasn't for the payments I have to make to Mancuso.

Most people don't realize just how much start-up capital is needed when you start a business. At least I didn't. None of the local banks were willing to lend me what I needed to get the business up and running. So I was forced to pursue non-traditional lending options. You might be more familiar with the term 'loan shark'.

Joey "the Nose" Mancuso is the non-traditional lender I was forced to turn to. The Mancusos are one of the original families who founded the world-famous Fisherman's Wharf.

Although he appears to be a legitimate businessman, Mancuso is actually San Francisco's number one crime boss.

He does try to differentiate himself from the stereotypical mobster. He actually goes to great lengths putting on the act. He has several legitimate businesses, is good friends with the mayor, and even gives publicly to several charities. Heck, Mancuso would be a real standup guy; if you didn't count the loan sharking, gun running, prostitution, gambling, and narcotics.

I know. Not the smartest of moves on my part, turning to a loan shark. I mean, hey, there's a reason they're called loan sharks, and not your friendly neighborhood money lender, or loan guppies.

It's just that I didn't want to be one of those guys you hear, forever whining to whoever'll listen. You know the type, they're always saying "I could have been a...", or "if only...". You know what I mean, we've all heard 'em. "I could have been my own boss, but I never got the money." "I could have been a star, but I never got a break." "I could have been an astronaut." "I could have been president." "I could have been a contender.

Coulda', woulda', shoulda'…

In my opinion, it's the things we don't do, not the things we actually do, that we wind up regretting later. I really believe that.

At the end of my life, when I look back on things, I'll be able to deal with "it didn't work out, but hey, I gave it my best shot".

What I wouldn't be able to live with, would be if I never had the balls to even really give it a try. So I rolled the dice, and turned to Mancuso for a loan. And now, along with all my other bills, I make monthly payments to Mancuso. Those payments barely even cover the interest.

Finding a way out of this mess was easier said than done though. Mancuso wanted his money of course, but his reputation was important to him as well. He wouldn't want it getting out that people could just trounce his enforcers, and get out of making payments. Not that I was trying to weasel out of paying Mancuso. I had the money, sort of.

You see, I had enough money for Mancuso's payment, but it would have left me short on rent, with nothing left over to buy groceries with. True, my landlord wouldn't send goons to try and rough me up if I was late, but a man still has to eat, right?

I was still trying to come up with a solution as I dragged Rhino Man's unconscious body down the hallway. When we reached the stairwell, I paused for a moment.

I really didn't relish the thought of lugging Rhino Man's dead weight down those babies. Luckily, he saved me the trouble, and started to come around.

"Ah, good morning, sunshine. Now I hope you've learned your lesson. That whole ugly incident could have been avoided if you'd just waited a minute." I produced an envelope stuffed with money. "You see, I have Mancuso's payment right here. I was just in the middle of something."

Rhino Man ignored the envelope, and instead tried to regain his feet. He brought himself into one of those three-point stances football linemen use. By the time my mind had registered that little tidbit of information, Rhino Man launched himself forward with a surprising burst of speed that caught me off guard.

He slammed me into the wall hard enough to rattle my teeth, and knock the wind out of me. Then, using his weight to keep me pinned to the wall, he slammed three good upper cuts right into my midsection.

Rhino Man may not have had any combat training, but he was plenty strong, and those body-blows hurt like hell. He gave me two more for good measure, and I felt my insides turn to mush.

"Wait," I somehow managed to croak. "What gives? I just handed you the money."

In answer Rhino Man slammed me with another devastating blow to the midsection, ensuring my silence. Then he clamped his left hand around my throat, and slammed me back against the wall.

"Don't worry asshole, I'm still gonna' take your money. But first, I'm gonna' make sure you have some hospital bills next month too!"

As he kept me pinned to the wall with his left hand, Rhino Man hauled way back with his right. Maybe he did it for dramatic effect, hoping to scare me a bit before he pummeled me. More likely it was just his lack of training. Either way, it gave me all the time I needed.

I brought both of my hands up hard, and slammed into Rhino Man's wrist, while I simultaneously dropped down with all my weight. Kind of like the clean and jerk motion you see power lifters use.

The body mechanics are different, but the two moves look kind of similar. I wasn't going to be able to lift massive amounts of weight with my technique, but it did break me free of Rhino Man's grasp, while simultaneously getting my face out of the path of his incoming punch.

His fist slammed into the brick wall, where my face had been an instant earlier. Rhino Man howled in pain, and cradled his now injured hand to his chest, which left his face wide open.

I took advantage of his gift, and launched a quick left jab squarely into his already injured nose. He cried out even louder and brought up both hands to protect his face.

Jeez, this was almost too easy.

Thanks to the fact that Rhino Man had obscured his own vision, he never saw the kick coming; the one I'd ruthlessly launched at his groin.

Wham! Right in the balls!

The cojones, by the way, are also impossible to build up at the gym. In fact, a lot of gym rats shrink 'em. You know, the dangers of 'roids and all.

Rhino Man collapsed into a crumpled heap on the floor, moaning.

I wasn't quite through with him yet though.

I used my foot to give him a little push that sent him crashing down the stairs, and into the main lobby of the building.

It was only one flight, and not a particularly long one at that, but it was still fun to watch while it lasted.

I stooped to pick up the envelope of money and did my best not to grimace in pain while I did so. Having sufficiently steeled myself, I boldly strolled over to Rhino Man.

I took my time going down the stairs, and scanned the area to make sure we didn't have an audience.

We were alone.

I straightened my blazer, and checked both it and my dress slacks for blood. They were my only set of nice clothes. Not the best getup for a fist fight I suppose, but they did give me the look of a business man. The blazer also offered the added bonus of concealing my Colt 1911, .45 caliber pistol, which I kept tucked away in a shoulder rig.

"Weren't you listening when I said this whole ugly mess could have been avoided?" I gave him a kick in the ribs to accentuate my point.

I don't usually kick a man when he's down, but Rhino Man had just demonstrated that he had a propensity for both violence and revenge. I wanted to discourage any irrational thoughts of payback he might have.

It seems harsh, I know, but again I wouldn't normally do this sort of thing. It's just that experience has taught me that when dealing with guys like Rhino Man, whose reaction after our first encounter was to try and send me to the hospital (his words), that physical stimulus seems to have a greater impact than flowery prose.

It's best for all parties concerned, if that kind of brute has a healthy fear of any repercussions that rash actions on his part might incur. "Let's try and avoid a repeat of today's occurrences here pal."

"You should try to remember, that it is NEVER," I gave him another kick in the ribs, "EVER," yet another kick, "a good idea to try and get physical with ME, pal. It will always end badly for you. Besides, next time you might not find me in such a good MOOD." I gave him one last kick for good measure. That time though, instead of in the ribs, it was right behind his ear, ensuring it was lights-out for him.

I took another quick look around. By that time, I was paying more attention to the view through the glass double doors that led out to the street.

I saw a car parked out front. It was a sleek, black sedan. Way too upscale for my neighborhood. There was a guy in a two-dollar suit slouched lazily behind the wheel. If his body language was any indicator, he hadn't noticed what just happened inside.

It was the only car parked out front, and I doubted Rhino Man had walked all the way here to see me. So odds were in my favor that the bored looking guy was probably his ride.

A crazy idea came to me! The beginnings of a plan, and if it worked, I figured I just might be able to get Mancuso his money, and avoid any retaliation for what I did to Rhino Man.

Or I just might have been on my way to an early grave. I wasn't sure which.

I headed outside and toward the parked car, before I could change my mind.

Chapter 4

Nefarious Schemes

Stark white candles, which appeared to have been burning since the dawn of man, littered virtually every surface in Daraku's office. They did little to brighten the room, however. Rather, they seemed to cast dark and flickering shadows everywhere. If it was at all possible, they made the space feel even more forbidding.

The walls were lined with shelves; shelves that held more than just books. Takeshi saw that some of them held jars and vials, which were filled with all sorts of powders and herbs. There were others that appeared to contain pickled organs or perhaps even severed body parts. Takeshi saw one filled with fingers, another loaded with ears, and another still, full of eyeballs, the eyestalks still attached and floating like kite-tails in the thick liquid.

In one dark corner, there was a set of shelves that was stacked with glass tanks and mesh cages. There in the shadows, vile creatures slithered and crawled.

"Close the door. We shall require privacy," Daraku said as he seated himself behind a massive ebony desk, its surface strewn with pieces of ancient, yellowed parchment.

Takeshi watched as Daraku settled into his regal, high backed chair, like an emperor settling into his throne. It was upholstered in red velvet, and accented in intricately carved ebony to match the desk. Since the wizard had not motioned for him to sit in one of the three smaller chairs facing the desk, Takeshi remained standing.

"Little has been gained from questioning the prisoner," Daraku stated coolly.

So, the monk has not succumbed to torture then, Takeshi thought. "I cannot say I am surprised lord Daraku. Even if he *did* know the Horn's whereabouts, it is unlikely that he would give up such important information. The Hikari may be sanctimonious fools, but they are not weaklings."

"I have broken many a brave man before, but it is of little consequence. I have discovered another means of locating the Horn." Daraku gestured towards the worn looking scrolls and pieces of parchment scattered upon his desk. Upon closer inspection, Takeshi noticed that there was an ancient tome that lay prostrate upon the desk. Although he couldn't say why, it was somehow disconcerting to look upon. He quickly shifted his gaze back to Daraku.

"During the course of my research, I have discovered a very rare treasure indeed, one that could lead us to the Horn. It is a book penned by the legendary god-emperor, Di Ku Gaoxin Shi. A very powerful sorcerer who mastered, and rode upon dragons! Within its pages are the secrets to summoning mighty devils, much greater than the lesser demon you saw earlier. I believe that one in particular will be able to tell us the whereabouts of the Horn."

If that nightmare was a lesser demon, I most certainly do not want to encounter one of these greater devils, Takeshi thought. "How may *I* be of assistance in such matters, lord Daraku?"

"It is no easy task, I assure you. This will require a blood sacrifice!" Takeshi had seen the wizard kill various animals in his macabre rites before. Numerous chickens, goats, and even the occasional bull had met its end under Daraku's sacrificial blade.

"So, you wish me to procure a special animal to prepare for sacrifice?" Takeshi made no attempt to mask the disdain in his voice, as the task was clearly beneath him. He was chief assassin of the Kagé, not a sniveling errand boy!

"Don't be daft, Shinobi! I would not require you for such a task. The life blood of some mindless animal will not suffice for a summoning of this magnitude! No, this must be perfect in order to succeed. This devil will require genuine suffering and loss, true despair. For that reason, the victim cannot be a mere, dumb animal. It must be a sentient being, one with a soul. This will require *human* sacrifice. Yet even that is not enough, it cannot be just any human. It must be the right *kind* of human."

"I still do not see how I can be of assistance in this matter."

"Ah, but you can. You, Takeshi, have slain more Hikari than any other."

Takeshi was a bit surprised. It was rare for the wizard to pay such a compliment.

"In this *current* generation, anyway."

Ah yes, that was more like it, a compliment that bore the seeds of an insult; the insinuation that his generation of ninja was less capable than previous generations.

"Still, it is no easy feat. As you so aptly put it, the Hikari may be sanctimonious fools, but they are not weaklings. They are in fact, quite capable warriors. For you to have vanquished so many, it is not enough that you are more skilled than your opponents. You must know your foe. Know him as only an enemy could. So Takeshi, I must know if our Hikari guest will be a suitable sacrifice. You must help me ascertain if he will make the perfect gift. You see, he has the potential. The blood of a defeated foe, especially one who is good and pure as our monk friend, could be a delectable treat for this devil."

"You say 'could be', as if there are other important criteria that I might help you identify."

"Very good Shinobi, you have gotten to the crux of the matter. The essential component is despair! The feeling of hopelessness is what this devil will require most of all."

"I see. Then let me ask you, the tortures you have subjected him to, would they have broken most men?"

Daraku stroked his beard as he pondered this question. "I believe that they would have, yes."

"Were they purely physical?"

"Ah, excellent question Shinobi! Very good, very good indeed. There are far worse things that a man can be subjected to than physical pain. The answer to your question is no, but I do want our guest to retain his sanity."

"I will have to witness one of your sessions, to be sure I suppose. But my initial feeling is that the monk will not suffice as the splendid gift you are hoping to present to this devil. Not if you are seeking hopelessness and despair. The Hikari cling tenaciously to their code of honor and ideals. It gives them both purpose and hope."

"I feared as much. In that case, another sacrifice must be found."

"Perhaps you can have one of your minions procure a drug addict, or perhaps a prostitute. I would think theirs is an existence of utter hopelessness, and crushed dreams."

"To a certain extent, yes, but I have found that most of them have developed a certain numbness. I think we shall kidnap a child. It will give us the added bonus of sheer terror!" Daraku smiled wickedly to himself at the heinous thought.

Takeshi barely masked his feelings of contempt. To show no mercy to a defeated enemy was one thing. A true warrior is always prepared to forfeit his life if necessary, but to prey upon children! That was the reprehensible act of a coward, completely devoid of honor. He could not stand to be in the presence of the vile sorcerer any longer.

"If that is all lord Daraku, I have other matters to attend to."

The wizard seemed preoccupied with his perverse thoughts. "Yes, yes, very well Shinobi. You are dismissed."

Takeshi immediately spun on his heels and exited the room. He felt to be there any longer would somehow contaminate him, as if exposed to an infectious disease.

As he made his way back up the stairs, Takeshi pondered. *The wizard may be a necessary evil now, but once the Horn is ours, I think it might be best if Daraku were to meet with an unfortunate accident of some sort.*

Chapter 5

Walking a Thin Line

As I crossed the street, I got a closer look at the guy inside. He had dark brown eyes and jet-black hair that was slicked back. He had a pencil thin mustache, the kind that was popular back in the 40's, like Clark Gable used to wear. He didn't have that debonair look about him like Gable did, though.

He seemed much more mousey. It was his nose. It somehow gave him a rat-like appearance. It was hard to tell how tall he was while sitting down, but he was definitely thin. So thin in fact, he looked brittle compared to Rhino Man.

My mind automatically assigned him a nick name as I crossed the street towards the car: Rat Boy. Yep, Rhino Man and Rat Boy, quite the pair.

Once again, I scanned the area to make sure there wasn't an audience to witness the stunt I was about to pull. I'd crossed the street and was almost to the car before Rat Boy noticed me. He quickly straightened up from his slouch, and reached inside his suit jacket for something.

He might be going for a gun, I thought, realizing that I might have just taken the express lane to that early grave. But his hand stayed inside his jacket, so if it was a gun, he wasn't drawing it just yet. It was more of a precautionary measure on his part. Although this eased my nerves just a bit, I pretended as if I hadn't even noticed that he was reaching inside his jacket at all. I casually strolled up to the car and rapped on the window with my knuckles.

Keeping his right hand inside of his suit jacket, he rolled down the window a crack with his left. "What do want?" He barked, sounding annoyed.

"Excuse me sir. I'm sorry to bother you, but do you happen to know a really big fella wearing a white tank top?"

I saw his eyes widen for just an instant before he caught himself and put his tough guy persona back on. "I don't know who you're talking abou-"

I cut him off before he could finish. "Because he just took a nasty tumble down the stairs."

He immediately dropped the pretense of not being associated with Rhino Man. "He did what!?" He took his hand back out of his suit jacket.

"Yeah, he's pretty banged up. He's such a big guy, I can't carry him out by myself. Do you think you can help me get him over here to the car?"

Rat Boy mumbled something under his breath, but started to get out of the car.

By the time he had the door open, I had my Colt 1911 pistol out of my shoulder rig and pointed right at him. He froze, still as a statue. I motioned with the pistol for him to slide over. He obliged of course, and I got into the car.

Without taking my eyes off Rat Boy, I closed the door to give us some privacy.

Then, keeping the 1911 on him, I relieved Rat Boy of his own piece with my free hand.

It was also a Colt, model 1908, pocket hammerless .380 ACP. Relatively small and easily concealed, the model was a favorite among gangsters. Rat Boy didn't have bad taste in guns.

I slipped it into my pants pocket.

"Take it easy. Your pal is still breathing. I just roughed him up a bit is all. You'll fare better if you can remember your manners."

Rat Boy gave me an incredulous look.

"Trouble believing the big ape lost a fight? Yeah, I don't think he saw that one coming either. I guess he thought because he was big, he was also invincible. You'll get to see that I'm telling the truth for yourself." I shifted a bit in my seat. "The point is, it didn't have to go down that way. You see? I have the money." I tossed the envelope full of cash into Rat Boy's lap.

He glanced at the money and then back at me. He didn't have to say a word. The expression on his face said it all. But he said it anyway. "If you had the money why did Renzo get physical?"

So that was Rhino Man's name. Renzo the Rhino. It fit.

"Your buddy was so eager to fight, he didn't even give me a chance to hand it over. I don't know if he was having a bad day, or if he's always this irritable. It would be wise for him, you, and all your friends, to remember that trying to rough me up is a very bad idea. Bottom line, this whole ugly mess could have been avoided. You seem like a reasonable fellow. There's no need for this to escalate any further with you now, is there?"

Rat Boy glanced nervously at the barrel of the .45 pointed at him.

"Oh yeah! I'm reasonable all right, *very* reasonable. No need for this to escalate, noooo need at all."

"Good, very good. I'm glad to see that I'm finally dealing with an intelligent and reasonable fellow. You'll find there are certain perks for being reasonable."

Rat Boy arched an eyebrow at this, but his expression seemed to be more curiosity than disbelief. I had his attention. That was good. "That stack of cash there is one hundred dollars light, but there's no need to panic. I have a client who is paying me for a job tonight. They require a bit more privacy than my average client, so they're paying after hours, at a different locale than my office."

I noticed Rat Boy's expression turn from curiosity to one of doubt. I had to show him the silver lining in all of this, and fast. "Now I realize this would require a second trip on your behalf, so in addition to the missing hundred, I was going to include an extra three hundred dollars to make up for the inconvenience. Your pal Renzo didn't give me a chance to explain that. Now Mr. Mancuso, being the sound businessman he is, would certainly see that an extra three hundred dollars is worth a slight delay; even if that was beyond your muscle-bound friend Renzo's ability to understand."

Rat Boy's expression softened a bit, but I could tell he wasn't sold yet.

"Now seeing as how you are a much more intelligent individual than your buddy Renzo, I think it only fitting that you should be compensated accordingly."

I saw Rat Boy's expression turn back to one of curiosity. I had him back on the line. Time to set the hook.

"So I figured, why not add an extra three hundred dollars for you? That is, if you could help sell the idea that the added cash is worth the slight delay, and it makes up for the misunderstanding between Renzo and me. No one needs to know you are being handsomely compensated of course. It will be our little secret."

You could practically hear the wheels turning in Rat Boy's head as he mulled it over.

"Come on. When have you ever made an easier three hundred bucks? Besides, consider the alternative." I waved the 1911 a bit to emphasize my point, which seemed to help Rat Boy make up his mind. He was suddenly nodding his head up and down enthusiastically.

"Ok, we have a deal."

I smiled impishly. "Good. I'm glad you could see reason. What's your name, pal? I like to know who I'm doing business with."

"Calvino, but this doesn't mean we're all chummy. In fact, word can't get out that this ever happened."

I smiled, thinking: *Calvino the Rat. It doesn't have quite the ring to it that Renzo the Rhino does, but oh well.*

"Of course, Calvino. I understand your need to keep things under the radar. As I'm sure you understand my desire to keep things copacetic with Mr. Mancuso. I'd like to avoid any more unfortunate misunderstandings in the future, like what happened to your poor friend Renzo."

I saw fear resurface on Calvino's face. "What did you do to Renzo anyway?"

That was good. I needed Rat Boy to have a healthy respect for me.

"Oh, nothing too serious: a broken nose, a few broken ribs, some other assorted bumps and bruises. Oh yes, and his family jewels are going to be quite tender for a while, I'm afraid. Yes, he's in pain, but he should recover, *eventually.* It's like I told you, it's not a good idea to try and get physical with me. It will end very badly for whoever tries it. But you, Calvino, you are much more reasonable."

I gestured with the .45 again and he nodded his head up and down enthusiastically.

"Good. That is why you'll end up three hundred dollars richer, instead of having a bunch of broken bones. Now meet me back here at midnight. I'll have the additional cash for you and Mr. Mancuso." I kept the 1911 trained on him, and patted my pants pocket with my free hand. "Oh, you'll get your piece back too."

Without taking my eyes off Calvino, I holstered my 1911.

I'd made my point. Besides, I didn't think he posed much of a threat to me unarmed. I seriously doubted he'd try anything physical, after our little chat.

It turned out I was right, and I left the car without incident. I jogged back across the street, mumbling to myself.

I walked a slippery slope there. Yes, the extra cash would probably smooth things over with Mancuso. The thing was, I didn't have the extra cash, and I'd just lied about the client. There was no payday coming. I had just dug myself six hundred dollars deeper into debt.

So, it was a good thing I had a plan. Sort of. The word 'plan'
implies something which has been thought out. This was more like a
desperate grasp at straws while flying along by the seat of my pants.
You see, the reason Mancuso's payment was a hundred dollars light,
was because I knew of an underground gambling establishment that
had a poker game with a five-hundred-dollar minimum buy in. If I
combined what I shorted Mancuso, with what I was going to use for
rent and groceries, I could cover the buy-in.

I'm good at cards, so I figured my odds were better than
average that I could win what I needed. The beauty of it was Mancuso
owned the place. So, in a round-about way, I'd be using Mancuso to
pay off Mancuso.

Of course, there was the distinct possibility that I wouldn't
win enough to cover my rent, groceries, and the extra three hundred
I'd promised Calvino. Or that I'd even win enough to pay the extra
three hundred I said I'd pay Mancuso. Heck, there was even a chance
that I'd lose what I was using to buy into the game. The more I
thought about it, my plan had more holes in it than Swiss cheese.

But why focus on the negative?

I climbed the stairs and turned the corner, heading down the
hall towards my office. As I halfheartedly made my way, preoccupied
with thoughts of the fateful card game that would take place later that
night, I heard a phone ring.

I broke into a run, sprinting down the hall when I realized
that it was coming from my office. I couldn't afford to miss a call from
a client.

I didn't care who saw me running down the hall like a crazed
lunatic.

Professional image be damned. I needed the money!

44

Chapter 6

The Horn of Ryujin

Takeshi surveyed the board room. He quietly took in the numerous conversations taking place around him.

To an outsider, it would have appeared no different than any ordinary business meeting. Several Japanese tycoons, clad in expensive suits, seated at a long table, discussing the latest quarter's projections.

These were not captains of industry however.

No. Gathered at the little conclave, were the highest-ranking members of the Kagé - a centuries old ninja clan, and one of very few dynasties to survive into modern times.

The Kagé however, were not content to merely survive.

Master Oh-maga, head of the Kagé, cleared his throat.

Instantly the room fell silent.

It was hard to guess Oh-maga's age, although upon close inspection, his hair betrayed a few streaks of gun metal grey intermixed with the black. His face had the slightly weathered look of a man in his late forties, or early fifties. But he had the broad shoulders of a young man in his prime. His posture and his movement exhibited a vigorous spirit, and masculine forcefulness few men in their twenties could match.

His very aura exuded physical prowess.

Every man in the room, except Daraku, was a martial arts master. Yet, they all gave respect and showed obvious deference to Oh-maga.

"I will quell the rumors now. What you have heard is indeed true. The Horn of Ryujin is within our grasp at long last. The mighty weapon that was once used to decimate the Mongol hordes will be ours once more! This will change everything. Under our influence, Japan can once again ascend to her rightful place as a world power!"

The assembly did not want to draw any undue attention, so it did not burst out into cheers. But it was evident that the mood in the room had changed from one of anticipation, into that of elation.

"Tanaka, are our allies in the government ready?"

Tanaka was another well-seasoned, yet robust looking man, with a walrus like mustache and a commanding presence. Yet he too, snapped to attention when Oh-maga called his name, and gave a brisk bow before answering.

"Yes, my lord. As soon as we have the Horn, our men in the House of Representatives will put to vote an amendment to the constitution, allowing Japan to raise an army once more, thus paving the way for Japan to re-forge her empire of old. We have a slim majority, but a majority none the less. It will pass to the cabinet for ratification. Once there, however, problems arise. We have influence over only six of the fourteen members. Not enough to ensure success."

Oh-maga nodded stoically at this. He turned his gaze to Takeshi. "Can this be dealt with?"

Takeshi followed Tanaka's example, standing at attention and bowing before he replied. "Yes, my lord. The two cabinet members most likely to oppose the amendment will be *unable* to participate in the vote. The measure will pass."

"Good." Oh-maga then turned his gaze to a man seated across the table from Takeshi. The man had a shaved head, and wore a perpetually sour expression.

"Motobu." Oh-maga said the man's name and nothing more. Upon being addressed, Motobu rose to his feet and bowed to Oh-maga.

Motobu's expensive suit did little to conceal his broad shoulders, barrel chest, and tree trunk like limbs. He was massive by Japanese standards; standing six-foot-two, and weighing two hundred and thirty pounds. He dwarfed his fellow countrymen, who averaged just five-foot-seven inches in height.

"Our factories are ready, and can start mass producing military vehicles and other machines of war immediately." Motobu remained standing but said nothing more. The scene became awkward, and the mood uncomfortable. All eyes in the room were now fixed on Motobu who did not take his seat but rather continued to stand, saying nothing. Oh-maga cut the pregnant silence short. "Is there something you would care to add, Motobu?"

"My lord, we risk much. This ancient artifact has been lost for one hundred and thirty years, and has not been used in over seven hundred! The centuries can embellish mundane events into the stuff of legend. Even if it is all true, and the Horn wiped out the Mongol fleets, how can we be sure that it will be as effective against modern warships, as it was against the rickety sailing vessels of the thirteenth century?"

Daraku rose from his seat. "I assure you the tsunami the Horn would produce, can sink even a modern US aircraft carrier!"

Motobu glared contemptuously at Daraku. "How can you possibly claim to know such a thing!?"

Daraku's eyes widened at being addressed in such a manner.

With a snarl on his lips, Daraku back handed the empty air in front of him, as if swatting an invisible fly. Motobu was sent flying backwards, and crashed violently into the wall behind him, some ten feet away.

Composure regained, Daraku gave Motobu a withering look. "You see Motobu, it is because I have a certain way with magic."

Enraged, Motobu sprang to his feet, and charged forward.

Daraku made another gesture, lowering the palm of his hand, as if he were pressing down on something.

Motobu instantly collapsed in a crumpled heap, as if gravity had suddenly increased tenfold where he was standing. He writhed about on the floor, though whether it was out of outrage or agony, was unclear. He was clearly unable to rise, and he began to shout for Oh-maga to intercede.

"Motobu, enough! Daraku, release him!"

"As you wish," Daraku replied calmly. He made another gesture in the air with his hands, and Motobu was able to regain his feet once more.

Motobu stood panting, staring daggers at Daraku who smiled wickedly in response, obviously egging him on.

Wishing to avoid any further hostilities, Takeshi rose from his seat. Bowing to Oh-maga, he inquired, "My lord. If I may interject?"

Oh-maga nodded, allowing Takeshi to continue, glad for the distraction.

"Although Motobu's manners were lacking," he said, hoping to placate Daraku, "I believe his concerns are valid. The better our understanding of the Horn's capabilities, the better our chances of success shall be." Takeshi looked again to Oh-maga, and seeing another nod from his master, took his seat.

Oh-maga turned his gaze to Daraku. "Takeshi is right. Enlighten them."

"But of course, lord Oh-maga." Daraku replied. "A modern aircraft carrier battle group can indeed weather severe storms. But the reason you never hear of one being swamped isn't due to their sea worthiness, so much as their early warning capabilities. Modern radar allows them to avoid truly dangerous weather. With the Horn however, we will be able to conjure forth truly devastating storms with absolutely no warning, rendering their radar useless. The Americans, or whoever dares to oppose us, will find themselves caught in the throes of super typhoons and tsunamis, with no chance of escape!"

Takeshi began to rise from his seat, but with a wave of his hand, Oh-maga stopped him. "No need for ceremony, speak your mind Takeshi."

Takeshi nodded his acknowledgment, and then turned his attention to Daraku. "We all know the Americans have much more than aircraft carriers that they can bring to bear. What happens when they send nuclear warheads!?"

There it was. The elephant in the room had finally been addressed. The Japanese, having endured nuclear fire decades before, still feared it, generations later. The entire room turned to see how Daraku would respond.

"The answer lies with modern technology. We can use it to enhance the effectiveness of the Horn. In addition to being able to blanket a large area in devastating storms, the Horn can also produce terrible funnel clouds, which can be targeted with pin point accuracy. Using radar, we can track incoming missiles and then use the Horn's tornadoes to re-direct them to crash into the sea, or Korea. Perhaps even China. The same funnel clouds can be used to swat jet fighters from the sky. The point is, gentlemen, once we combine the Horn with modern technology, even America's military might will be no match!"

Oh-maga smiled approvingly as he saw realization dawning upon his generals. The sheer power that would be theirs to command was truly staggering. "Now my friends, we must take back the Horn of Ryujin, and reclaim our rightful place as masters of Japan!"

That time, the men did not restrain themselves, and the room broke into cheers. Oh-maga indulged them for a moment, but soon motioned for silence. "Daraku, tell us where we may find the Horn."

"The Horn is in America, lord Oh-maga. San Francisco, California, to be more precise. Utilizing resources available only to someone of my particular talents, it was made known to me that a Dr.

Nia Lockhart, an American professor of anthropology, at San Francisco State University, has stumbled upon the location of the Horn. I will assist your people if need be, but I should think that the Kagé are capable of retrieving the Horn from a mere college professor."

Takeshi spoke. "We should not be lulled into overconfidence. Correct me if I'm wrong Daraku, but doesn't legend say that it is our age-old enemy, the Hikari, who have the Horn. How is it now in the hands of an American anthropologist? I think the Hikari will need to be dealt with."

Daraku sneered. "Obviously the Hikari hid it in America. Now this Dr. Lockhart has discovered its whereabouts."

Oh-maga spoke. "Takeshi is right. We can be sure that the Hikari will try to spirit the Horn away again. We cannot afford for it to be lost for another one hundred and thirty years."

Motobu stood. "I can have a war band in route to San Francisco within the hour. I will lead them myself!"

Takeshi stood as well. "I think our interests will be better served if we use subtlety, my lord. I can lead a covert team to retrieve the Horn. It would be best if the Horn was taken with no, or at least very little collateral damage. That way the Americans will remain in the dark until it is too late."

Oh-maga considered Takeshi's words. He finally nodded, satisfied that he had a suitable answer. "Both of you shall go. Takeshi, you will be used first, as our scalpel. If the Horn should elude you, then Motobu will be used as our hammer."

Daraku sighed. "I suppose you are right lord Oh-maga. It is best to take no chances. The Hikari have proven to be formidable adversaries. If by chance, neither the scalpel, nor the hammer is enough, perhaps you will need, what is it the Americans say? Ah yes, an ace in the hole."

Oh-maga nodded. "You will accompany them Daraku. Now assemble your respective teams, and leave at once. Time is of the essence! Takeshi…"

"Yes, my lord?"

"Although we do not want to alert the Americans with a trail of blood, if this Dr. Lockhart stands in our way; her life is forfeit."

"Understood my lord."

Chapter 7

Shame on Shane

I burst into the office, and snatched the ringing phone from its cradle. "White Knight Detective Agency," I said, in my smoothest businessman's voice.

I know I'm a one-man shop, but hey, the word 'agency' has a nice ring to it. Also, it sounds very professional. I hoped I didn't sound out of breath to whoever was on the other end of line. That probably *wouldn't* sound very professional.

Luckily, they didn't seem to notice.

On the other end of the line, in an annoyingly nasally tone, I heard, "Yes, my name is Brandy Hooska, and I need to hire a detective."

"You've called the right place, ma'am. How may we be of service?" Again, I use 'we', instead of 'I', because it sounds more impressive.

"It's Shane: my lousy, no good, sorry excuse for a husband. He's been cheating on me, and I wanna' catch him in the act."

Oh boy. I sighed on the inside. *Another one of these cases.* "I see. Well, we have extensive experience in such matters, ma'am."

"Good, because he's going to do it again tonight. I'm sure of it! He just called to tell me he'd be working late again this evening, but I don't know who he thinks he's fooling. I know damn well he's just hooking up with some college girl slut! I need you guys to catch him in the act, tonight! My car is in the shop, so he's not worried about me surprising him. His guard will be down. I don't know when I'll get a better opportunity to catch him red-handed!"

Again, the inside sigh. *Why tonight, of all nights? As if I didn't have enough on my plate, with the whole Mancuso mess. Well, I do need the money. Maybe I can still make it work.* "That's short notice ma'am, but we could assign a man to follow him, and get photographic proof. That is, if we have one available. Let me check the roster. Just a moment please."

I held the receiver near some papers and noisily shuffled through them. Don't laugh. A bit of theatrics like that adds value to my services, and makes the client feel special. At least I'm pretty sure it does. I read it somewhere anyway. "Good news Mrs. Hooska, you're in luck! It looks like Gideon Jones is available, and he's our very best."

"Great! That slimy, two-timing bastard, will finally get his!"

Man, that lady was pissed! "Yes, Mrs. Hooska, of course there is the matter of payment. We'll need a retainer before we begin."

"Fine! Just as long as I catch that son of a bitch with his pants down. But you'll have to come over here to get it. My car is in the shop, and Shane is in no hurry to get it fixed. He knows if he did, I'd follow him and catch him. Then I'd cut his little pecker off!"

Jeez. I rolled my eyes. *This lady is something else.* But money didn't seem to be an issue, so I thought that maybe I could squeeze more than usual out of her. Ordinarily I didn't ask my clients for a retainer, unless I thought I might incur a lot of expenses. Usually I charged an hourly rate, which varied, depending on what kind of case it was, and what I thought the client could afford.

But if I thought it was possible that I might have to catch a plane to tail somebody out of town, or out of state, which has happened, or that something else might become costly, I'd charge a retainer. Around four to five hundred dollars usually did the trick. Mancuso definitely qualified as a lot of expenses, and Mrs. Hooska sounded like she might be willing to pay more. It was a win-win.

I ran some quick numbers in my head. *Let's see. I was short one-hundred on my Mancuso payment, plus an additional three-hundred to smooth things over with Mancuso for roughing up Rhino Man. Then there's the three hundred for Calvino for facilitating things. That makes seven hundred. Plus, I can use a little extra for groceries, and maybe a trip to the video store. Am I forgetting anything else? Nah.* "The retainer will be eight hundred dollars ma'am."

"Eight hundred dollars!? That's outrageous!"

"Well ma'am, it costs a bit more when the job is given priority over all the other cases, and it's on short notice to boot. You did say you wanted to catch him in the act, and it would have to be *tonight,* correct?"

"All right, fine. Come on over and I'll write you a check."

Shit! Mancuso definitely won't take a check. "I'm sorry, Mrs. Hooska, but retainers must be in certified funds: cashier's check, money order, or even cash." I was making the stuff up as I went along, but it sounded good.

"Listen, I can't get to a bank. My car is in the shop, and I don't keep that kind of cash lying around."

Shit! Oh well, maybe I could still wring something out of her.

"Well," I shuffled some more papers next to the phone. "If you could give us at least six hundred in cash tonight, we could accept the rest via check."

There was silence on the other end of the line as Mrs. Hooska considered my offer, and I mentally crossed my fingers. I was beginning to worry that I'd lost her, when she broke the silence.

"I don't know if I have that much cash here at the house. Hold on. Let me check."

I heard her put the receiver down noisily, and then, nothing. I watched three minutes tick slowly by on the clock. But just as I was about to give up on her ever coming back, she did.

"I have five hundred and sixty-seven dollars, and ninety-eight cents. That's it."

Less than I was hoping for, but certainly better than nothing. "Please hold the line for just moment, Mrs. Hooska. I need to check with management, to make sure we can accept that small of an amount."

I watched the clock again, and let four minutes tick by before talking. Hey, turn-about is fair play, right?

"Good news, Mrs. Hooska! We can make an exception. We'll accept what cash you have tonight, and allow the rest to be paid via check, when the job is done.

"Good! How soon can you be here?"

"What's the address ma'am?"

"2237 Farnsworth Lane."

"And your major cross roads?"

"Willard and Parnassus Avenue."

That was down in Cole Valley. "Ok, Mrs. Hooska. Mr. Jones should be there in about an hour."

"Good." With that, she hung up the phone. I followed suit, and rummaged through my desk drawer, looking for my road atlas. San Francisco is a big place, and I wasn't too familiar with that neck of the woods.

I found my Thomas-Guide, and familiarized myself with the area. Then, I planned a route before finally taking the atlas, my camera, and some other assorted stake-out gear, and heading out the door.

I'd put myself on a tight schedule there: tailing Mr. Shane Hooska, a poker game, paying off Mancuso. I was in for a busy night. Oh well, it was par for the course. It seemed like things were always either really slow, or I was running around like a chicken with my head cut off. Rarely was it anywhere remotely in-between.

An hour later, I stopped by Mrs. Hooska's place, and picked up my retainer. While I was there, I got a bit of unexpected good news. Mrs. Hooska told me that the lying, cheating, no-good Mr. Hooska, taught Psych. 101 at the university. She was sure he was getting himself some college girl tushy on the side. Well, not exactly in those words, but that was the gist of it.

Shane's alleged infidelity wasn't the good news though, the bit about it taking place at the University was.

The underground poker game was happening in the back room of 'Baci', an Italian restaurant right by the University. It was directly across the street, and a few blocks down.

My plan suddenly looked like it might work out after all!

Chapter 8

Unwelcome Intrusion

The sun was already beginning to set when I left Mrs. Hooska's place, and headed down to the university, where she was sure the extra-marital acts were taking place.

It was completely dark when I pulled into the west parking lot. I took advantage of the privacy darkness afforded me and switched outfits.

I exchanged my dress clothes for a tee-shirt, jeans, and my Nike running shoes. It was a much more practical outfit for what I was about to do, compared to the more professional get-up that I had on for my meeting with Mrs. Hooska.

I completed the ensemble with a light windbreaker that zipped down the front and had a hood. I wasn't expecting rain, but it was black. That made me harder to see at night. It also did the job of concealing my Colt 1911 in my shoulder rig.

I took out a pen-light, and studied a map of the campus that Mrs. Hooska had given me.

Once I was pretty sure of where to find the psychology department, I clicked off the light, and waited a bit for my eyes to adjust to the darkness. Then I grabbed the little backpack that held my camera, and two extra t-shirts, one green and one yellow.

The backpack would help me blend in on campus, and you never know when a quick and simple wardrobe change will come in handy. Something as simple as a different colored shirt can help you slip away unnoticed.

More than once, I have been in the unfortunate situation where unsavory characters were looking for the guy in the green shirt, trying to pick him out in the crowd. They paid no attention to me, walking in the opposite direction, wearing a yellow shirt.

Once I was all set, I headed out.

I tried to keep a low profile as I made my way past the dorms. But I didn't tip toe about, and actively try to sneak around. That would actually draw attention to myself. If you want to go unnoticed, don't do anything out of the ordinary. Most people are too absorbed in their own affairs to take much notice of the world around them anyway.

College kids were no different, it seemed. Probably pre-occupied with studying, or partying, or chasing co-eds. Whatever it is that college kids do. If it looked like I'd accidentally caught the eye of someone, I simply proceeded on, as if I belonged there, and they took no further notice.

It worked like a charm.

I soon passed the dorms and made my way to the sector of the campus where all the classrooms were. This part of the campus was deserted, so I switched gears. I went from strolling about as if I belonged, to sticking to the shadows and staying out of sight.

If the map was correct, the psychology department was just around the corner, behind the building where I was now.

I found a spot deep in shadow, stopped, took my camera out of the backpack, and slung the strap over my head. Then I crouched down low, and crept around the corner.

I was not prepared for what I saw.

Something was definitely wrong. Like cat and fish making-out wrong! I was expecting the same old, same old. I slip in unnoticed, set up in a clandestine spot, and take some pictures of some schmuck cheating on his wife. Not the most glamorous of jobs, but hey, it would mean a payday.

I thought I'd see a sole light in an otherwise dark building, and upon closer inspection, I'd find Shane and some little missy who was trying for an "A" the hard way. I would take some pictures, Mrs. Hooska would have her proof, and I would have my money.

What I got was something else entirely. Not just unexpected but wrong!

I don't know how else to put it.

There were about a dozen guys, dressed all in black, wearing hoods and masks, running around slicing each other up with swords!

Like ninja!

I'm serious.

Now not only is this the wrong century for that kind of thing, but the wrong continent as well.

I'm no linguist by any stretch of the imagination, but I do know English when I hear it. What they were jabbering, was not English. It was Japanese. Not to be confused with the sing-song cadence you hear used down in Chinatown either. Nope. I've heard the techniques and commands barked out, for over fourteen years now, at the Golden Eagle Dojo. That's the martial-arts studio where I train.

My vocabulary is limited. I'm able to count to twenty, and say very rudimentary things like: yes and no, please and thank you, you're welcome, high and low, punch and kick, the Japanese names of various techniques, but not too much beyond that. It's a martial arts class after all. The focus is on self-defense, not language. Sensei still wants to teach us a bit more than just punches and kicks though. He wants to share some of the rich traditions, and history of the art. Consequently, I know a little Japanese, and whatever these guys were yelling at each other, was definitely Japanese.

Like I said earlier, I have a fourth-degree black belt in both Karate and Judo. Being able to defend yourself is a valuable skill set to have in my line of work. It has turned out be very handy on several occasions over the years. Like with Rhino Man. In most scenarios, I can do more than just hold my own. The other guy had better be armed or pretty damned big, strong, and fast, to pose much of a threat to me. I'm not trying to brag, but outside of elite military special forces, professional fighters, and high ranking martial artists, which combined make up a tiny segment of the population, there aren't too many people out there who can take me in a fair fight.

That being said, I wouldn't willingly tangle with these guys, not in a million years. They weren't just good, they were *scary* good. Their form was perfect, and their speed was blinding. It was clear that they understood, and had mastered distance, timing, and feints. They wheeled about in a mesmerizing dance of death.

Fascinating as it was though, Mrs. Hooska wasn't going to want to pay for these kinds of pictures. It was time for me to exit stage left as quickly, and as quietly as possible.

Shit! It occurred to me that I would have to refund her most of the retainer. I needed the money too.

Can somebody please tell me why the fates always seem to be conspiring to keep me broke?

Then it dawned on me. Maybe Mrs. Hooska wouldn't pay for pictures like these, but one of the newspapers probably would! Hell, maybe I could wrangle a payday out of this night after all.

The things I do for money.

Any sane person would be getting the hell out of dodge, but here I was, sneaking up closer. *Come on Gideon you can do this! You sneak up on people and take their pictures without them knowing it all the time. That's it, just a little bit closer. Holy Jesus, he just cut that guy's arm off! What a great shot! Hot damn, but I'm gonna get paid!*

I made my way even closer. *That's it boys, keep it up.*

I risked a few steps closer, my camera to my eye, snapping pictures the whole time. Click, click, click, more great shots. *Loving it boys, loving it!*

I was probably pushing the envelope on safety, but I crept up even closer, and got more great shots, from a different angle this time. Click, click, click. I could see the money rolling in now. This was going to be a great payday after all!

That's it boys, show off for the camera. Click, click, click.

The fight ranged all over, and I moved so I could keep up with the action, taking more shots as I went. Click, click, click.

That's it! Fabulous darlings, just fabulous! You're doing great, keep it up! Yes, that's it, make love to the camera. Love it boys, I really do! Now make me hate it. Wonderful! You're all gonna be stars, and I'm going to have a nice fat wallet.

Then it happened. Life went all slow-mo. Nothing good ever happens when life goes all slow-mo.

I could see the silvery blade slicing through muscle, sinew, and bone like a hot knife through butter, separating the man's head from his neck and shoulders.

The disembodied head sailed through the air, and hit the ground, where it made a disturbing sound, like a soggy cabbage. It tumbled and rolled, like some sort of ghastly misshapen bowling ball. It left a grisly trail of blood behind it as it went rolling along. And it kept on rolling, until it stopped right at my feet.

I stole a quick glance down, and then looked back up to see the masked man staring right at me. The mask was made of some type of black fabric that matched the rest of his outfit, and was in two pieces. The lower half covered his face from the nose down, kind of like ones that the old west stage coach robbers used to wear, only tighter, and more form fitting. The second piece covered his head, from just above the eyebrows and back, so that only a narrow strip for the eyes was left uncovered.

It was unmistakable. He was a ninja! A real, honest to God ninja! Just like the ones in the movies!

We just stared at each other for a fraction of a second, but in slow-mo time it seemed much longer. Then the ninja quickly switched from a two-handed grip, to a one-handed grip on his sword, so he could reach inside his jacket with his free hand. Then he threw something at my head!

My arms instantly shot up to protect my face, and just in time to catch some type of circular blade in the forearm. I looked down at the thing protruding from my arm. It was a shuriken. A goddamned throwing star for fuck's sake! I couldn't believe it was actually happening!

It was only a superficial wound, and it only stuck into my arm a little more than half an inch deep maybe, nothing life threatening. The way it was designed, it couldn't get much more penetration than that.

It still smarted though.

In the approximate .9 seconds that it had taken my mind to process this information, the ninja had nearly covered the 30 feet that had previously separated us.

That's when my martial arts training took over.

Fourteen and a half years of sparring had ingrained in me the innate knowledge that a man moving backwards was slower than a man moving forwards. So, obeying the instinct to backpedal the hell out of there would only get me dead.

Stepping off the line of attack, to the left or right, might be a little better, but I didn't want to risk that either.

I had already seen these men fight, and they were too good. If my timing was even just a shade off, it would enable the ninja to track my movement while simultaneously swinging a three-foot sword as sharp as a razor blade at me.

That would not have ended well for yours truly, so I did the unexpected. I jumped into a judo dive roll, right towards my attacker's feet, and just under the arc of the oncoming sword blade.

The momentum of the roll took me past him. In the time it took the masked man to spin back around, and take two steps in my direction, I had drawn my Colt 1911 pistol and put three rounds in the ninja's chest.

The rapport of a 1911 .45 caliber pistol is quite loud, and there was a sudden, but brief and awkward moment where all the ninja were staring at me. I like to imagine that underneath their masks, all of them had their mouths open out of surprise.

Then it was raining throwing stars.

Throwing stars may not be lethal, but believe me when I tell you, they hurt like hell. I must have had four or five of the damned things stuck in me. Then they bum rushed me while throwing even more!

I stood my ground, and let out a manly battle cry. Sure, to the untrained ears of the uninitiated, it could have possibly been mistaken for a yelp of fear. But trust me. It was a manly battle cry.

I squeezed off four more shots at them. They weren't particularly well aimed. I pretty much just prayed and sprayed in their general direction.

That's usually all it takes though. Few and far between are the men who can stand tranquilly still while shots are being fired at them. All the while, calmly thinking to themselves, *this guy isn't taking his time to aim, odds are pretty good he'll miss me.* I mean a lucky shot'll kill you just as dead as a well-aimed one.

About half of the ninja scattered. The other half remained eerily cool under fire though. With their swords raised high, they came running at me in a zig-zag, or 'serpentine' pattern, making them that much harder to hit. All the while, they were yelling their own war cry, just like you see in the movies.

Ok, you want to play for keeps, fine. I'll show you what happens when you bring a sword to a gun fight, assholes.

"Okay then! Let's dance," I shouted, as I drew a bead on the ninja closest to me, and made sure to lead him a bit because he was in a sprint.

BAM! The shot rang out and the ninja went down.

Not wasting a second, I got another one in my sights!

CLICK! This incidentally, is the single worst sound you can ever hear in a gunfight.

Shit.

I was out of bullets! And by then, they were almost on me.

Now, I train with my side arm regularly. I can eject a spent magazine, and get a fresh one in, pretty damn quick. I was sure I could do just that, and squeeze off another shot before the remaining ninja hacked me to pieces with razor sharp swords.

So I ejected my spent magazine, and slammed a fresh one home. All while I ran as fast as I could in the opposite direction.

Thank God I'd changed into my running shoes. Those guys were fast! But then again, so was I.

My morning routine of running the hills of San Francisco really paid off. I sprinted like a track star, in the general direction of the dorms.

Chapter 9

The Shinobi Sprint

I was trying to get to a more crowded area, in hopes that the ninja would be less likely to try and kill me in front of an audience.

It didn't seem to deter them any though, and I wasn't losing them even though I was really pouring on the speed, so I started crying out at the top of my lungs. "Help! Help! They're trying to kill me! Call the police! They're trying to kill me!"

It wasn't very brave, but it did the trick. We quickly drew a crowd, and the ninja peeled off into the shadows.

I slowed down my pace to a fast jog, but I kept yelling. "Somebody call the cops they killed a guy!"

I continued on towards the parking lot, all the while yelling, "It happened in front of the Psych. Department! He's dead! They killed him! Call the police!"

I slowed my pace to a walk, as I headed back towards my car. I no longer wanted to draw attention to myself. It was time to slip away in the confusion.

That's when I spotted them, silhouettes patrolling the parking lot. Damn, those assholes were good.

I turned back towards the campus.

I'd just have to leave another way, and come back for my car later, preferably in broad daylight.

Then I spotted more of them. Two figures, dressed all in black cutting through the crowd like shark fins through water. No swords or masks but they were of oriental decent and I was pretty sure they were ninja.

Shit! What was I going to do? The ninja didn't give me any time to think as they quickly made their way through the crowd in my direction.

They would be on me in a few seconds.

I bolted!

I wasn't sure of where I was headed, but I sure as hell wasn't sticking around there. As I took off like a cat with his tail on fire, with the ninja right on my heels, it dawned on me.

Mancuso's card game!

It was only a few blocks away, and they wouldn't be able to follow me in.

I changed course and headed south, towards Fulton Street.

After the first few blocks, panic began to set in. I wasn't losing them. I was running full out, at break neck speed, and those guys were keeping up. We had already run clear across campus, and a couple more blocks down Fulton Street. I was finding out the hard way, that even if you're a runner in good shape, you just can't keep going at a full out sprint for that long.

My lungs felt like I was breathing Tabasco sauce, and my heart was beating faster than a crazed drummer on speed. I was afraid it would burst from the strain at any moment.

The traffic was whizzing past us as we ran down the sidewalk. I thought of waving or screaming again to attract attention, but the streets were devoid of pedestrian traffic, and it was doubtful that anyone in the cars speeding by would hear.

Hell, since we were all dressed in black, they probably didn't even see us.

It seemed I was out of options. I drew my pistol and whirled around to face my pursuers, prepared to go down in a blaze of glory. I hoped I might get lucky, and take two or three of them with me before the others cut me down.

I tried to get one of the ninja in my sights, but the little bastards had learned from last time. They immediately started zig zagging again; only this time even faster, and more erratically. Some were even dive rolling into summersaults, then popping back up again in a different spot. It was like trying to get a bead on a single kernel of corn in a popcorn popper.

The glare from the headlights of the oncoming traffic made things even more difficult. It looked as if I wasn't going to get a clear shot.

In close quarters, my gun wouldn't be of much use. I was physically exhausted, and I sure didn't relish the thought of tangling with these guys hand to hand, much less hand to sword. So as the ninja closed in for the kill, I played my ace in the hole, and dove right into the oncoming traffic.

Horns blared, tires squealed, and cars sped by almost as fast as the life that was flashing before my eyes. Crazy you say? Crazy like a fox! Who would be insane enough to follow me into traffic? Ninja, that's who! Tenacious little bastards!

I'd like to say my years of martial arts training paid off, and my highly tuned cat-like reflexes enabled me to escape unscathed. But the truth is, we don't practice a lot of car dodging techniques down at the dojo. A more accurate description of what happened would be that I ran like hell for the other side of the street, while I prayed as hard as I could a fast-moving car wouldn't make a hot mess out of me.

Luckily for me, sprinting through traffic didn't seem to be in the ninja's training curriculum either. Because as I made a mad dash across the street, I heard the squeal of tires, followed by the bone crunching thud of a faster moving car slamming into a slower moving ninja behind me.

Pandemonium ensued as a truck slammed into the rear of the car that had just hit its brakes in a vain attempt to avoid hitting the ninja. The car spun out of control, right into the other lane of oncoming traffic. The already badly damaged vehicle was instantly T-boned, and sent back into the other lane.

It quickly deteriorated into a multiple car pile-up, taking out at least one other ninja in the process, maybe two. I couldn't tell for sure. I only risked a quick glance over my shoulder, as I continued to run down the alley which led to the rear entrance of Baci.

I wiped the sweat from my face, and tried to slow my ragged pants for air to a semblance of normalcy.

If I knocked on the door out of breath, all sweaty and wild eyed, odds were, they wouldn't let me in. I quickly scanned the alley and spotted a dumpster. I stashed the windbreaker, my camera, my 1911, and its shoulder rig in my backpack, and put them behind the dumpster, under some cardboard and assorted trash.

A camera would be an odd thing to bring to a private card game, and Mancuso's men definitely wouldn't let me in while packing heat.

Speaking of heat, I took Calvino's little Colt 1908 pocket hammerless and shoved it down the front of my pants. A tough guy was much less likely to grope another man's crotch, even when patting them down looking for firearms. It turned out homophobia has its advantages.

Lastly, I changed out of the T-shirt I had on, which was now soaked with sweat, and put on one of spares I had with me. The green one because it was the color of money; symbolic of all the cash I'd be winning tonight.

Once done, I knocked on the back door.

A little panel slid open revealing a pair of dark, beady eyes. They gave me a quick glance, and then a gruff voice barked. "We're closed!"

"I know, but I phoned in an order for some cannoli. They said to pick it up in the back." This was the code phrase for entrance to the poker game.

"Let me see your green, pal." I opened my wallet, and held it up to the sliding panel for the man to see. It was full of the five hundred and sixty-seven dollars from Mrs. Hooska's retainer, plus the hundred I had held back from Mancuso's payment, and four hundred more that I had set aside for rent and groceries. I even mixed in a stack of twenty-six one dollar bills I had been saving for a trip to the strip club for good measure.

Don't judge. Everyone has a weakness. Mine happens to be boobies. Besides I think I speak for every red blooded American male when I say; once you've seen one woman naked, you want to see the rest of them naked! Except for maybe the really old ones, and the morbidly obese.

Where was I? Oh yeah, I'd mixed the ones into the middle with the rest of the bills, to make the wad of cash look even bigger.

All told, it was one-thousand and ninety-three dollars.

I had to admit, it made a fat stack of cash that looked impressive in my eyes. It seemed to work for whoever was behind the door too.

The panel slid shut, followed by the sound of several dead bolts clicking, and then the door swung open.

Chapter 10

Poker Night

I was escorted into the kitchen of Baci, where four guys sat on folding chairs around a card table, playing spades, and listening to a portable radio. They looked out of place alongside all the stainless-steel pots and pans, counter tops, cabinets, and stoves. Out of place, and bored as hell. My guess was, they were the security detail for this little shindig.

The guy who let me in locked the door behind us, then one of the three remaining guys from the table begrudgingly stood up, and started to pat me down, checking for weapons.

Even though he seemed bored, he gave it more than a half-hearted effort. I didn't want to risk him finding the 1908 pocket hammerless, so I thought I'd better do something to tilt the odds in my favor.

I lewdly thrust my pelvis forward, and started to gyrate my hips. "Hey sweetheart, don't forget to check here. I'm sure you'll just love what you find." There was a look of utter disgust on the guy's face, and he shoved me away from him. "Fag!"

"Hey! You were the one who was groping me, pal!"

"I was checking you!"

"Out? Yeah, I could tell you were checking me out."

"For weapons, asshole!"

"Hey, let's leave my asshole out of this, homo." That really ticked the guy off. It looked like he was ready to come to blows, and I was afraid I'd taken it a bit too far. But luckily one of the other guys intervened, and stood in-between us, to restrain his friend.

"Steve, take it easy. Settle down, he isn't worth it." The guy who was being the voice of reason glanced over his shoulder and gave me a withering look. "Get to playing cards, smartass, and get the hell outta' here." Then he shoved me away from Steve, and continued to roughly herd me through some swinging double doors that led out of the kitchen.

I was taken through the deserted main dining area, to a room in the back, which looked like it might have been used for private parties.

On that night, most of the tables were pushed back against the walls, with chairs stacked neatly on top. All except four tables in the center of the room, that were arranged in a diamond formation.

Those tables were occupied by men playing some serious poker. There were six men to a table, plus a dealer. The latter being easily identifiable, as they were wearing matching white dress shirts, and silver vests.

Most of the room's occupants were smoking either cigarettes or cigars, and as a result, a thick haze of smoke hung in the air. There was another guard standing in the entry way. My escort left me with him, and headed back towards the kitchen.

I noticed there was a fully stocked bar at the back of the room, where a young bartender, who I guessed to be in his early twenties, was going through the motions of wiping glasses with a rag, looking bored out of his mind. Next to him was a big guy in a light blue dress shirt, sporting a Smith & Wesson .357 magnum in a shoulder holster. No jacket or blazer to cover it up, so the whole world could see he was packing heat.   Probably there to keep things honest, I imagined. There were two big aluminum suitcases sitting conspicuously on the bar next to him.

The guy in the entryway gave me a nod, and pointed to Mr. Blue Shirt. "You can buy chips and cash out at the bar."

I thanked him, and strolled past the men playing poker, and on over to Mr. Blue Shirt.

"Good evening." I flashed my best nice-guy smile as I opened my wallet, and laid my cash down in front of him. Apparently immune to my charms, Mr. Blue Shirt merely grunted as a means of a response, before opening one of the suitcases. It was full of multi-colored clay poker chips, all stacked in neat, little rows.

"Whites are five dollars, reds - ten, blues - twenty, greens - fifty, and blacks are one hundred. There's a five-dollar ante per hand to play. If you win a hand, you have to wait another two before you cash out. When you do cash out, the house gets ten percent. Cheating automatically donates all your chips into the pot, and gets you walked outside for an ass-whooping. If you survive, you're banned for life. Any questions?"

"No sir. Seems pretty cut and dry to me."

Mr. Blue Shirt nodded in agreement, and started counting out my money. He exchanged it for poker chips, which he stacked in rows in a little slotted tray. He stopped abruptly, halfway through the stack. "Ones? Seriously?"

"Hey, they spend too pal." I said defensively.

Mr. Blue Shirt shook his head, and continued to count out chips. When he was finished, he opened the second suitcase, which was filled with an obscene amount of cash, and added mine to its contents. He handed me back three one-dollar bills.

"Your change," he said, making no effort whatsoever to mask the disdain in his tone.

For some reason, his tone really bugged me. Maybe I was hyper-sensitive after being chased by ninja. *What an ass*, I thought. I could feel the irresistible urge to annoy him suddenly building up within me.

"Wait a second." I began digging into my pockets.

I then produced a handful of change. I plopped it down in front of him, and proceeded to count it out. I wanted to get him back for mocking my ones.

"Twenty-five, fifty, seventy-five, one dollar, one-twenty-five, one-fifty, one-seventy-five, one-eighty-five, one-ninety, one-ninety-five, one-ninety-six, one-ninety-seven, one-ninety-eight, one-ninety-nine, and two dollars!" I pushed the three singles, and the two dollars in change over to him.

"You've got to be kidding me." Mr. Blue Shirt sighed.

"Hey man, money is money."

Mr. Blue Shirt rolled his eyes, and with a genuinely pained expression, exchanged the money for another white chip.

My desire to pester was not yet fully sated and I wondered if I could manage to annoy him further. I surveyed my stack of chips and frowned. It didn't seem very large. I counted them out. Yup, there was one thousand and ninety-five dollars' worth. I tossed him a black chip. "Color me down please."

"What would you like?" Mr. Blue Shirt was getting pissed.

"Let's see." I placed my hand on my chin. "Hmmmm, give me two twenties, four tens, and four fives."

He gave me the requested chips, and shut the suitcases, signifying he was done.

I shrugged my shoulders, gathered up my chips, and strolled over to the table closest to the bar.

There were two empty seats, and I chose the one that would give me a view of both the entrance, and Mr. Blue Shirt. Call me jumpy, but I don't like sitting with my back towards an armed stranger; especially one I've just pissed off.

"Good evening, gents." I greeted the other men sitting at the table. There were four of them.

One guy was so heavy, he looked like he could be a stunt double for Jabba the Hutt! Seriously, if he gained any more weight, he would start pulling smaller fat people into his orbit!

Then there was an older guy, who was probably in his late sixties or early seventies. His face was so wrinkled, it looked like someone peeled an apple and left it out in the sun all day. The old man smoked like he was on fire, and drank like he was trying to put it out. He'd take a drag on his cigarette, and then sip his whiskey. Puff of cigarette, sip of whiskey, and so forth, and so on, non-stop.

The third guy looked like your quintessential biker. He was a big dude who had a shaved head, a mustache, and a goatee. It was a long one too. It was long enough to braid, which he did. The thing stretched all the way down past his chest. He was wearing a black Harley Davidson t-shirt with the sleeves cut off. It showed off his arms, which were covered in muscles and tattoos.

The fourth guy looked like he stepped directly off the pages of GQ magazine. He was wearing an expensive looking tailored suit, complete with a silk tie, and pearl cufflinks. His blond hair was parted in the middle, and feathered back. Not a single strand was out of place. He wore a Rolex watch, and his finger nails had recently been manicured to perfection.

As was my habit, I immediately assigned them all nicknames. Porky, Gramps, Harley, and Yuppie.

The dealer was the only one who answered my greeting out loud. The rest merely nodded in reply. "Good evening sir. The game is five card draw, nothing wild. Ante up if you want in."

I tossed a white chip in the center of the table, along with everyone else.

Ahhhh. The resulting, distinctive sound they all made as they hit each other and the table was music to my ears. I raked in the cards dealt to me casually.

I love poker. The game is more strategy than chance. It takes so much more than just knowing the rules, or even the odds, to be good at it. You have to play against the other guy's hand, more than just playing your own. Since you can't see their hand, you must be able to read the other players.

That's the real game: looking for the 'tells' of an opponent who is actively trying to cover them up, ferreting out the truth of another guy's act, deciding if the number of cards a guy takes, or the amount that he's betting, is a clue, or just a smokescreen. In a way, it's similar to what I do as a private eye. Detective work!

It's why I love the game, and probably why I'm so good at it. Better than most, I dare say. So, being the good detective that I am, I'm more focused on getting to know my opponents style of play in the beginning of the game, than I am on winning hands.

I look to see how they hold their cards, how often they look at their hand, how close, or far they sit from the table. Do they talk a lot, or are they quiet? Do they play with their chips, or drum their fingers? If so, when? All these things can tell you as much as a facial expression. Sometimes they can even tell you even more.

I casually fanned out my cards and looked at my hand. I had the ten of clubs, the nine of hearts, the eight of spades, the seven of diamonds, and the three of hearts. I mulled it over for a second, and decided to try for the straight, even though the odds were long. I was more concerned with how the people at the table would react to my taking just one card, than if I actually got the six or jack that I needed to make the straight.

But first came the betting.

Porky had the bet, and threw in a red chip for ten dollars.

Then it was my turn. I raised, but only five dollars. Again, it was more to see people's reaction, than a display of confidence in my hand.

Then came Harley and Gramps, who each called me.

Then Yuppie, who raised it another twenty-five dollars. *Show off...*

Porky folded, but Harley, Gramps, and I called. I looked to see what everyone's posture was like. The dealer asked us if we wanted any cards at that point. Harley and Gramps each took three. Yuppie and I only took one. Again, I took note of my opponents' reactions, even Porky's. It didn't matter that he was already out.

Porky raised his eyebrows, just a little.

Harley stroked his mustache and goatee.

Gramps was unreadable, and Yuppie was smiling like a shark. I didn't read too much into that, though. It could have been an act.

I didn't even look at my cards as I soaked it in.

I did this partly to read the people at the table. Mostly I was readying myself, so regardless of what I drew, good or bad, it didn't show on my face. I didn't want to give anything away with my expressions.

Harley leaned back in his chair, just a little.

Gramps took a longer pull on his cigarette than usual. He also skipped his customary sip of whiskey.

Yuppie never took his eyes off me.

"Your bets gentlemen," the dealer announced, motioning to Gramps. The bet was his, since Porky folded.

Gramps sipped his whiskey, and tossed a blue chip onto the pile for twenty dollars.

Harley folded, and Yuppie raised thirty dollars.

I glanced at my hand for the first time since drawing the new card.

The jack of clubs! I had a straight!

I was confident that my face gave nothing away. I made a mental note of my posture, and counted three Mississippi's before reaching for my stack of chips.

I wanted to create a routine that I kept, regardless if my hands were good or bad. I took two blue chips, and tossed them onto the growing pile in the center, raising Yuppie forty dollars.

Gramps folded.

All eyes were on Yuppie, who continued to smile. "Call." He sounded supremely confident.

There was three hundred dollars in the pot. "You've been called sir," the dealer declared.

I turned over my hand.

Yuppie shrugged and tossed his cards down face up. Three aces. Good, but not good enough to beat a straight.

The pot was mine!

Chapter 11

Party Crashers

Three hundred dollars baby! More than enough to make up for the one hundred and thirty-three I was short to Mancuso and company, after Mrs. Hooska's retainer. I just had to ride out two more hands and call it a night.

I glanced at my watch as I raked in my chips. It was eight-thirty. I had plenty of time to meet Calvino.

I started arranging the chips into neat little stacks by color.

"Ante up gentlemen," the dealer said.

I tossed in a white, five-dollar chip, along with everyone else. As I did so, something in the entryway caught my eye.

I glanced over to see the guard clutching his throat with both hands, in a futile attempt to stop the crimson torrent of blood that gushed past his fingers. He staggered forward, then crashed into one of the tables. Cards and chips scattered everywhere.

Pandemonium ensued as people jumped up from their seats, and shouted all at once.

Amidst all the commotion, I couldn't see who had attacked the guard.

I glanced back to the bar, and saw Mr. Blue Shirt's eyes grow wide with panic as he went for his .357 magnum. Just as the hand cannon cleared leather, a shuriken struck him in the face, and lodged in his cheek bone just below his left eye. Mr. Blue Shirt recoiled in pain, and his finger that was already on the trigger, involuntarily squeezed off a shot that went wild, and hit the overhead lights.

There was a shower of sparks, and the lights flickered on and off rapidly, like a strobe light. It made for a surreal, nightmarish scene as two ninja moved through the smoke-filled room, cutting people down indiscriminately as they forged ahead.

I heard another shot, and dropped to the floor, not trusting Mr. Blue Shirt's aim. From there, I low-crawled for cover as fast as I could manage, fishing out Calvino's Colt 1908 pocket hammerless as I went.

The two ninja worked in tandem. The first hung back, and cut people down as they made a break for the exit. The second singled out Mr. Blue Shirt, and started cutting a path through the room towards him.

More elusive than a wisp of smoke on the wind, the ninja closed the distance between them. He avoided three more shots from the .357 magnum as he did so. Then, with a lightning fast swipe of his sword, he took off Mr. Blue Shirt's hand at the wrist. Screaming in agony, Mr. Blue Shirt staggered backwards until he collided with the bar.

Then, in a desperate play, Mr. Blue Shirt grabbed one of the aluminum suitcases on the bar, and hurled it at his adversary's head.

The ninja easily dodged the impromptu missile. It sailed past and hit the wall behind him, where it burst open, spilling poker chips everywhere.

Undaunted, Mr. Blue Shirt flung the second suitcase at his attacker.

To his dismay, the ninja struck the suitcase in midair with a spinning back kick. The suitcase flew open and spun off, showering the room with dollar bills in the process.

I paused long enough to stuff a few handfuls of the bills into my pockets.

Hey, don't judge. Life doesn't often present you opportunities like that. I looked up as I grabbed more handfuls of cash, just in time to see a blood-streaked sword blade emerge from the back of Mr. Blue Shirt's skull. I took that as a sign to stop shoving money down my pants, and made a bee-line for the exit.

The people in the room who were still alive, scurried about like roaches after the lights had come on. I saw one of the dealers skirt around to the left of the ninja who was blocking the entryway. Yuppie simultaneously made a break for it to his right, trying to split the ninja's attention. In a blur of motion, the ninja cut both men down.

Harley had picked up a chair, bellowed a war cry, charged forward, and swung it at the ninja's head. The ninja blocked with his sword, and then, with a counter strike, reduced the chair to kindling.

Moving surprisingly fast for a big guy, Harley leapt backwards, narrowly avoiding another swipe of the ninja's sword.

A tear in Harley's T-shirt, along with a thin line of blood, showed he hadn't escaped the ninja's blade entirely. Harley glanced down at the flesh wound, and looked back to the ninja. They locked gazes and he smiled darkly. "Let's see how well you do without that sword, pal!"

Damn! You just have to admire balls like that, I thought.

Apparently, so did the ninja. After a brief pause, he sheathed his sword.

Immediately, Harley shot forward. The ninja rushed to meet him, but came in low. Using a spinning motion, he stuck his leg out, and swept Harley's feet out from under him.

The big biker crashed to the ground. The momentum from his charge sent him sliding along the floor. The ninja closed in, but Harley came up with the severed leg of the chair, and using it like a billy club, rained down blows on the man. Clearly caught off guard, the assassin attempted to block the blows with his forearms.

Quickly recovering, the ninja kicked Harley in the groin. The big man doubled over, and the ninja immediately followed up with a flying knee that caught Harley under the chin. The big man lay sprawled out on the floor, stunned. The ninja drew his sword, and moved in for the kill.

That's when I put four .380 rounds into his chest with the Colt 1908 pocket hammerless.

Before the first ninja had even hit the ground, the second one charged forward.

I adjusted my aim and fired off a shot. It was as if he had Spidey senses, or the ability to read thoughts. At just the right moment, he went into a forward dive roll and dropped down, narrowly avoiding my shot.

I tracked his movement, and left just enough room to account for his rate of speed. I squeezed off another shot. The slippery devil abruptly changed direction just as I fired, again avoiding the bullet by the narrowest of margins.

The little Colt 1908 carried seven rounds. I had just one shot remaining. I didn't like my chances if I ran out of bullets.

Keeping the gun trained on the ninja, I started backing out of the room. Using a sparring trick that I'd learned at the dojo, I kept my eyes focused on his hips, and not his head, thereby minimizing the chances of him faking me out with a feint. The ninja switched to a one-handed grip on his sword. The last time I saw one of them do that, I got hit with a shuriken.

So I stopped moving backward and exhaled, readying myself to take the shot.

As if he sensed my intentions, the ninja froze. We just stood there for a moment in a standoff, eyeing the other, looking for some sort of sign. A few seconds ticked by, but in my heightened state of awareness, it seemed like a nerve racking eternity.

It's much harder than Hollywood makes it out, taking a life. Even that of an enemy who is actively seeking to end yours. Unless you're a psychopath, it just isn't easy to kill another human being. Stone cold killers are few and far between. Without realizing it, a man often grimaces, or sneers before he attacks. At the very least, he widens, or narrows his eyes. Whether he's throwing a punch, or pulling a trigger.

I couldn't afford to give my enemy such a warning.

For the second time that night, I was playing poker. Only now the stakes were much higher. It was my very life that was on the line.

I slowed my breathing, and made my face a blank mask. I wasn't about to give the ninja a 'tell'.

Then, calmly and smoothly, I pulled the trigger.

I saw the spray of blood, and the ninja went down. I didn't even wait for the body to hit the floor before I spun on my heels, and beat feet towards the exit.

I'm a big fan of the old saying, "he who fights and runs away, lives to fight another day". Or in this case, "he who is gone before the police arrive, saves himself mucho-much heart ache".

I needed time to sort things out. What had I stumbled upon there? Ninja?! Were those guys really ninja? I mean, for crying out loud, last time I checked, this was nineteen eighty-five, not fourteen eighty-five! Even if I assumed those guys were the real deal, which certainly seemed to be the case, what were they doing fighting each other! More to the point, why were they doing it on a college campus in the good old U S of A, and not in Japan, or at least somewhere else in Asia?

Whatever was going on, it was something big! Big enough that they wanted me dead for just stumbling upon it.

I stepped over the corpses of the guys who had been the security detail in the kitchen, careful not to step in the growing pool of blood, a grim reminder that those guys were willing to butcher anyone who saw them. To what lengths were they willing to go to eliminate the guy who had pictures of them?!

I grabbed my back pack from behind the dumpster, and after a quick change into the yellow shirt, I headed back towards the campus to retrieve my car.

I needed to get the hell out of there, and plan my next move.

Takeshi picked himself up off the floor of the restaurant. He had barely been able to move in time to avoid a fatal wound. Thanks to his training, he dropped the instant before the American had pulled the trigger. The bullet had been aimed at his heart, but struck inches higher, and tore through his trapezius muscle instead.

The fact that the American had hit him at all was impressive. A countless number of Yakuza had tried before. All had failed. The American was highly skilled indeed. The man had managed to take out his entire team!

Showing up when he did, just as they were battling the Hikari? The timing of the American's appearance was far too suspect to be mere coincidence. He had to be some sort of agent of the enemy.

It was as they had feared. The Hikari were somehow aware of the plan. What other explanation was there? They had showed up to stop his team from taking the notes of Dr. Nia Lockhart, the American anthropologist who had stumbled upon the location of the Horn. They had apparently brought a hired gun with them.

It was unlike the Hikari to bring in outside help. The war that the Kagé and Hikari waged was a secret one. Perhaps they were willing to risk exposure to keep the Kagé away from the Horn. Whatever the reason, the Hikari's plan had worked. The Kagé still didn't know the exact location of the Horn, and they had just lost their entire covert ops team!

Ignoring the pain in his shoulder, Takeshi picked up the sword of his fallen comrade, along with the spent shell casings of the American. No evidence could be left behind that could point to the Kagé, or that anything nefarious had taken place.

He took a bottle of liquor from behind the bar, emptied its contents, and lit it on fire.

The blaze would further mask their presence. It would appear only as a fire that had resulted from drunken carelessness; an unfortunate accident, nothing more.

Takeshi had already hidden the swords of his other fallen brethren, so the clean-up was complete.

Damage control wasn't enough.

They couldn't afford to let the Horn slip through their fingers, and Takeshi seriously doubted Motobu's war band would be successful where his special ops team had not.

No. As much as he disliked doing so, they would have to turn to their 'ace in the hole'.

It was time to seek the aid of Daraku.

Chapter 12

The Perfect Woman

The meeting with Calvino went off without a hitch. As it turned out, I'd managed to stuff three thousand one hundred and eighty-three dollars down my pants at Baci's, so I had almost tripled what I walked in with. More than enough to smooth things over with Mancuso and company. It wasn't enough to write home about, but it was a real nice payday for a change. I was overdue for one. Besides, that was money hard earned, if you ask me.

After making my payment to Mancuso, I headed back to my place, a little house in the Noe Valley. It's not much, but it's home.

I had a small dark room set up at the back of the house.

A lot of my jobs are like Mrs. Hooska's, and involve taking pictures you don't want dropped off at the local photo hut.

I started the process of developing the film.

While the pictures soaked in their chemical bath, I hopped into the shower.

Running for your life is quite a workout. I stood there, letting the hot water wash away the sweat, and soothe my aching muscles. It felt good; so good, I was planning on staying there until I was old and grey. I quickly changed my mind once I ran out of hot water.

I hurriedly toweled off, and threw on a pair of sweats and a t-shirt.

I went over the pictures, still in awe. There were some really nice action shots, and I imagined the newspapers pay a pretty penny for them.

With a Herculean effort of sheer will, I resisted the urge to sing "We're in the Money", and instead studied the photos, looking for some sort of clue.

Then I noticed something.

Only half of the ninja were in black. The other half were dressed in dark grey. I wasn't sure what that meant, but it was something I'd missed earlier. I mulled things over methodically. Ninja were Japanese. Maybe the Yakuza, the Japanese equivalent of the mafia, were trying to muscle in on the Triads, the *Chinese* equivalent of the mafia.

Maybe this was some sort of turf war.

I had a contact down in China Town, Jimmy Chen. I could ask him.

Not much happened down there that Jimmy didn't know about.

It wasn't much to go on, but it was a start. Since things had slowed down a bit, I realized I was starving. I made myself a turkey sandwich, with lettuce and tomato, and poured myself a glass of milk. Then I set up a TV tray, and plopped down on my couch to relax, and watch the boob tube.

That late at night though, all the big network channels were showing those colored bars, along with that god-awful beeping noise, signifying they had stopped broadcasting for the day.

That left a couple of UHF channels: 44 and 36.

Channel 44 ran Creature Features at that hour. It was a B-rated horror flick starring Vincent Price and an army of cockroaches. Channel 36, had Kung Fu Theater. Shaolin Monks were battling ninja.

After my night, neither seemed very relaxing.

I popped an X-rated VHS tape into the VCR instead.

Aahhhh boobies, much better.

I wolfed down the sandwich, guzzled down the milk, and settled in to enjoy the show.

I fell asleep half way through, and had nightmares that naked women were chasing me with samurai swords. I woke up with a start. I was drenched in a cold sweat, and sported morning wood. Not really knowing what to make of that, I put on my Nikes, and headed out the door for my morning run.

As far as I was concerned, working out had saved my life. That and firearms of course. So, as I ran, I made a solemn vow to myself to never skip my morning run or evening sessions down at the gun range. Ever!

When I got back, I poured myself a tall glass of orange juice, and gulped it down. Then I made myself a mushroom, spinach, and Swiss cheese omelet. It was rather yummy, if I do say so myself.

After breakfast, I showered, ironed my clothes, and headed down to the office.

Traffic wasn't bad, and I was in a good mood. I sang along as "Money for Nothing", by Dire Straits, played on my car radio.

I drove a 1979 gun-metal grey Chevy Nova. Nothing too flashy, but I liked it that way, unassuming. It blended in well on stakeouts. I'd done modifications, for some added horsepower though. I'd also put in quiet mufflers, so she was fast and silent. I'd dubbed her the 'Grey Ghost'.

I pulled into my reserved spot in the underground parking garage, and deliberately took the stairs instead of the elevator. My office was only on the second floor, I didn't want to be lazy.

When I got there, I glanced proudly at the door-plaque that read:

White Knight

Detective Agency

I did that every morning while I put my key in the lock.

I like going into the office. It's my home away from home.

I wanted clients to get the impression that this was the workplace of both a consummate professional, and quintessential badass when they stepped through the door.

I toyed with the idea of hiring an interior decorator, but thought better of it. I didn't have the money for starters. Besides, what would some creampuff with a degree in interior design know about being a badass?

I chose a place with hardwood floors. They seem more badass than carpet somehow. When you first walk in, on the right, there is a little waiting area. There are chairs, and a coffee table that has issues of Bloomberg Business Week, and Guns & Ammo. I hoped the magazines would subliminally reinforce the whole badass but professional image.

I've never been so busy that clients actually had to wait, but if it ever does happen, I'm ready. Until it does, I want to give the impression that I'm a busy man, with need of a waiting area.

That's why I also have a receptionist's desk to the left; for the receptionist I'll be able afford someday, when I get busy enough that I need one. Until that day though, I made sure that the desk had a phone, stacks of file folders, and even a coffee mug. It looks as if I have a receptionist, but one that just stepped out on a break or something.

There's no door separating the receptionist slash waiting area from my office, but it's designed in such a way, that you'd have to stick your head around the corner to be able to see in.

If you do, you'll find that my office is much larger than it appears. To one side is a bank of large filing cabinets, and to the other is a water cooler, small fridge, and a coat rack where my trench coat and Fedora hang with care. Some people may find it cliché, but I pay them no heed. I'm old school. No private eye's office should be without a trench coat and fedora. Next to the coat rack, was the all-important coffee station; complete with an overhead cabinet stocked with sugar, coffee filters, spoons, mugs, and even more coffee. No vile powdered creamer though. Yuck! I use only the real deal, which I keep in the fridge.

I'm not joking when I say *all important* coffee station. My good friend caffeine has seen me through many a late-night session, and early start. A fresh pot is brewing so often, that even when one isn't, there is still a faint but pleasant aroma of coffee in the air.

There's no art adorning the walls of my office. Instead I have my private investigator's license, matted and framed, hanging along with several newspaper headlines proclaiming in extra-large bold print:

MISSING CHILD FOUND

MURDER MYSTERY SOLVED

FUGITIVE BROUGHT TO JUSTICE

Things of that nature.

None of those cases were mine, but since I had them framed and hanging on the wall, clients most likely assume they were.

My desk is in the back of the room, and just like me, it's old school. A great big, massive thing of beauty. Rich polished mahogany, not the pressed particle board crap you see nowadays.

Behind it, taking up the entire back wall from floor to ceiling, is a colossal set of bookshelves, each filled with handsome leather-bound tomes. They were all hand-picked, solely for their looks, not content. There were some law books, a set of encyclopedias, and the odd novel; so long as they were stately looking but inexpensive. I wanted to impress my clients, nothing more.

The bottom left hand drawer of my desk is full of dog-eared paperbacks that I read when things are slow. They weren't nearly as impressive to look at, so I keep them tucked away, out of sight.

I sat down at my desk, and punched Jimmy Chen's number into the phone. Jimmy answered on the third ring. "Ni hao".

"Jimmy, how ya doin'?"

"Gideon, it's good to hear from you." He said, switching to English without the slightest trace of an accent. Jimmy is a second generation American, and runs a little souvenir shop down in Chinatown.

One day, a couple of years back, some tough guy wannabes, probably looking to impress the local Tongs or Triads, were harassing his customers. Jimmy tried to chase them off, but they started to rough him up. He fought back, but it was four on one. I just happened to be walking by. It was none of my business really, but I just hate bullies. So I jumped in, and together we gave them a good thrashing. As recompense for the things that were broken in his shop during the fight, I liberated cash from the thugs' wallets.

It turned out to be a sizable hunk of change, which more than paid for the broken knickknacks. So Jimmy closed shop early, and the two of us went down to the local watering hole to celebrate our victory. It was the beginning of a beautiful friendship. Now Jimmy and I get together every couple of weeks for some beers, and to play dominos.

Jimmy is good people. He was truly grateful for my help, and has referred more than a few clients my way over the years. As a result, I now have a good rep down in Chinatown. Jimmy is also a good source of info. He sees and hears things that, unless you were Chinese, you'd probably miss.

"You ready to get your ass handed to you in dominos again?" He teased.

"You wish. You got lucky last time. Don't get cocky."

"Luck had nothing to do with it. You are outmatched! It's a good thing you are better at private eye work, than games of skill."

"Speaking of private eye work, I need a favor."

"Sure thing. What can I do for you?" Good old Jimmy, saying yes before he even knew what I needed.

"I was hoping you might be able to check on a hunch for me. Keep your ear to the ground for any word of the Yakuza trying to muscle in on the Triads."

"That shouldn't be too hard."

"It's probably nothing." I said as I swiveled around to face my bookshelves, careful not to get tangled up in the phone cord. I just love my swiveling, high back, leather chair. It's wonderfully comfortable, and I picked it up for next to nothing at a garage sale. You can find some real nice things on the cheap, if you go to the right neighborhoods.

Suddenly, I heard the unmistakable sound of high heels clicking on the hard wood floor, and I swiveled back to face my new visitor.

I managed not to stare, with my mouth wide open, salivating.

But it wasn't easy.

She had the kind of looks that would ruin marriages, make a priest give up religion, or make an animal-lover club baby seals.

Some women are beautiful because of their face, others, because of their body. This woman had both. I had to force my brain to focus on something besides the sudden and powerful urge to make babies. So I took note of her wardrobe. She wore a light gray woman's suit. It was tailored to accentuate every curve. The skirt showed just the right amount of leg to make it damn near impossible not to look.

It was well worth the look though. She had smooth, shapely legs that started in heels just high enough to give you ideas, and ended in hips that made you want to grab a hold of them and pull her in close. She had a narrow waist, and shoulders wide enough so she looked strong, yet still oh-so feminine. She wore a white silk blouse beneath her blazer with a neck line just low enough, you wanted to look just a little bit lower.

If you did, you were in for quite a view. She had the breasts of youth, full and exciting. Big, wonderful beauties that pushed against her blouse balking at the need for restraint.

Her face was a thing of supernatural beauty. It was flawless, as if some master craftsman had improved upon nature itself. She had high, chiseled cheekbones, yet they were still soft in appearance, not sharp and angular.

She was fair, but not pale. Her complexion had a healthy glow. It was rich and creamy, without blemish. She had the most amazing lips, full and plump, the color of fresh strawberries. And she had big beautiful blue-grey eyes that reminded me of a stormy sea.

Her lovely face was framed by long, cascading, red hair that came to a stop just past her shoulders. It was the rich, auburn color you just couldn't get from a bottle.

Although my heart was beating like a drum within my chest, it was no longer mine. She'd stolen it.

"Gideon, are you still there?"

With a heroic effort, I tore my gaze away from the goddess, and returned my focus to Jimmy. I cradled the phone receiver between my chin and shoulder, listening to Jimmy. I opened my ledger with one hand, and motioned for my new visitor to sit at one of the two chairs facing my desk with the other. I wanted my new client to think I was a busy man.

"Well Mr. Chen, I'm afraid we only have a slot available at 2pm on Monday afternoon. Will that work you?"

"Gideon, what are you talking about?"

"Wonderful! We'll see you on Monday at two. I'll go into more detail then." I jotted down a reminder for myself to call Jimmy back and explain in the ledger, then hung up the phone.

I turned my attention back to the new visitor. "Sorry about that. What can I do for you Ms...?"

"Doctor, Dr. Nia Lockhart."

Doctor! She had the face of an angel, a body that made you want to sin, *and* brains? I wanted to make babies again.

Dr. Nia Jones. That had a nice ring to it.

"My apologies doctor. How may I be of service?"

Her perfume was intoxicating, making it hard to focus. As if her breasts weren't distraction enough.

"I need you to help me locate an artifact, Mr. Jones."

Artifact? That was an odd choice of words. She had my full attention, not that she didn't already have it. Suddenly it was because of what she said, not her looks.

"Artifact. Now there's a word you don't hear every day. The more common word would be object. Yet you used artifact. Why is that, I wonder?"

She had the faintest trace of a smile on her luscious lips when she answered me. "Well, I suppose the fact that I'm a professor of anthropology at San Francisco State University might color my speech a bit. My use of the word artifact was a deliberate one."

Professor!

Suddenly the drumline from "Hot for Teacher", one of the new hits from Van Halen's latest album, <u>1984</u>, was pulsing through my head.

Focus Gideon, focus! "Deliberate? Do tell."

Chapter 13

Counter Strike

Motobu wore the traditional, all black uniform of the ninja, sword slung across his back, minus his mask. He paced restlessly back and forth, like a caged animal. He was a warrior. To wait idly by, doing nothing, while others took action, was nerve racking to say the least. He detested relying on others for anything. Leaving the fate of this all-important mission in the hands of anyone else, even a man as capable as Takeshi, was akin to torture for Motobu.

The fact that he and his men had to wait alongside Daraku made matters exponentially worse. For starters, the pompous sorcerer had chosen a horrid base of operations; an empty warehouse by the water, in the area of town known as Dogpatch.

Admittedly, the place provided privacy, but it was extremely run down. It was so dilapidated, it should have been condemned. The building was chilly, dank, and rat infested.

Would it have been so bad to have more modern facilities?

The wizard took a perverse pleasure in vile surroundings. Daraku's secret office in the sub-basement of their corporate headquarters was no better. It was more than the surroundings though. It was Daraku himself. To be humiliated as he was in front of the other masters, by the wizard was unforgivable, yet Daraku did not stop there.

The wizard sat, lounging in an old, weathered chair, looking completely out of place in the dingy surroundings. His attire was better suited for a night on the town. He was sharply dressed in a black silk shirt, pleated black trousers, and expensive black dress shoes. Daraku sat there with a devious smile on his face. He constantly made snide remarks and thinly veiled insults, deliberately trying to goad Motobu into losing his temper. Worst of all, it worked.

"Your ceaseless pacing will not speed the Horn to us any sooner, Shinobi," Daraku remarked.

Motobu stopped long enough to stare daggers at Daraku. "Unlike some, I am a man of action," Motobu tersely replied and resumed his pacing.

The wizard smiled impishly, delighted that he had struck a chord. "Ooooh a man of action? Perhaps if you were to quicken your pace from that ponderous lumber. It might help. It would be more befitting a *man of action* at any rate."

Motobu froze in mid step, his back towards the wizard, afraid that if he faced him he'd lose control. Now was not the time for rash actions on his part, he reminded himself. Motobu took a deep breath, restraining himself, and then resumed his pacing.

"Perhaps you are right, Motobu. To quicken your pace might tax you physically. It would be too much like calisthenics, and such activities are best left to those in better shape than yourself."

Motobu shook with rage. He wondered if a shuriken to the face would distract the wizard long enough for him to close the distance between them, and run the wizard through with his sword.

Daraku sensed Motobu's outrage. Grinning like the Cheshire Cat, he goaded him further. "Then again, maybe a few jumping jacks wouldn't be such a bad idea. Tubby."

The last remark was just too much for Motobu, a martial arts master, and general of the Kagé. To be insulted like that in front of his men! He could not let such an outrage go unanswered.

Motobu spun to face Daraku, a shuriken in his hand. But just as he extended his arm for the throw, Takeshi seemingly materialized out of thin air and restrained him while whispering in his ear, "Now is not the time."

Daraku seemed disappointed by the intervention. "Ah, Takeshi. Your timing is fortunate, for Motobu at any rate. You have the Horn I presume?"

"I do not. It was an ambush. The Hikari were waiting for us, and they had a gunman with them."

"Where is the rest of your team," Motobu asked.

"I was the only one to survive."

Motobu's eyes widened with surprise. Takeshi's men were all highly skilled. That none of them had survived was shocking.

"Were you able to follow them?" Daraku interjected.

"Not for long. They made good their escape."

"The Horn is lost then!" Motobu wailed.

"Perhaps not," Daraku said, stroking his beard in apparent thought. "How long ago did your battle with the Hikari take place?"

"A little more than an hour ago, possibly closer to ninety minutes. Why?"

Daraku ignored the question, and instead asked another of Takeshi. "Did you kill any of them?"

"Nariko beheaded one, but Hikari casualties are not important. Capturing the Horn should be our pri-"

"Did *you* kill any?" Daraku interrupted.

"No. Only Nariko struck a killing blow, but I fail to see how that is impor-"

"Did you wound any?"

"Yes, but-"

"Give me your sword, quickly!"

Takeshi did as he was asked.

Daraku snatched the weapon from him and closely examined the blade. "Yes, yes. It's not much, but it should do the trick."

"What is enough? What are you talking about lord Daraku?"

"Blood, Shinobi! You have a foe's blood on your blade. If that foe yet lives, so much the better."

"I do not understand lord Daraku."

"I can use the blood to construct a spell to lead us to the wounded Hikari warrior."

"And thereby to the Horn as well, hopefully." Takeshi raised an eyebrow.

"Very good, Takeshi. You see, Motobu, use of one's brain will often produce better results than blind action."

Motobu grunted. Whether it was a concession or a rebuttal, one could not tell.

"The tracking spell is a complicated one. I will have to work through the night to have it ready by dawn. I think I will prepare a surprise for the Hikari as well." Daraku took his leave and started towards his field office. His stride dripped purpose. He called over his shoulder as he went. "Ready your war band Motobu, and let us hope that your thirty-six men fare better than Takeshi's six. For soon, you will have the action you so greatly desire."

"Pompous ass," Motobu muttered.

"We have need of Daraku, *for now*," Takeshi whispered.

The warlord eyed the ninja suspiciously. His emphasis on 'for now', was not lost on Motobu, did he have an ally in Takeshi? "But once the Horn is in our possession…" Motobu deliberately left the sentence unfinished, drawing out the last word.

Takeshi picked up on the hint. "The Hikari are formidable warriors. I lost my entire team. It is highly unlikely *all* members of your war band will make it back tomorrow. Is it so far outside the realm of possibilities that Daraku should fall in battle as well?"

Motobu nodded. A smile similar to the one Daraku had worn earlier, spread thinly across his face. "No, that is not outside the realm of possibilities at all. In fact, I think it is a *distinct possibility*."

Chapter 14

The Game is Afoot

"An artifact is exactly what it is Mr. Jones. An *ancient* artifact, that if found, will not only ensure the person who finds it a place in history, but have repercussions that reach far beyond academic circles."

Hot damn! It was too good to be true. A real, honest to God mystery! It's why I got into this line of work. I had begun to think a real mystery didn't exist; that they were myths, fairy tales. All the years I'd been in the business, I'd never once ran across a real mystery. Oh sure, I had my share of jobs. They were insurance work, or cases like Mrs. Hooska's, but not mysteries. Finally, a real mystery comes my way, and it's delivered by a beautiful damsel no less!

I said a quick mental prayer. *Please God, let her be in distress, just a little. That way I can ride to the rescue! The name of my company is White Knight Detective Agency for crying out loud! Sorry God, I didn't mean to be pushy.*

I admit, I was excited, but I didn't want to seem too eager. I wanted to come off like solving mysteries was something that I did every day and no big deal. So I thought I'd play a little hard to get, so to speak. "Well, Doctor Lockhart, as it happens, I am quite adept at locating missing objects. That being said, are you sure I'm the right man for the job?"

She arched an eyebrow at the question.

"I'm not saying no, but *ancient artifacts*? You make it sound like you might need an archeologist, not a private investigator. I'm Gideon, not Indy."

She smiled at that. Ah, a woman who appreciated my sense of humor. She *was* perfect.

"Well Mr. Jones, I'm afraid it's a bit more complicated than simply digging for buried treasure."

"Is it now? How so?"

She paused for a moment and chose her next words carefully.

"I'm not the only one looking for this artifact, Mr. Jones."

A race then! This keeps getting better and better, I thought.

"I see. Please continue."

Her expression changed at that point. It was only for an instant, but I caught it. Part of being a good private eye is having the ability to read people, especially when they don't want you to. The good doctor Lockhart was putting on an act. She wanted to come off as the learned professor who was all business. She tried to hide the fact she was also frightened.

"The others looking for this artifact, they want to make sure they are the ones who find it." My, my, this was getting interesting. I leaned forward in my chair to see if she would look me in the eye.

"Most people in a race want to win, Doctor." She met my gaze.

"True, but when most people say they want to eliminate the competition, they are speaking figuratively." Hot damn a damsel in distress!

"Are you saying your competition will kill you to be sure you don't beat them to the artifact?"

In answer to my question, she rummaged through her purse. She produced a rolled-up piece of paper, tied with a black ribbon.

"That's exactly what I'm saying." She untied the little scroll, and laid it in front of me, on my desk. It was oriental calligraphy. I'd seen its likes before, at the martial arts studio where I train. Unfortunately, I had no idea what it said.

"I'm sorry Doctor, but I can't read kanji." She made an odd face at my use of the word.

"You at least know the proper name for their alphabet, it's more than can be said of most Americans."

I hoped that impressed her a little bit. "I take it you know what it says though."

The frightened expression returned.

"It says, 'stop seeking the Horn, or we will see to it the shadows take you to Hell'."

Ok. That explained why she was scared. That would unsettle almost anyone. *What slimy sack of shit would threaten a poor girl like that? Whoa, Gideon, slow down! You know you've got a soft spot for a girl in trouble. Don't let your guard down. Sure, she may sound sincere, but you know from experience, that can mean next to nothing. You've learned the hard way not to put too much stock in your judgment when it comes to a pretty redhead, or blonde, or brunette for that matter. Stay objective!*

"Well, that *is* frightening, but it could just be a scare tactic. There may be no real intent to cause you any harm. In fact, it doesn't actually say they're going to kill you."

"Which is essentially what the police told me. But answer me this, Mr. Jones; if someone threatened your life, wouldn't you take it seriously?"

Touché, gorgeous. "I'm not saying you have no reason for concern doctor. But I'm going to need some more information. For starters, what exactly is this thing you're after, and why are there people willing to go to such lengths to keep you from getting it?"

Her body language changed dramatically when I asked the question. She no longer seemed scared. I wouldn't go so far as to say she was relaxed, but it definitely seemed as if we were on a more comfortable topic now. Back to business. "I am a professor of historical anthropology and East Asian studies. My area of focus has always been the Mongol Empire, the largest empire the world has ever known. At its height, it stretched from Asia to Europe, encompassing nearly 23% of the world's land mass and over 28% of the world's population. The Mongols were the ultimate warriors. They were the first non-Chinese people to conquer all of China. Their armies were unstoppable. They defeated the Hindu States, the Persian Kingdoms, the Muslim Caliphates and Sultanates, and the Russian Principalities. They even bested the European Knights. The list goes on and on. I've always wondered why these masters of warfare would send invasion fleets to Japan during the storm season to be wiped out by typhoons? Not just once but twice! Part of mastering war is mastering logistics. That's not a detail they would have missed. They should have known better. It didn't make any sense, so I looked for a reason. It became something of an obsession of mine. My search for answers eventually led me to Japan. It was there I learned the Mongols didn't make any mistakes. It turns out neither attack was launched during storm season. In fact, they were at times of the year when storms were a statistical improbability.

My research revealed Kublai Khan and the Mongols had timed their invasions perfectly. The Island of Japan was preparing for the worst. The warring clans set aside their differences and joined forces to present a united front. Even so, they were outnumbered. Undaunted, the Samurai warriors were prepared to fight to the very last man."

Never one to miss an opportunity to impress a lady, I nodded knowingly. "Ah yes, the Samurai Code of Bushido. The Way of the Warrior. For a Samurai to die in battle in the service of one's lord and the people, was the ultimate honor."

More than just a trace of a smile crossed her lips, and she nodded her head in approval.

"Very good Mr. Jones. Most Americans are not familiar with Bushido."

My heart did a somersault. Never in my wildest dreams did I think my love of the martial arts and its history would impress chicks. I'm fascinated with Bushido and its Western counterpart, the chivalric code of the European knights. I try to live my life by a similar code of honor.

My primary goal however, was to land a client, not a date.

That was a secondary goal.

So instead of blushing and saying aw shucks, I merely shrugged my shoulders nonchalantly at her compliment.

Her smile didn't fade, and her eyes seemed to say 'you're not fooling anyone'.

I had to work on my poker face.

Jeez Gideon, focus! Don't look at her tits. "Please Doctor, by all means continue."

"Well, although the Samurai were more than willing to face a numerically superior force in battle, and the accompanying likelihood of death without flinching, the majority of Japan was far less eager. There was a big movement by the Shinto priests for the people to besiege the gods in prayer for aid, especially the god Ryujin. Ryujin, the dragon god, was the tutelary deity, or patron guardian and protector of the sea in Japanese mythology. This Japanese dragon god symbolized the power of the ocean."

I wasn't sure where she was going with all of it, but she managed to pull me in, and I found myself hanging on every word. It was evident she was passionate about the topic, and her energy was infectious. The students in her class should consider themselves very lucky, not just because of her looks. Although I'm sure her male students thanked their lucky stars for that. Way beyond that, she was a master orator who managed to take a potentially dry topic and make it fascinating.

"Just as the rival Samurai clans united for battle, so did the people of Japan unite as a nation in prayer. They believed that their prayers were answered. It was thought the out of season typhoons were the work of Ryujin, protecting the people of Japan in answer to their prayers. The conspicuous timing of the storms led to that line of thinking, no doubt. However, through my research, I discovered it wasn't just the timing of the typhoons that lent credence to this belief. Not only were the storms out of season, but they were said to be much larger, and more powerful than any other typhoons ever witnessed. Again, all of it could easily have been written off as embellishment and mere coincidence if the Mongols had not tried to invade Japan a second time, with the exact same results. Two massive invasion fleets, the first numbering over one hundred and fifty-five thousand men, and the second even larger, numbering over one hundred and seventy thousand, were wiped out by the devastating typhoons. The second storm, coming again after the nation united in prayer, cemented in the minds of the Japanese people, the belief that the super-typhoons were the work of the dragon god of the sea, Ryujin. So the storms were given a special name – 'kamikaze', which means divine winds. Americans associate the word 'kamikaze' with the suicide pilots of World War II. Those pilots were named after the kamikaze storms – the legendary divine winds that had saved Japan from foreign invasion, not once, but twice."

You could tell that the good doctor Lockhart had transitioned fully into teacher mode. It was as if she was lecturing on her favorite topic at the university. I happen to be a bit of a history buff. I always found stories about people, regardless of what time period they lived in, more engaging than the abstract topics, like math, back when I was in school. So the history buff in me liked Doctor Lockhart's lecture. The private eye in me was wondering where she was going with all of it. What did thirteenth century invasion fleets, and storms in Japan, have to do with twentieth century America? How did it all tie together?

"It is in fact very common for pre-industrial cultures to believe in gods and their intervention and aid, especially in times of crisis. That the Japanese turned to their gods in prayer was not especially noteworthy. Something did grab my attention however; a specific ritual, performed by an obscure sect of priests. You see, most references to these, miracles if you will, stated people prayed to Ryujin for aid, and nothing more specific. Before the first invasion attempt, Shinto priests beseeched the people to pray. Before the second attempt, the Shoguns ordered that the people pray. Again, it was nothing specific. That's why, when I stumbled across the mentioning of a specific ritual in my research, it caught my attention. The account told of an obscure sect of priests who worshiped Ryujin as their patron deity. They used something called the Horn of Ryujin in their ritual to conjure up the storms. The Horn was described as a huge conch shell, embedded with three large precious gems: a sapphire, an emerald, and a black pearl."

There it is! The note said: 'don't seek the Horn', and now I find out that it's full of large precious gems! This is starting to make more sense.

There was a subtle change in the doctor's body language again. It looked as if she might be coming out of teacher mode. "That was it, nothing more. It certainly didn't seem important at the time, just an obscure mention of a ritual and a brief description of the Horn. It only caught my attention because it was more to go on than a vague reference about praying to Ryujin. I didn't pay it much mind, and it got filed away with other notes. Recently however, it seems to connect with a project closer to home. I'm researching the Tin Hau temple here in San Francisco. The original, smaller temple was built in 1852 in China Town, soon after the Chinese started immigrating to American with gold rush fever. At the time, there was no place to build but up in Chinatown. In the 19th century, laws restricted where Chinese San Franciscans could live and work. They had to build atop barber shops, laundries, anywhere they could find along Waverly Place. In 1854, however, special dispensation was granted to a group of monks, and construction of the grandiose temple we recognize today, broke ground. Today, it's one of the city's tourist attractions, but back then, it was a bit of a controversy. It was only allowed because it was outside of the city limits at the time."

Ok, she'd started talking about things that happened in America, instead of Japan. And they happened in the eighteen hundreds, instead of the twelve hundreds. I guess that was a bit of an improvement, but I still didn't know where she was going with all of it.

"It was a considerable undertaking, and it wasn't only the monks who were involved. It was a large segment of the Chinese community as well. At any rate, during my research I came across the diary of a man who was involved in the construction of the temple. He was a local carpenter, and craftsman. In it, I found the most astonishing entry: a description of the Horn of Ryujin! Although he didn't call it that, it matched perfectly with the obscure passage from centuries earlier. A great conch shell embedded with large gems: a sapphire, an emerald, and a black pearl!"

Now we're talking sweetheart!

"According to the carpenter's account, he was enlisted by the monks to build a secret chamber. This chamber had many intricate, hidden compartments, and it was protected with booby traps. Great lengths were taken to keep the project secret. The construction was done in the dead of night, and during the day it was camouflaged to look like debris. The very existence of the chamber was unknown to all but a select few. The purpose of the chamber was a mystery, even to those building it. In the carpenter's diary, he tells how curiosity got the better of him. After construction was completed, he snuck into the temple to see what was kept there. That is when the carpenter discovered the Horn. He assumed it was something of great value, but had no idea what it actually was."

Sweet jiggling jugs! I couldn't have dreamed up a better mystery if I tried. It was fantastic! I wasn't the only one all worked up. I could tell Doctor Lockhart was excited too.

"I knew I had potentially stumbled upon one of the greatest anthropological finds of the century! I immediately went to the temple with my findings. They categorically denied the existence of such an artifact, even when I presented evidence of firsthand accounts to the contrary. I was not about to be so easily thwarted, so I started perusing other avenues, asking around Chinatown. I don't give up so easily, not without a fight at least."

That filly had fire. I liked her! Brains, boobs, gumption, she's the total package! I had to be careful not to get a boner in front of her.

"At first it seemed as if my inquiries would yield nothing but frustration. Then I was contacted by a research team from Japan, who was looking for the Horn as well. I was elated! It seemed to validate my theory, and prove I wasn't on some sort of wild goose chase. I had hopes we could pool our resources, and collaborate in some fashion.

It turns out this Japanese group wasn't familiar with the concept of teamwork. They plied me for information, but weren't willing to reciprocate. Also, they didn't strike me as the academic type. Call it women's intuition if you will, but they gave off the wrong vibe. This became especially apparent when I didn't hand over all my work to them. Their thin veneer of civility quickly melted away, and they became outright hostile. They even threatened me. Luckily, we were in a public place, or I think it would have turned ugly. I was more disappointed than frightened. The next day I found my office in shambles. Someone had ransacked the place. I reported it to the police, and they seemed very interested at first. Apparently, there had been a violent clash between rival Triad factions that spilled onto the campus the night before. It happened in front of the psychology department, which is right next to the anthropology department and my office. It was gruesome. They found a man beheaded. But the police decided the two incidents were unrelated. When I returned home from work that night, I found my apartment was torn apart as well. That's when I found the death threat. I know they were looking for the diary. They need it to find the Horn. Thank God I accidentally left it at my intern's place."

Holy coincidences Batman! Well I could confirm that a man was beheaded in front of the psychology department. I don't think it was warring Triad factions though. I heard those guys speaking Japanese not Chinese. And there was the lovely Dr. Lockhart, saying that her rival research team was Japanese. It was very conspicuous timing. Were the ninja and the rival research team one and the same? Maybe the fighting wasn't a turf war, but the Yakuza and the Triads competing for the same priceless artifact. Were the two incidents even related? It was just too early in the game for any answers.

Chapter 15

Stinking Badges!

I stopped my musings when I noticed Dr. Lockhart staring at me. She looked as anxious as a kid on Christmas Eve; if that kid happened to be a gorgeous, big breasted swimsuit model.

"Well, Mr. Jones? Will you take the case?"

I smiled the kind of smile a man gives a stunning damsel in distress. "Oh yes, Dr. Lockhart. I'll take the case."

She returned my smile with interest and it lit up the room.

I felt a stirring in my nether regions as my baser instincts started taking over. Stupid, inconvenient desire to reproduce. I forcibly locked those thoughts away in the deep, dark recesses of my subconscious, where they belonged. The case was beginning to sound like it could be the mother of all cases. I intended to handle it with an appropriate degree of professionalism, regardless of my irrational desire to see the client do jumping jacks wearing nothing but a healthy application of suntan oil.

"We have two priorities, and the first is your safety. If they came up empty after ransacking both your home and office looking for the diary, we must assume the next thing they'll try is making a grab for you. They'll try forcing you to tell them the Horn's location. You'll have to lay low for a while." She nodded grimly.

"I can stay with family for a few days."

"No, that's the first place they'd look. Let's give them a false trail to follow. Call your work and tell them there's been a death in the family. You'll be in New York for a few days attending the funeral. With any luck, they'll be out of our hair on a wild goose chase. But we still need to be careful. You should stay in some out of the way motels for a few days. Use an alias to check in, and pay with cash." I wrote my home phone number and home address on the back of one of my business cards, and handed it to her. "Check in at least twice a day. If you see, or even sense anything out of the ordinary, trust your instincts and bolt. Get the heck out of there to somewhere public, and give me a call regardless of the time. I have one of those new electronic pagers, so I'll know you've called, even if I'm not near a phone."

She took the card and nodded, looking very much like a frightened child on the verge of tears. I felt anger seething up inside of me. I am very old school. I subscribe to the belief that women are wondrous creatures that make life worth living. One should treat them with dignity, and respect, and hold doors open for them and such.

When they are disrespected, taken advantage of, or in this case threatened; I see red. I want to rush to their aid, and rain down much hurt and pain upon the scum bags who would dare do such a thing. I know it's the 80's. Women's lib is big, and notions like mine aren't. Thinking like that, coupled with the urge to rush in first and think later, has landed me in hot water before. But damn it, it's who I am. I got into this business to help people. It's why I named my business 'White Knight Detective Agency', and I'm not about to change. Not now, not ever! I was going to help Dr. Lockhart find the Horn, or die trying. I'd make the people who threatened her pay in the process. I placed my hand over Nia's in an effort to comfort her.

In a reassuring tone said, "Don't get too worked up, Doctor. This is probably overkill on my part. I would rather err on the side of caution when it comes to your safety."

She put on a brave face, and gave me a smile that didn't quite make it all the way up to her eyes. "I understand. Thank you. I can't tell you how much this means to me."

I needed to lighten the mood before I went all weak in the knees, so I tried a little humor. "Don't mention it. Besides if anything happens to you, how am I going to get paid?"

She laughed. It wasn't a belly laugh or anything, but she laughed all the same. She either appreciated my sense of humor, or was succumbing to my manly charms. Quite possibly both. Hey, a guy can dream.

"The second thing we need to do is get that diary from your intern and put it somewhere safe, ASAP! Oh, there's also the matter of my fee," I added sheepishly.

Tenured professors must do ok for themselves, because Nia, I mean Dr. Lockhart, didn't bat an eye when she wrote out a check for my fee. After the formality was taken care of, we picked up the diary from her intern. I had her go over the part where the carpenter mentioned the Horn's hiding place at the temple, taking copious notes in a little Steno pad I keep handy. Then, she checked into a little motel. I was off on the case!

I think the lovely Doctor was on the right track when she went to the temple to find the artifact. She just assumed, as some academic types do, they would all be as delighted as she was to find out about the Horn, since it would make history and all, and would enthusiastically volunteer to help her find it.

I'm not saying the good doctor was stupid by any means, although I've seen many a well-educated idiot. Having book smarts does not necessarily mean you have street smarts, or even common sense. People from different walks of life have different perspectives. Dr. Lockhart lived in the world of academia. I on the other hand, lived and operated in a world with much less decorum and positive thinking. You ever hear of Murphy's Law? Whatever can go wrong, will. Well in my book, Murphy was an optimist! Not only *will* they go wrong, but it will be at the most inconvenient time and in the most inconvenient manner possible. That kind of perspective helps keep one alive on the mean streets, and serves me well as a private eye.

Nia, I mean Dr. Lockhart, assumed the monks would want to find the artifact. But what if they wanted to keep the thing a secret? I mean, the carpenter's diary made it sound like they were going to great lengths to keep the thing hidden. Just because one hundred and thirty years had gone by, didn't necessarily mean anything had changed. If that was the case, then you couldn't just ask pretty please to see the Horn. Nope, a situation like that called for a little snooping.

It just so happens, in my line of work, I do quite a bit of snooping. Over the years, I've gotten pretty good at it. The trick to a successful snoop is to appear legitimate. The easiest way to do that is to flash a badge. I'm not saying it's right, but it does make things quite a bit easier. I know what you're thinking. What reason would the police have to go sniffing around if no crime had been committed? And you're right. The police would have no reason to do something like that, but the police aren't the only ones who carry badges.

That's right. There are many state, county, and city government officials who carry badges besides the police. Hell, even department of health representatives like food inspectors carry a badge! One of the many government agencies that employ badge toting officials is the fire department. Now most people, when they hear fire department, think of the guys who ride around in the nifty red trucks and use the big hoses to put out burning buildings.

They also have people who do less glamorous jobs, like inspect buildings, and ensure they are up to fire code. It just so happens, the Tin Hau Temple is a tourist attraction. Nowhere near as popular as the Golden Gate Bridge, Fisherman's Warf, or Alcatraz, but it brings in a stream of revenue I'd wager is pretty darn important to the monks. I was also willing to bet they wanted to stay up to code, in order to keep the stream of tourists and their donations rolling in.

As luck would have it, I am in possession of just such a badge and ID that proudly proclaim, in a very convincing and official-looking manner, I am a building inspector for the San Francisco Fire Department. Under the guise of an inspector ensuring the temple was up to fire code, I would do some snooping and see if I could dig up the Horn!

The badge would get me in the door, but I didn't want to wander around aimlessly once I got there. Luckily, I had a plan. All I needed was to get my hands on the blueprints to the temple.

The blueprints to every building must be filed with the city, regardless of how old they are. Getting them is easier said than done though. It involves a lot of red tape, and as with pretty much anything that is run by the government, there is bureaucracy involved. It's not a fast and easy process.

That is, unless you have a contact on the inside with a weakness for pie! This time it was pecan pie, but more often than not, it's Boston Cream. Whatever Larry is in the mood for. It doesn't really matter to me. Whatever he asks for, I will deliver the goods. If I do, he makes things happen. Larry is a clerk down at city hall, but don't let his title fool you. The man can and will move mountains for a good Bumbleberry pie.

It's a good thing to have friends in low places sometimes.

Hmmm, I like the sound of that, it's kind of catchy! *Friends in low places.* Someone should make that into a bumper sticker or a song or something.

Anyway, Larry was able to get me the blueprints just before city hall closed. From there, I drove out to the Tin Hau Temple. It was out in San Bruno Mountain State Park, near Daly City.

I showed up at the temple just before dark, badge and blue prints at the ready. I apologized for showing up so late, announced that the temple was my last stop for the day, and flashed my badge. I walked in like I owned the place, saying that I was running behind, and wanted to get it over with quickly.

They were very accommodating, and showed me around as I asked to see smoke detectors and fire extinguishers. All the while I checked to see if there was any discrepancy between the blue prints and what I saw, that might give away the Horn's hiding place.

I must have arrived just before evening prayers, or chanting, or whatever they called it. As I stood in a large antechamber, monks in orange robes filed in from everywhere to congregate in a big chapel-like area with a huge decorative altar. Candles burned everywhere, and the room smelled of sweet incense. The monks knelt in neat, orderly rows. All was quiet for a moment, until somewhere, one of them rang a bell. That was apparently the signal for them all to start chanting, because, well, they all started chanting.

It reminded me of a scene from the TV series Kung Fu, except no David Carradine.

My guide led me away from the chapel area and down a hallway. As he walked he diligently pointed out what he thought I wanted to see. I tried to pinpoint our location on the blueprints. In doing so, I noticed an odd sized room not too far from where we were. It seemed a tad too small to be a common area, but a tad bit big for a living space, or storage area.

I excitedly deduced that it could be a hiding place for the Horn.

I stopped and pointed it out to the monk. "What is this little area here? A supply room? I'll need to see if it requires a smoke detector."

The monk smiled. "Oh, that is our Buddha. Come with me, I will show you." The monk then took me to a part of the temple that held the biggest statue I've ever seen inside of a building - a gargantuan Buddha that must have been twenty-five feet tall, and nearly as wide. It looked as if the room had been built around it, and there was a special dome to make room for its head.

It was surrounded by little burning votive candles in clear glass holders, and smoldering sticks of incense. There was also a huge assortment of flowers, some fruit, and bowls of water. I must have looked puzzled, because the monk offered a friendly explanation. "They are offerings for the Buddha."

"Well, I suppose as long as they're in those little glass containers, they don't pose much of a fire hazard." The moment the last word crossed my lips, all the soft yellow flames suddenly flared bright red.

Chapter 16

Celestial Warning

Onosai was kneeling in seiza position in front of the altar, bathed in soft candlelight, and in deep meditation. His breathing was slow and measured. He was calm and centered, slowing slipping away from his present reality. The sweet smell of the burning incense and the steady drone of his brother monks chanting faded further and further away. Before long, his consciousness would no longer be tethered to our plane of existence.

The darkness his physical eyes perceived was slowly replaced by swirling white mist as he opened up his sixth chakra, or third eye; the spiritual eye that seeks to see and know all truth, and is the center of divine wisdom. Onosai's spirit-self now followed a path through a landscape that seemed to be made up of clouds. Up ahead, there was soft golden light, though Onosai could not see its source.

As he made his way towards the light, the incline of his path increased dramatically. Soon he was ascending a long, steep, winding staircase. When he finally reached the top, he saw the source of the light. A massive structure that appeared to be a temple, or perhaps a fortress of some kind, was engulfed in flames.

A lone figure stood somberly, watching the inferno.

Onosai drew closer. As he approached, he saw that the man wore long flowing robes, like his own except that instead of orange, they were grey. He had a shaved head just as Onosai did. The two men were quite similar, except the other man appeared much older

Onosai, who was only thirty-three. Onosai greeted him warmly. "Hello friend, what is it that you are looking at?"

The old man smiled at Onosai before answering his question.

"I gaze upon the past. Hopefully not the future."

"What do you mean, sir?"

"I mean to give you a warning, Onosai."

"You seem to know me, but I do not recognize you."

"Ah, you may not recognize me, but you do know me."

"Forgive my ignorance sir. Please enlighten me."

The old man bowed. "I am Himura Hiro."

Onosai's spirit-self gasped in surprise. Grandmaster Hiro was the founder of his particular sect of the Hikari order. The younger man bowed deeply out of respect. "What is the warning, master?"

"Seek the aid of the Chosen One, for the Kagé have come for the Horn!"

Onosai's eyes snapped open. All around him his brother monks milled about in panicked confusion. The many candles that lit the room were now burning bright red, like magnesium road flares. It was the warning that someone was trying to breach the wards. The magical defenses surrounding the temple prevented hostile spells, and hostile beings of a magical nature from entering.

Onosai leapt to his feet, and bellowed, "Arm yourselves and make ready. They are coming for the Horn!"

Under cover of darkness, the war band crept up to the wall that surrounded the temple grounds. It was easily twenty feet high, but the ninja scaled it as if it were child's play.

Once on the other side, they had scarcely taken two steps when Daraku raised his hand signifying a halt. The war band immediately froze in their tracks.

Takeshi scanned the area, but saw no Hikari guards or patrols.

Motobu verbalized what he thought. In a barely audible whisper, he hissed, "Why do we stop? I see nothing."

Daraku narrowed his eyes, clearly perturbed. "They have a ward! A magical defense that prevents me from assisting you with any spells."

Motobu did not even attempt to hide the joy the wizard's words brought him. "My war band can take back the Horn without the aid of your magic."

"Master Oh-Maga disagrees, or he would not have sent me."

Takeshi intervened, before the situation got completely out of hand. "Can you defeat this ward, lord Daraku?"

In answer, Daraku's eyes rolled back in his head, showing only the whites of his eyes. He mumbled incoherently, and after a moment he stopped, his eyes returning to normal.

"Yes. There is a weakness I can exploit, but it will take time."

"We will move forward then, while you disable their defenses."

Daraku, who was dressed in the same field uniform as the ninja, withdrew a silver talisman from within the folds of his black garb.

"I will send aid once I've broken through. Try to stay alive until then, Shinobi." Daraku abruptly sat cross-legged upon the ground, and started his incantations.

The temple grounds were a massive Zen Garden with the temple proper sitting at the center. Silent as ghosts, the ninja moved stealthily past beautifully manicured trees and shrubs, little koi ponds, small islands with boulders strategically placed, and patterns raked into the sand. The beautiful garden drew many a tourist, but the ninja were immune to its charm. They slunk past in the dark, intent upon mayhem.

"Holy shit!" I jumped back in surprise as all the candles suddenly lit up like a massive red fireworks display.

I turned to my guide-monk. I hoped for some sort of explanation, but he appeared as startled as I was.

From the chapel area, someone shouted something in Chinese.

The monk's eyes widened like the devil himself had appeared out of thin air and said boo!

"What's going on?!" I demanded, as a large group of monks ran past us.

My guide just stammered unintelligibly in response.

The same group of monks who had just run past, ran back in the opposite direction. On the second pass, they were armed with an impressive assortment of swords and spears.

"What the hell?!? Tell me what's going on pal!"

He answered in a very pronounced Chinese accent. "Very dangerous! Not safe, you hide." The monk pointed to a door off to the right. "Lock door, no come out 'til we say!" Then he ran off in the direction the unarmed monks had first gone.

I stood there in stunned silence. What had I just gotten myself into?

My guide ran back down the hallway, brandishing a sword. "You hide now. Hurry!"

"Oh, don't you worry pal, I'll hide all right," I said to myself, as I drew my Colt 1911.

It looked like my instincts were right. The monks had the Horn, and those ninja were probably making a play for it. If I was lucky, I just might be able to sneak off with the Horn in the confusion. I would take precautions of course.

I racked the slide of the pistol back, and chambered a round.

Chapter 17

The Hammer and the Anvil

In a bold attempt to set up a hasty ambush, Onosai quickly marshalled the monks to either side of the large, ornate, wooden doors that adorned the main entrance to the temple. As soon as they banded together, the double doors flew open, and the ninja war band poured through like deadly baby spiders from an egg sack.

Amidst the din of crazed battle cries and the ring of steel on steel, the two groups fell upon each other.

Motobu blocked an overhead strike. His counter sliced diagonally through his adversary's chest and resulted in a crimson spray of blood. Takeshi lightly parried the thrust of a spear. He kept his sword held forward, and let his charging opponent impale himself upon his blade. Onosai quickly decapitated a ninja before he completely made it over the threshold. Then, dropping low and twisting at the hips, he swung his sword in the opposite direction, to eviscerate another.

The battle was chaos incarnate, a maelstrom of flashing steel that left a grisly trail of blood in its wake. Neither side gave quarter, intent upon wiping the other out of existence. The two forces struggled back and forth, the irresistible force contending with the immovable object.

Although the monks were not caught completely off guard, not enough of them were in position to keep the ninja out of the temple. The fight was savage. Fierce war cries intermingled with shrieks of agony as blades were plunged into torsos, and limbs were hacked completely off.

The stalwart monks fought valiantly, yet Motobu's war band proved to be more formidable. Even though the monks did not die easily, the indomitable ninja killed them all the same. It seemed as if the ninja would prevail but for Onosai, who fought more like a force of nature than a mere mortal. His blade whirled faster than the eye could follow, mowing down ninja in its wake. The master's Herculean effort bought enough time for more monks to enter the fray, until it appeared that despite their greater skills, the ninja would be overwhelmed by a sheer force of numbers.

Motobu was harried by a spear wielding monk. He blocked lightning fast thrusts with his sword, but was unable to close enough distance to counterstrike with his much shorter weapon. Then, narrowly avoiding another thrust from the monk, Motobu switched to a one-handed grip on his sword. He grabbed the haft of the spear with his free hand, immobilizing it just long enough for him to lop off the end of the monk's weapon with his sword arm.

Motobu quickly closed the distance with an overhead strike aimed at the monk's face, which the monk parried with what had just been reduced to a staff. But the monk was not quite fast enough to prevent Motobu from driving the tip of the broken spear, which he still held in his other hand, into the side of the monk's neck. It punctured the carotid artery and drew forth a geyser of blood.

In doing so however, Motobu left his flank unguarded and a monk took advantage of the opening. He cut into his left deltoid with a swipe of his sword. Motobu howled in rage, and his counter strike took off the monk's hand at the wrist. But yet another monk attacked with a spear and stabbed Motobu in his right pectoral. Incensed, he batted the spear up with his sword blade, and rushed under its point. The monk tried to back pedal away, but Motobu was faster, and ran him through with his sword.

Then, using the dying monk as a shield, Motobu charged forward and bowled over a group of three monks who were clustered together. They fell in a tangle of limbs. Before they could right themselves, Motobu beheaded one and stabbed another through the chest. He would have dispatched the third as well, if not for his fellow monks coming to his aid.

Motobu's berserker advance was checked and outnumbered. He was driven back, slashed down his right forearm, and under his left eye.

Takeshi's fighting style was almost the polar opposite of Motobu's. Where Motobu was savage strikes and overpowering blows, Takeshi was deceptive feints and false openings that lead to lethal counters. After beheading a foe, Takeshi stayed frozen a fraction of a second longer than he needed at the end of his movement. He appeared overextended. A monk took the bait, and rushed in for the kill. Takeshi swept the monk's blade aside with a circular motion, giving himself just enough opening to snap his own blade back inward, slicing open the monk's jugular. The monk dropped his sword. He clutched instinctively at his throat in a futile effort to staunch the flow of blood which poured past his fingers, and out his open mouth.

Shouting a battle cry, another monk thrust a spear at Takeshi's head. Takeshi barely had time to move his sword blade up, redirecting the spear tip an inch to the right. He received a nasty gash along the side of his head, but avoided being skewered. Then, Takeshi rushed in, his sword blade riding the inside of the monk's spear, and embedding itself in the monk's eye socket. Several more monks rushed in, and Takeshi was forced back until he was next to Motobu, the only other ninja left standing.

Onosai had just run a ninja through with his blade, and looked up to see the only two enemies remaining. The pair was slowly making their way to the temple doors, to their escape. Without hesitation, Onosai sprinted to the doors, and slammed them shut with a resounding boom that echoed throughout the temple. Then, taking a key from within the folds of his robe, he quickly locked them.

Everyone froze, and the room fell deathly quiet.

Motobu broke the silence. "It would seem there is no escape for you now little monks! Who shall I slay first?!"

The group of monks that stood before him remained frozen in place, none too eager to face Motobu.

"Come now, don't be shy. Hurry to meet death before your place is taken!" He added in a barely audible whisper to Takeshi, "Guard my back while I get the key." Motobu pointed his sword towards Onosai. "How about you then? You seem to have the spine your brothers lack. I challenge you to single combat, monk!"

Onosai calmly strode forward in response.

"You do have backbone, very good. What is your name monk?"

"I am Master Onosai, of the Hikari. What is yours, Shinobi?"

"I am Master Motobu, Hammer of the Kagé."

With a calm demeanor, looking as if he were about to take a stroll in the gardens, rather than preparing to engage in mortal combat, Onosai took a few steps forward. "Give us room brothers. Witness the hammer as it shatters upon the anvil."

Beneath his mask, Motobu wore the fierce grin of a predator. *Finally, a warrior worthy of testing my mettle against.*

The monks did as Onosai instructed and formed a ring around the two combatants. Meanwhile Takeshi, unnoticed, slowly inched his way towards the doors.

The two men advanced upon each other but stopped short, just out of their weapons' respective reach. Then, as if on cue, the warriors bowed to each other in unison. Although their eyes never left one another's, mutual respect was evident in the gesture. The two stood, staring in silence for a moment, and then suddenly, the fight was on.

Motobu was the aggressor, immediately pressing the attack with a flurry of strikes aimed alternately at the left and right sides of his adversary's head.

Onosai parried and countered in turn, and the pair circled each other. Each rained blows and counters upon the other in rapid succession, too fast for the audience of monks to follow.

Then Onosai, changing levels, suddenly dropped low and scored a strike on Motobu's leg, slicing into his left quadriceps.

Motobu ignored the wound, and struck out at Onosai's head, but the Hikari master parried the blow, and rolled clear. Motobu pursued, lashing out with his sword, but again the monk was ready, blocking and countering. The exchange continued for a few passes.

Motobu initiated attacks that culminated in nothing more than the clanging of swords. Onosai blocked, countered, and disengaged each time, forcing Motobu to shift and place weight on his wounded leg.

Soon the tactic paid off, and Motobu was forced to favor his wounded leg. Onosai pressed his advantage and launched a flurry of strikes that Motobu, with his injury, was not able to propel himself away from in time. Although he managed to block three of the lightning fast blows, the fourth slipped past his guard and laid open his left forearm.

Motobu knew he could not afford to fight Onosai's fight. He had to switch tactics, and soon. Bellowing a war cry, he rushed in like a bull and threw an attack he knew the monk would have to deal with, for the sole purpose of closing distance and catching his opponent in the bind.

It became a grapple, and Motobu, having superior leverage, disarmed his opponent. He smiled triumphantly beneath his mask. "Well fought Onosai, but it is over."

At the prospect of losing one's sword, facing a larger, stronger opponent, most men would have panicked and retreated. Master Onosai pressed in closer and jammed his thumb into Motobu's eye. Then, taking advantage of his unbalanced opponent, reaped his legs out from under him.

Onosai followed him to the ground, knife in hand. "Yes, it is over. Farewell Motobu." Without another word, Onosai plunged the knife into the ninja master's jugular.

Onosai sprung back to his feet. He faced Takeshi, and calmly uttered, "Thus perishes the Hammer of the Kagé."

Takeshi was at the temple doors, and attempted to pick the lock. He turned to face Onosai and the other monks, sword in one hand, the other behind his back trying to pick the lock.

Onosai's voice was not loud, but held the authority of a teacher addressing a pupil. "It is too late for escape, Shinobi, but there is no need for you to die. Throw down your weapon, and surrender. We will spare your life."

Takeshi made a show of tossing his sword into the air, catching it by the blade, and presenting it handle-first toward the monks. All the while, he clutched a smoke pellet in his free hand. It was a small glass bead, not much larger than a child's marble. When it struck something with enough force, it would explode; the glass shattering, and mixing its contents in the process, causing a chain reaction, igniting the smoke element.

Takeshi threw the pellet against the temple's stone floor, and was lost in the resultant billowing cloud of smoke. Just then, the temple doors exploded inward.

Chapter 18

Oni

A nightmare from the depths of hell burst into the room, smashing the heavy oak doors of the temple into kindling in the process.

The hideous beast was over nine feet tall. It had a powerful build not unlike that of a silverback gorilla with its heavily muscled arms longer than its legs. The Oni was hairless, with brown and grey skin the color of rotting meat. It had fingers that ended in wicked curved talons more than eight inches long. They looked capable of shredding concrete. Its head was vaguely canine, with a snout, except its maw opened impossibly wide, revealing rows of teeth like a shark's, nearly as long as it's claws.

The thing had several eyes, all lidless and red, burning with hate.

The demon charged forward. A swipe of its claws nearly cut a monk in two, spilling his intestines onto the floor.

Lightning fast, it snatched another monk in its claws and pulled him in close. It bit down savagely on the monk's head and shook him violently back and forth like a dog with a chew toy. The monk's head ripped free, and those nearby were covered in gore.

Screaming in terror, the remaining monks scattered.

I rummaged through the temple, looking for the Horn's hiding place. I used the blueprints as a guide. Several times I had to hide as monks rushed to join in the fight. I could hear the battle rage in the distance. It made one hell of a racket, but I was grateful for the distraction.

It's much easier to snoop around, when you don't have to worry about being quiet.

Despite the fact the monks were distracted, I was coming up empty. According to the blueprints, the only place likely for the secret room mentioned in the carpenter's diary seemed to be the area where the statue of the Buddha was. I started making my way back in that direction. The sound of running footsteps forced me to duck down a hallway to avoid detection.

They still seemed to follow me, so I made a mad dash for the nearest door.

I found myself in a dining area, with long tables and bench seats. I heard the footsteps close behind, and ran out another doorway at the opposite end of the room.

I didn't stop. Instead I sped up; weaving in and out of entryways, diving through doors, and sprinting down a couple of hallways until I was sure of two things. First, I was no longer being followed. Second, I had become hopelessly lost.

As I made my down a long corridor, I noticed I could no longer hear the sounds of battle. I must have wandered too far away, or it had ended.

The corridor ended at a closed door. I turned the knob gently to see if it was locked. It wasn't, so I slowly pulled it open, just a crack. I put my face right up next to it and looked to see what was waiting on the other side.

It seemed I had made my way back to the other side of the temple. Through the crack in the door, I saw the opposite end of the large antechamber in front of the chapel area, where I had originally entered the temple. By that time, it was littered with corpses.

Several dozen dead monks and ninja lay strewn about the floor in grisly poses. There was blood everywhere. There must have been close to a hundred dead bodies.

The monks had apparently come out on top, because about twenty of them still stood, and had backed one last ninja up against the big double doors that led to the garden outside.

One of the monks said something in Chinese. It looked like the ninja was surrendering as he flipped his sword around, and started to hand it to the monk handle-first.

It was a trick though! He threw something on the ground with his other hand and disappeared in a cloud of smoke, like a stage magician. Except when the smoke cleared, it wasn't a scantily clad magician's assistant standing in his place.

It was...

The reporter switched off the tape recorder. "Mr. Jones, are you ok? You're as white as a ghost."

"Yeah, but no... some things you see, you wish you could *unsee.*"

The reporter looked sympathetic. "My police contact said it was an especially gruesome crime scene; the worst he'd ever seen.

He's a twenty-year veteran, not some rookie fresh from the academy. People getting hacked to pieces with swords? It couldn't have been easy to watch. We can take a break if you want."

"That's not it, Mack. Sorry, I mean Mark. Maybe for this next part the tape recorder should stay off." I could see curiosity warring with sympathy on the reporter's face.

"Did you want to share something off the record?"

"This police contact of yours. Did he say anything about the crime scene not making any sense?"

The reporter leaned a bit closer. "Maybe..." Mark's voice was nonchalant, but his body language radiated eagerness and excitement.

"Like some of the victim's wounds were inconsistent with injuries sustained from bladed weapons?"

Mark froze.

"Did he say some of the bodies looked like they'd been mauled by some sort of wild animal?"

Mark didn't say a thing, but from the look on his face, it was obvious his police contact told him exactly that.

"Do you mind if I call you Mac? It seems to fit you better somehow. Besides, every Mark I know is an asshole. You seem like a nice guy."

The reporter smiled. "Sure, Mr. Jones, you can call me Mac."

"Good. Then Mac, call me Gideon. Mr. Jones makes me nervous. Feels like I just ran a red light, or I'm late on my taxes or something."

"Ok, Gideon it is."

"Mac, do I seem like a normal guy to you?"

"Normal is subjective, but yes, you seem normal enough."

"I don't seem like some wild eyed crazy who's gone off the deep end?"

"No, you don't seem crazy."

"Do I seem like a stress monkey who's only half a banana away from going ape shit?"

"What?"

"Like I'm not crazy *yet,* but I'm in the neighborhood. I can *see it* from where I'm standing."

"You mean, do you seem so stressed out it looks like you could be on the verge of a nervous breakdown or a psychotic episode?"

"Yeah, like I haven't snapped, but the rubber band sure is stretched awfully far."

"No Gideon, you don't seem like a man on the edge about to lose it. Where are you going with all of this?"

"In my line of work, I've seen it all Mac. I've seen the good, the bad, and the ugly. None of it prepared me for what I saw when the smoke cleared. I'm not crazy, and I wanted to make sure you knew that, because what I saw that night *was* crazy. Not funny crazy, or odd and puzzling crazy. No. It was the stuff of nightmares crazy. The kind of shit that could make a man lose his grip on sanity."

"What did you see?"

"When a man sees something like what I saw, he's not really over-eager to share because most people will write him off as a grade-A nut bag. Nothing good ever comes of that."

"I think we've already established you're not crazy, Gideon."

"I haven't told you what I saw yet, Mac."

"Go ahead, I'm listening."

"Off the record? No tape recorder?"

"Off the record. The recorder stays off."

I closed my eyes and tried not to shiver. It all came flooding back. The thing was massive, maybe ten feet tall, and it ripped through the heavy oak doors like toilet paper. It had arms like King Kong on steroids, but they ended in claws that would have made Freddy Krueger jealous. And the face… My God, that face. That thing was uglier than a warthog's mother-in-law. Imagine Dr. Frankenstein shaved a werewolf and somehow unhinged its jaw, so that it could open it wider than a hippo's. Its teeth were as long as butcher knives. Instead of two eyes, the thing had more like ten, all over its head, all red, and eerie as hell.

The monster started tearing the monks apart, literally.

It tore out one of the monk's guts with its claws as easily as you or I might tear into a glob of jello. Then it bit another monk's head clean off. The poor guys tried to make a run for it, but the thing was just too fast. It chased them down, tearing and rending with its terrible claws.

One monk almost made it the door I was hiding behind. When he got close, I recognized him as my guide from earlier, the one who told me to run and hide. He had almost made it to me, when the monster grabbed him by the ankle, and dragged him back. The creature lifted him into the air, and dangled him over its open mouth like an hors d'erve. The look of sheer terror on the monk's face, it got to me.

This gentle soul who gladly showed me around the temple, regardless of the late hour, good natured and smiling – about to meet his end in the jaws of some living-horror, eaten alive. It was too much. I just snapped I guess. I couldn't stay cowering behind a door while some nightmare from hell ravaged those poor holy-men.

Before I even realized what I was doing, I had my 1911 out in front of me in a two handed grip, advancing as I put round after round into the thing's chest.

I don't think I managed to hurt it too badly, but I sure as hell pissed it off. The thing dropped the monk and charged me, mouth open, roaring.

That thing's roar might give me nightmares for the rest of my life. I can't liken it to anything I've ever heard before. It was creepy beyond words. It was unnatural, unnerving as all hell, and it made my blood run cold.

Certain that I was about to die, I planted my feet and took aim at its head. That's when everything went all slow-mo. Time grinded to a halt, and my universe narrowed down to the front sight of my pistol, centered neatly between my rear sights.

I had good sight alignment.

Forcing myself to ignore the charging monstrosity, I took half a heartbeat, and aimed. I placed my front sight dead center on one of its menacing red eyes.

I had good sight picture.

I smoothly squeezed the trigger. The report and recoil of the gun barely registered. My laser focus was on that one, big, disturbing red eye. My focus paid off. My aim was true, and the eye exploded like a nasty pus-filled pimple.

Chapter 19

Hounded

The monster howled in pain, and reflexively brought one hand up to its face covering the ruined eye, while simultaneously swinging a vicious back handed strike at me with the other hand.

I saw it coming, and leapt backwards to avoid the blow. The thing was just too damned fast, and although I avoided the brunt of the wallop, it managed to clip me with its finger-tips.

Thank God it was just a glancing blow, because it felt like I'd been rammed by a semi-truck! I think a full force punch from the thing would've been fatal. Even though the thing only hit me with its fingers, the force of it still knocked me off my feet, and sent me sailing through the air.

I crashed through the jagged remnants of the double doors. The monster may have torn through them like paper, but they seemed pretty damn solid to me.

I felt a searing pain down my left arm as a foot-long splinter ripped open my shirt sleeve. I collided with the shattered mess, and kept on going.

From there, my Judo training took over. I tucked my chin to my chest and exhaled, relaxing my body. I prepared to slap down with my arms to help absorb some of the energy of the fall, and thereby lessen the impact. In Judo, this whole falling down business is called ukemi, a Japanese word which translated into English, means break-falling, or breaking ones fall. I've taken more falls in my judo training than I can count. The very first thing they teach you in Judo, is how to fall, and you never stop practicing.

It makes sense, since a big portion of the art is off balancing your opponent, and then throwing him. If you're going to practice that over and over, you'd better train yourself to fall properly. Do it in such a way it minimizes the impact when you hit the ground, so as not to injure yourself. Believe me, the ground can hit you a heck of a lot harder than a punch or kick, if you don't know how to fall right. Good thing for me, I do know how to fall right.

I'm grateful for adrenaline and endorphins, because I've never been hit so hard, or thrown so high and fast in my life!

If I had not fallen correctly, I would have been a mangled heap of broken bones! Even though my ukemi is good, and I fell correctly as I've trained to do, it still hurt like hell! At least my training ultimately resulted in nothing being fractured, splintered, ruptured, or snapped.

I laid on the ground for a second or two, feeling very much like a bug who'd just smacked into the windshield of a car going a hundred miles per hour. I would have liked nothing more than to have laid there quite a bit longer, but as my eyes re-focused, I saw that hideous behemoth coming for me. Just to make things worse, somewhere between the shambling monstrosity and the forty odd feet it had sent me sailing through the air, I'd lost my handgun.

I didn't want to pick myself back up again. Being back handed forty feet through a set of big wooden doors, not only hurts, but it takes a lot out of you.

At some point, *way back when*, our ancestors knew what it was like to have to run or fight for their lives on a daily basis. Now there's something primal hard-wired down deep in all of us.

Seeing a ten-foot-tall, one-thousand-pound nightmare of muscle, claws, and teeth, rekindled that in me. I'm not talking about motivation, or digging down deep for will power. What I'm talking about isn't mental, it's physical.

There are certain automatic physical responses that can help you survive a dangerous situation. Your nervous system kicks into high gear, speeding up your reflexes, and heightening your senses. Your heart rate and blood pressure increase, delivering adrenaline and thirty other different hormones to do things like: dilate your eyes, allowing you to take in as much light as possible to sharpen your sight, or relax your smooth muscles, allowing your lungs to take in more oxygen than normal.

Non-essential systems, like your immune and digestive systems, shut down to allow more energy to be directed to your muscles, giving you more strength and speed - sometimes near super human levels. It's what enables a hundred and ten-pound mother to lift a three-thousand-pound car off their child in an emergency, or in my case, to pick myself back up after being flung forty feet, and run at nearly thirty miles per hour!

I tore through the garden as fast as an Olympic sprinter, weaved through trees and shrubs, and hurdled over small boulders. The creature ripped after me, smashing its way through obstacles I'd just dodged around, barely taking notice of them.

It was something straight out of a nightmare, racing through a dark forest with the boogey man hot on your heels, coming to get you.

I made it to the garden's decorative wrought-iron gate. It was at least twelve-feet high, and locked shut. I scaled it like a monkey, barely slowing down.

When I reached the top, I risked a backwards glance. The beast was almost on me. I leapt off the gate, instead of climbing down. I made sure to launch myself forward, knees towards my chest, and hands up. I made sure to plot out my landing.

I landed on the balls of my feet, bent my knees, tucked my head, and curled my shoulder. I let my forward momentum turn into a forward roll. I came out of the roll at full sprint. The monster smashed through the gate an instant later. The phrase 'running for your life', just doesn't have the impact that it should. Modern man has been at the top of the food chain for too long. He no longer has any idea what it's like to be hunted. It has been ages since man was terrified prey, run down by some voracious predator. I, however, was very much the frightened rabbit trying to get away from the big bad wolf, except I had no cozy rabbit hole to dive down.

We were in the parking lot in front of the temple, which was empty except for my car. As I ran towards my trusted ride with a nightmare intent on tearing me to bloody pieces in hot pursuit, my mind raced even faster than my legs. Odds were, I wouldn't have time to start the car before that thing was on top of me. The way it tore through the heavy wood doors of the temple, and the wrought iron gate, I seriously doubted my driver side window would pose much of a barrier to it as I tried to turn my key in the ignition.

I kept a twelve-gauge shot gun in my trunk sometimes, though. You never know when a little extra fire power'll come in handy.

I had my keys in my hand, desperately hoping it would be there. I didn't always bring it along, and I honestly didn't remember if I had it in there or not.

"Please be there, please be there," I wheezed as I turned the key and flung open the trunk.

The demon roared. It was so close, I felt the heat of its breath on the back of my neck, and the stench of blood assaulted my nostrils. My stomach clenched up tighter than a balled-up fist, and my heart sank when I saw that the shotgun wasn't there.

I should probably clarify at this point, that my trunk wasn't empty. It just didn't contain the Remington 870 Wingmaster, pump action, 12-gauge shotgun, loaded with slugs I was hoping for. What I saw instead, was my grandfather's old Ithaca Auto & Burglar. A double barrel sawed off shotgun with a pistol grip. It was a badass-looking, but mostly harmless antique from the 1920's. It was loaded with rock salt, a non-lethal load I used for scare tactics.

My blood ran cold.

I was about to die.

Until I'd shot it in the eye, the thing shrugged off .45 ACP rounds - ammunition specifically chosen by the American military for its stopping power. What was a little rock salt going to do?

I felt one of the demon's massive hands clamp down on me like a vise, and I snatched up the shotgun by reflex. It was a futile gesture, but if that was the end, I would go down swinging.

As the beast drew me towards its gaping maw, full of razor sharp teeth, I shot it point blank in the face.

What happened next, I didn't see coming.

The demon's face melted like I had dumped a bucket of hydrochloric acid on it. It dropped me and shrieked hideously.

I took my opening, and shot it once more, but that time the load hit center mass. Once again, the rock salt ate right through it, and left a basketball-sized hole in the demon's chest that bubbled around the edges.

The monster collapsed in a crumpled, foul smelling heap. Sickening, purplish-black fluids oozed everywhere. It smelled like one part septic tank, and two parts burning hair. I fought back the urge to wretch, and loaded two more shells into the Ithaca Auto & Burglar. I didn't know if there were any more of those things running around, but better safe than sorry.

A loud crackling noise like downed power lines coming from the garden caught my attention, it was followed by cries of agony.

I looked forward to facing one of those monsters again about as much as a root canal with no Novocain. But apparently rock salt was their Achilles heel. If I slinked off with my tail between my legs instead of trying to help, and people died as a result? I couldn't live with something like that.

So I grabbed a handful of rock salt shotgun shells, and stuffed them in my pocket.

Then, clutching the Auto & Burglar like a teddy bear, I ran back towards the screaming.

Chapter 20

The Devastation of Daraku

As I made it back to the ruined temple doors, there was a ghostly green light that flickered inside. The crackling sounds of electricity and screams were much louder.

I paused just outside the doorway and took a deep breath, as if steeling myself to take a plunge into ice water. Then, raising the shotgun, I burst around the corner.

Now, even though I'd just seen a freaking monster, I still wasn't ready for what was waiting for me inside.

Picture, if you will, Emperor Palpatine guest starring in a kung fu theatre episode. That's pretty much what I walked into. A bearded ninja strolled boldly through the temple, and shot green lightning out of his hands at terrified monks. They tried to charge at him with swords or spears, only to get zapped.

The ninja's back was to me, so he didn't see my grand entrance. By the time I got in, he was about to disappear down the hall towards the giant statue of the Buddha.

After seeing what the guy had done to the monks, I did my best to quietly stalk him, rather than rush in pell-mell.

I crept down the hallway. *Think stealthy thoughts, Gideon.* I turned the corner like a Special Forces operative.

I found a group of monks who were making a last stand in front of the giant Buddha statue. They hurled spears at the bearded ninja, who somehow swatted them out of the air long before they reached him. All he needed to do was gesture with his hands. He moved fast. In answer to their attacks, he shot his green lightning like a Sith master.

One particularly agile monk dodged a lightning strike. But the others were not quite as fast, and the bearded ninja took two of them down.

Then, the faster, more agile monk, whipped out a couple of fans with highly reflective surfaces, almost like mirrors. He used the fans to deflect the bearded ninja's lightning attacks. Whenever the bearded ninja shot at him, the monk used the fans to block, and the deadly green bolts merely bounced off the reflective surface of the fans.

At that point, the tide of battle turned. No matter which monk the bearded ninja would shoot lightning at, the monk with the mirror fans would leap to intercept. The remaining monks had the freedom to throw spears.

The bearded ninja was forced to stop his lightning attacks, and focus on defense against the incoming spears, a task which he was barely able to accomplish. A few throws nearly got through to him!

Harried, he was slowly being driven back. It looked as if the monks would win the day.

Suddenly, another ninja appeared out of nowhere, and attacked the monks from behind. In an instant, he had cut two of the monks down, but the fan monk again came to the rescue, and checked the ninja's sneak attack. Fans folded, the agile monk managed to block the ninja's sword blows. Whatever those fans were made of, it was sturdy stuff!

The fan-monk and the ninja went at each other the way ravenous wolves battled over a fresh kill. It was something to behold. Their skill was nothing short of amazing. They moved like they were equal parts martial arts master, gymnast, and highly caffeinated spider monkey!

While the two battled, the bearded ninja eliminated the remaining three monks with his lightning. Callously, he stepped over the still smoldering bodies, and calmly sauntered over to the giant statue of the Buddha. He stopped just inches short of bumping into it, and closely examined it for a moment.

He produced a piece of chalk from a well-hidden pocket in his ninja uniform, and drew a circle around himself on the floor.

Once this was done, he spread his arms wide, tilted his head back, and started shouting. His eyes rolled back so only the whites were showing. It was sinister as hell! The shouting, by the way, wasn't in Japanese or Chinese. In fact, I don't know what language it was, but it was harsh sounding and guttural. Although I couldn't understand it, somehow it seemed, I don't know: wicked, corrupt, *perverse!*

The bearded ninja was incredibly loud, as if he was bellowing into an invisible boom mike. It grew louder and louder. We were indoors, but somehow a sudden and powerful gust of wind swept in, and extinguished all the candles. The peculiar green glow that emanated from the bearded ninja grew in brightness. As it did so, cracks started to appear on the statue of the Buddha, and slowly spread outwards like a growing spider web.

When the bearded ninja's chanting grew louder, the other ninja broke off from his battle. He threw something on the ground and disappeared in a cloud of white smoke, like a stage magician.

That was when the place started to shake, as if caught in a powerful earthquake. Even though we were indoors, a thick fog rolled in along the floor and began to coalesce into a dark cloud around the statue of the Buddha, until the piece was obscured from view.

It quickly darkened until there was a billowing black cloud of smoke that crackled with green lightning. Rays of pale green light pierced the dark cloud, followed by a multicolored ball of yellow and green flame that belched upward. A writhing column of smoke trailed behind it. It smashed through the ceiling, like a massive fist of green fire, and punched its way out of the building.

An enormous boom reverberated through the room like a dozen thunder claps. Windows shattered. Dust, ash, and debris rained down.

I realized I was on my back, and my ears rang like I'd just fired a fifty-caliber machine gun without hearing protection. The bearded ninja was completely unaffected by the explosion, as if he'd been behind some sort of invisible shield. Whatever it was, it must've inadvertently protected me as well. By all rights, an explosion like that should have killed me.

The bearded ninja was still unaware of my presence, and was fixated on the smoking ruin of the exploded Buddha. He stalked towards the shattered shell of the statue, a fiendish expression across his face.

He stooped over, and sifted through the ruble. Suddenly he burst into a fit of crazed laughter. It made a cackle from a wicked witch seem cheery and lighthearted in comparison.

He held up a huge conch shell, encrusted with sparkling gems somehow unmarred by the explosion, high over his head in triumph.

It was the Horn of Ryujin!

He stood there, arms raised high, completely absorbed in his moment of triumph. He was totally unaware of me, sprawled on the floor at his feet. I took advantage of his distraction, and leveled the shotgun at him.

The instant he turned around, I shot him square in the face.

He didn't melt like the creature did. Being shot at point blank range with rock salt, although not fatal, will ruin your entire day.

The bearded ninja was knocked off his feet. He dropped the Horn and shrieked. Clutching his face, he rolled around in agony.

Meanwhile, I scrambled to my feet, rushed forward, and scooped up the Horn.

The shrieks of agony turned into a roar of outrage.

I spun around. The ninja's face was a bloody mess. I can only imagine how the salt must have burned. Judging by the murderous look in his eyes, it was quite a bit.

I wasn't quite sure if he was snarling in anger, or grimacing in pain. It was probably both, and for half a heartbeat, I started to feel sorry for him. Then green sparks began to drop from his fingertips, like he was gearing up for one of his lightning strikes. So I shot him again, right in the groin.

I don't care how much of a Billy Badass you are, no guy is such a badass he can ignore being shot in the balls.

At least that was the plan.

I know I pointed the shotgun at his package and pulled the trigger. I remember the roar of the shotgun. Suddenly, there was this very strong tingling sensation throughout my body. It quickly escalated into a burning sensation. My body was racked by instantaneous and impossibly strong and painful muscle cramps. I convulsed uncontrollably. I might have heard a buzzing or crackling sound, and I think I smelled something burning, but it was all secondary to the unbearable searing pain.

It seemed as if an army of fire ants were eating me alive.

The agony was unbearable, but it didn't last long. Everything went mercifully black.

Chapter 21

The Flavor of Magic

I was lying down. Of that, I was fairly sure. I was aware of very little else. When I came to, I felt like I'd just stunt doubled for the side of beef Sylvester Stallone beat in Rocky. Except that the ninja decided to mix things up a bit, and switched from his fists to a sledgehammer!

Every inch of me hurt.

Hell, even my hair was in pain.

The soreness that possessed me was complete. If I moved ever so slightly, it came crashing down like a giant sumo wrestler with rocks in his pockets.

So I just laid there, perfectly still for a while.

I worked up enough energy to crack open one of my eyelids, and instantly regretted it. Light felt like searing flames that shot through to my brain, ushering in a headache that made me completely forget my soreness. The body aches paled in comparison, and my headache sneered contemptuously at their feeble attempt to deliver pain.

Well, it appeared as if moving and looking around were out the question for the time being, so I concentrated on listening.

As soon as I expanded my awareness beyond my own suffering, I became cognizant of voices. They were too faint to make out at first, but as I concentrated, I was able to discern people whispering. They were having an argument. That seemed odd. Most arguments I had witnessed were conducted with raised voices, not whispers. They must have thought I was still out cold, and didn't want to wake me. I took advantage of their error, and played possum to gather intel on my situation.

"The prophecy is a myth, brother! A fairy tale told to children! It isn't real."

"Just like magic and demons? You saw the mark. How do you explain that?"

"It is a tattoo he probably chose because he liked its appearance, nothing more."

I had a tattoo of an American bald eagle and a dragon on my upper left arm. It must have been what they were talking about. I had seen dragon and tiger tattoos, but wanted my own special variation. To me, the dragon symbolized the spirit of the Asian martial arts I studied, and the eagle symbolized the badassness of America. The guy was right, it looked pretty darned cool. But I had no idea about any prophecy.

"And how do you explain that he was here when the Kagé attacked? That he killed a demon? That he was aware of the Horn's existence, and fought to protect it? No brother, it is too much to be mere coincidence. He is the Chosen One the prophecy spoke of."

I heard footsteps approach my bedside. "He is awake."

I cracked my eyelids open a bit, and winced against the too bright light. Everything was blurry. I shifted ever so slightly, and as my aching body protested the slight movement, an involuntary groan escaped my lips.

"Lay still, you have nothing to fear. You are among friends.
I am Master Onosai, and you sir, are no mere fire marshal."

I forced my eyes open and blinked rapidly. I toughed out the
discomfort until things came into focus. When they did, I recognized
the fan monk I'd seen fight earlier. That dude was a grade-A badass!
I wanted to stay on his good side.

"You are no mere monk, sir." I said as I struggled to sit up. Or
at least that is what I meant to say. It came out, "Aaa uur nn mmm
mmm uk rrr."

Onosai put a restraining hand on my shoulder. "Please remain
in bed a bit longer. Rest, and regain your strength." He turned to the
other monk who I recognized as my tour guide from earlier.

"Brother Lin, please bring our guest some tea." The monk
bowed and left the room. I was grateful for the hospitality, but I the
last thing I remembered was fighting the bearded ninja for the Horn.
What had happened to it?

"Horn… bearded ninja," I managed to rasp.

Onosai gave me a sympathetic smile as he stood by my
bedside. "Please wait until Brother Lin returns with the tea before
speaking friend." He then stared off into space for a moment before
he spoke. Several expressions played briefly across his face as
different emotions were warring for dominance within him. First
there was concern, then anger, regret, and lastly one of resolve. "The
wizard took the Horn. We have failed as keepers of the Horn. But
then, we did not know it had other protectors. Perhaps all is not lost!
Do you have a plan to regain it, Chosen One?"

"Ummmm, what?" My reply was indeed eloquent.

Then Brother Lin returned with the tea, and I was saved from the awkward moment as he handed me a cup.

I sipped gingerly at first, then gulped it down greedily. The stuff was amazing! Not only did it taste good, and soothed my dry throat, but it somehow eased my pain. It felt like super-fast acting, extra-extra strength aspirin. It even gave me a bit of a buzz.

"This tea is fantastic! Thank you!"

The monks smiled at the compliment. Then they stared at me expectantly, but said and did nothing.

The silence stretched on, and grew more and more uncomfortable, until I felt I simply must speak. "My name is Gideon Jones. I'm a private investigator. I've been hired to find the Horn of Ryujin. During my investigation I ran afoul of the ninja."

Onosai interjected. "You were the one at the university with the camera?"

Now, how the hell would he know that?! Wait a minute! Of course! The monks must have been the ones in grey that the ninja fought against. It was starting to make more sense. "Yes, that was me. After my run-in with the ninja, I was realized they had no qualms with murdering innocent bystanders to keep their presence a secret. To say these are bad men is an understatement. Of course, I had no problem siding with you against them in a fight. In my line of work, I've had to deal with bad men before. The Yakuza are not unique in their willingness to murder innocents. Neither the Triads' nor the Mafia's hands are clean of innocent blood. But that *thing* that tore through the doors, what the hell was that!? And the guy with the beard who could shoot lightning? What on earth is going on here!?

What is this talk of a prophecy, and me being the Chosen One? I swear to God, I have no idea what you are talking about."

Brother Lin gave Onosai the classic 'I told you so' look, but Onosai seemed unfazed. He calmly turned to Lin and said, "Brother, would you please excuse us? I need to speak to Mr. Jones in private."

Without saying a word, Lin bowed and left the room.

Onosai turned to me, and with the same demeanor one might use to discuss the weather said. "The answer to your question is simple, Mr. Jones. Magic."

"Magic?"

"Yes, magic. You were there. You experienced it firsthand. You fought both the demon and the wizard. How would *you* explain it?"

I opened my mouth for a snappy retort, but stopped short. How else *could* this mess be explained?

"Magic has always been with us. It is how this world, and the life on it, came into being. In ages past, man understood and accepted this simple fact. But that changed as mankind learned more of the realm of science. Knowledge of magic was slowly forgotten. Magic became legend and then myth. Now mankind is so enamored with science, until he can explain magic using science, he will continue to stubbornly deny its existence. Mankind has an uncanny ability to ignore inconvenient truths that are contrary to his belief system. Look how we once clung tenaciously to the belief the world was flat. Even after you experienced it, your first instinct was to deny it, and explain it away somehow. Those who operate inside the world of magic, know this kneejerk reaction, and exploit it. In fact, they rely heavily upon it. They know that if anyone tried to make society acknowledge the inconvenient and disturbing truths that you experienced firsthand tonight, without irrefutable proof, they would be labeled insane, and no longer be accepted or allowed to operate within society."

I sat there in silence as the truth of what he was saying hit home. There were things that went bump in the night. Everyone knew it on some level, but no one ever talked about it, except in ghost stories. Come to think of it, almost everyone had a ghost story, or knew someone who had one. It really is a proverbial jungle out there, and we are not at the top of the food chain. But if I ever *really* tried to tell anybody in earnest, they'd lock me up in the loony bin.

"Do not judge mankind too harshly. Some things are hard to explain, and are better experienced. How do you adequately explain the flavor of pistachio ice cream to someone who has never tasted it? You can tell them it has a similar flavor to the nut, but it is cold, sweet, and creamy. All of this is true, but do they know what it tastes like? Can they ever know without tasting it?" He let that sink in for a bit. "It is the same with magic. You can tell someone about it, and explain it in as much detail as you like, but until they experience it for themselves, they will never fully understand." He produced a large scroll from the folds of his robes. "You however, have already experienced it, and so, you are ready for a more detailed explanation than most."

He unrolled the scroll and motioned for me to look.

I did so, and saw the ornate oriental calligraphy, but as I am unable to read kanji I had no idea what it said. "I'm sorry, but I can't read kanji."

Onosai smiled, "And so it is for those who have not experienced magic, but you have. Look again, more closely this time."

It was an odd request and I said as much.

"Look Onosai, I mean no disrespect, but no matter how long I stare at the scroll, I won't be able to read kanji."

His smile broadened. "Humor me Mr. Jones."

I sighed, but did as he asked, and took another look at the scroll. To my surprise, as I did so, the symbols began to swirl, and reformed themselves from kanji, into the Roman alphabet. Moreover, it was in English, so I could read them. I gasped in amazement. "I can read it now! How did you do that!?"

"As I said Mr. Jones, magic. Now keep your focus on the scroll."

I did as I was asked, and stared at the scroll again. As I did so, the letters on the paper began to swirl once more, but they did not reform into different letters. This time they formed a picture instead. It was a picture of an oriental temple. It was incredibly vivid, and had more detail than any drawing or painting I'd ever seen. It seemed more vivid and real than a photograph. As I continued to stare, the world around me swirled like a psychedelic kaleidoscope, but the picture of the temple remained unaffected. My reality slipped away. I could no longer see Onosai, or the room I was in a moment before.

I was suddenly standing on a beach. Above me was the temple, perched high upon a cliff next to the sea. Only I wasn't standing, I was incorporeal. I started to float upward on the air, approaching the temple.

I started to panic, and I heard the voice of Onosai inside my head.

Relax Gideon. You are in no danger. Think of this as the ultimate movie, only you can do more than see and hear; you can smell, feel, and taste. You can even tell what people are thinking. This is Kanagawa Monastery. It was where the Kagé clan, the ninja with whom we fought last, first tried to take the Horn of Ryujin from the Hikari, my order. I need to give you some much needed perspective on you are caught up in. You must not enter this struggle blindly. You must learn of the prophecy.

Scroll II
Clan War

Chapter 22

Training & Discipline

Kanagawa Monastery, near Yokohama Harbor, Japan

1854

Hiro paused to catch his breath. The trek up the monastery steps was long and arduous.

The setting sun slowly slipped beneath the horizon, its last rays splashed blood red stains across the dark clouds as if mortally wounded. A faint breeze carried the sweet aroma of the cherry blossom trees in the courtyard, it mixed delightfully with the tang of the salty sea air. This bouquet was unique to Kanagawa Monastery.

Perched high atop a cliff, with its back to the sea, the monastery was an imposing site. It resembled a fortress more than a religious retreat, with its high stone walls, and formidable front gate made of two massive oaken doors reinforced with bands of iron. The enormous gate was flanked on either side by two colossal stone statues of fierce foo dogs, the mythical half dog half lion guardians of palaces and temples. By day the commanding structure was striking, but now, in the twilight of dusk, as darkness crept in, it had an ominous air about it.

To Hiro, however, it was heaven on earth. He loved everything about the monastery. Hiro viewed it as a mystical place,

169

teeming with wondrous, hidden treasures. He especially enjoyed the dualistic nature the monastery possessed.

The drab stone walls hid a small but beautiful orchard and breathtaking gardens. The outward appearance of the main building was functional, simple, and even a bit dull. Yet on the inside it was all beauty and refinement. There were grand and elegant altars burning fragrant incense, magnificent and captivating murals and tapestries, and intricate, bewitching carvings.

Even the building's inhabitants seemed to possess a dual nature. At first glance, the monks seemed austere in appearance and manner. Yet they were patient and kind. The monk's training regimen was rigorous and demanding, almost cruel, but their teachings were enriching, and enlightening.

The lectures of the masters were the highlight of Hiro's existence. Especially on the rare occasion that the Grand Master of the order, Master Ueda, taught the novices. In the young boy's eyes, those lectures were the monastery's greatest treasure of all.

Yes, Hiro was truly grateful for his position within Kamakura. He first stumbled upon the monastery a half starved little scarecrow, with nothing to his name. He was an orphan whose parents had been killed, along with most of his village, in a raid by marauding pirates.

The monks took pity upon the poor boy. They welcomed him in as one of their own, and gave him a place in Kamakura as a novice. He truly loved his new life there, except for his chores, which he was currently busy doing.

Hiro paused a moment longer, turning to catch the breeze. The crisp night air was a blessing, cooling his sweaty face. As a new novice, one of Hiro's responsibilities was to draw water from the well, and bring it up to the monastery.

He dreaded the task. The steps seemed infinite, and his legs hurt as he thought about the daunting chore. He feared he would collapse from exhaustion before he reached the top, and on that night, master Ueda would tell the novices about the prophecy.

He didn't want to miss that.

Hiro closed his eyes and focused. He thought back to his lessons, until he could hear master Ueda's voice as clearly as if he was seated at his feet during one of his lectures.

"These vessels, our bodies, are capable of much more than we ask of them. Through discipline and training, you will find the supposedly impossible is indeed attainable more often than not."

Hiro steeled himself for another moment. He willed his breathing, which was coming in ragged pants, to slow into deep, even breaths. He renewed his trek once again, at a much faster pace, master Ueda's words echoing in his mind.

Chapter 23

The Hikari and the Kagé

Toshibi clung precariously to the cliff face, along with one hundred of his brothers. He slowly crept closer to the top. The monastery was waiting for him there upon the summit. He felt the wind tug at his clothing, and was mindful of his hand holds. They would soon lose the light. Although a fall from that height would mean certain death, the swiftly approaching darkness held no fear for him. Ninja welcomed the coming of the night.

He let his steel neko-te or "cat claws" bite deeply into the rock and take his weight, instead of his own limbs, as he listened to the footsteps of the sentry above. It was the cadence of a bored man, shambling along, lost in a mindless routine; something he'd done hundreds of times before. Not the watchful, measured steps of one who was alert and on guard.

Toshibi grinned wolfishly beneath his mask. It was as Grand Master Kubota had said, the Hikari had grown lax and weak. The Horn was ripe for the taking!

Hiro raced across the courtyard, and caught up to the column of novices as they were entering the temple. Just in time! He slowed his pace to match the solemn procession, and fell in at the end of the line.

The sweet scent of cherry blossoms and the serenade of crickets were replaced by the heady aroma of incense and sandalwood, and the throaty chanting of monks. The boys made their way through a series of corridors, until they came to the classroom.

Brother Taro was waiting for them. With his shaved head and traditional gray robes of a Hikari monk, he seemed to be the archetype of the order. Bowing ever so slightly, he slid open the shoji screen door, or 'room divider', consisting of translucent rice paper over a frame of wood. Once the boys had entered, Brother Taro closed the door, and left them to their studies.

An awe-fueled silence overcame the whispering novices. For there, sitting cross-legged in the center of the room, back-lit by hundreds of candles which created the illusion of him encircled by a shimmering golden aura, was Grand Master Ueda.

He sat there, as serene as the Buddha himself, with a benevolent smile upon his face. In addition to the traditional gray robes of a Hikari monk, he wore a white cape-like garment embroidered with silver. It was the mantel of his office, denoting him as Grand Master of the Hikari order.

Ueda gestured for the boys to enter. They did so slowly, not out of reluctance, but rather out of reverence.

Ueda's beatific smile widened as he beckoned the novices to come closer. "Come young ones, there is no need to be timid as the doe. Better to be bold as the lion in the quest for knowledge."

Toshibi was a ghost garbed in black, blending with the shadows. He moved swiftly as the cheetah, yet as silent as the grave. He appeared from nowhere, more than crept up, behind the sentry. The monk tensed as Toshibi cupped his hand over his mouth to stifle any cry. He pulled him roughly back onto his tanto knife, and with a cold, efficient twist, he ended the monk's life.

Toshibi unceremoniously tossed the corpse over the ledge. No evidence could be behind. As he did so, he saw several other bodies hurtling toward the sea. Grim evidence that his brother ninja were dealing out death as well.

The novices formed a semi-circle around their Grand Master, in seiza position. They listened with rapt attention as master Ueda spoke.

"It is good to walk the holy and peaceful path in search of enlightenment and strive to do good, to make the world a better place. Yet, worse than naïve, it is negligent to assume there will be no opposition. To act as if there is no evil, to assume evil will lie dormant if you are merely righteous enough, is not the path of the enlightened, but rather the path of the fool. There is evil in this world. It must be actively opposed, not ignored. It is the way of the universe to seek balance. There can be no light without dark, no yin without yang, no good without evil. For we, the Hikari, there is the Kagé."

Chapter 24

The Ancient Struggle

Toshibi finally reached the main building. It was surrounded by a raised porch, and was lit by lanterns placed at regular intervals. Although he could see no guards, he had to be wary of the light. Detection was probably inevitable, but the longer they could go before an alarm was raised, the better their chances would be.

Toshibi replaced his tanto knife with a kusari fundo, a two-foot length of chain with a five-inch-long conical weight at each end. At first glance it was seemingly impotent compared to his bladed weapon, in his hands it was every bit as deadly. More importantly, it would leave no telltale blood behind when he killed.

Graceful as a jungle cat, Toshibi leaped onto the porch. His tabi boots made no sound as he crept across the wooden floor boards. He paused and flattened himself against the wall in the dark space between lanterns.

The silhouette of a monk could be seen in the shoji screen, looming ever larger as he approached the door. Toshibi readied his kusari fundo, making a loop with the chain. A monk clad in gray robes slid the shoji screen door open and walked onto the porch. He paused there a moment, and waited for his eyes to adjust to the darkness.

"Nobu, where are you? It's time for me to relieve y-"

The last word was choked off as Toshibi emerged soundlessly from the shadows and threw the looped chain over the monk's head. He yanked savagely on either end, closed the loop around the monk's throat, and strangled him.

The monk flailed wildly and clawed desperately at the chain, but could gain no purchase as it bit deeply into the soft tissue of his neck. His wind pipe was crushed. His eyes bulged grotesquely as he desperately fought for air. Then it was over. His lifeless body went limp and Toshibi, using his foot, rolled the corpse off of the lit porch into the shadows below.

"Long ago, when we first introduced the light of the Buddha to this land, in the Kofun period, it was a dark place indeed. Strife and violence ruled the day. The clans were in constant war with each other, and burial mounds dominated the landscape. The Shinto priests were not as they are now, paying homage to benevolent nature spirits. No. Darker, evil spirits held sway then. The Kagé were among the worst of those who embraced the dark ways. They were vile demon worshipers who preyed upon the weak. The Kagé subjugated and enslaved multitudes. They were at the zenith of their power then, and the cause of much suffering and misery. The Hikari sought to free the people from this bondage of course, but the Kagé would not release their hold on the people. As long as there was wealth and power to be gained, the suffering of others was nothing to them. It was what caused us to realize evil *must* be opposed. There are times when you *must* fight. It was then the war began. It raged for centuries, and it was not fought only with fist and foot, sword and spear, and bow and arrow. It was also fought with magic."

Ueda saw the looks of surprise, doubt, and even denial upon the faces of the novices. "Be careful young ones. Do not be so quick to reject and dismiss that which you do not yet understand. There was a time when people thought gunpowder and firearms to be the work of demons. There are those who do not understand, or know how to manipulate Qi, as you are learning to do. They dismiss it as nonsense. A closed mind is a tragic thing. Endeavor to keep yours ever open in your quest for knowledge."

Ueda's smile returned as he saw the novices contemplating his words.

Toshibi darted down the hallway, and although he increased his speed, his footfalls still made no sound.

He slowed as he came to a blind corner, and turned it in such a way as to expose himself as little as possible. The precautionary measure paid off, for turning the corner at the same time, were two monks.

They froze at the sight of Toshibi, totally taken by surprise.

That barest of instants was all Toshibi needed. He lashed out with the kusari fundo, the weighted end striking one monk in the face.

The other monk tried to kick Toshibi, but the ninja angled himself behind the first, using his body as a shield.

Toshibi grasped the weighted ends of the chain so an inch was protruding from each clenched fist and used them as striking implements. He hammered the monk that he was using as a shield in the temple, and the back of the head.

The monk went down, but his companion lunged forward with a punch aimed at Toshibi's face. Toshibi was faster though, and he entangled the striking limb with the kusari fundo. Using his attacker's momentum, he pivoted and leveraged him into a shoulder throw that landed the monk on his head, breaking his neck.

The first monk was on his feet and turned to run. Before he took three steps, Toshibi whipped the kusari fundo around the retreating monk's ankle, and yanked backwards.

Toshibi's quarry fell flat on his face, and the ninja was on him in an instant. Using the kusari fundo, he strangled the terrified monk.

Chapter 25

Vestiges of Magic

"As your training progresses, you will learn that there is the seen world, and the unseen world. Both worlds exist, and both are very real, yet the unseen world is largely ignored, even dismissed. This is indeed sad. Do we say there is no such thing as the wind, simply because we cannot see it? *Of course not.* The rest of the unseen world is no different. It is every bit as real. It does not cease to exist simply because we cannot see it with our eyes. You have started to learn of Qi, the life force, or energy flow in all living things. Just as blood flows through the body in our veins, so does Qi flow through our body along set lines, or channels. It is why our hearts beat. It is the energy that powers our muscles so that we are able to move. It is even why our minds are cable of thoughts and dreams. In other lands it is known by other names. Prana is one such name, and it is believed to be centered in certain points on the body, called Chakra. Whatever name it is given, it is indeed real. As a real thing, it can be harnessed, controlled, and manipulated. Qi can be used to enhance our body's abilities. It can elevate our ability to heal. It can boost one's speed, and greatly increase one's strength and endurance. Qi is capable of a great many things. Magic is similar. There are channels, or lines of energy in the world that can be tapped into. It is a dangerous undertaking, for these channels tend to be wild and erratic, and difficult to control. So the ability to wield magic has always been a rare thing. Now, that knowledge has almost passed from the world entirely. But long ago, it was not so, and there were those who walked the earth, wielding that knowledge and power.

Wizards they were called, or Sorcerers, and they did many wondrous and terrible things that have become the stuff of legend. One of those things was to imbue certain objects with great magical powers."

Toshibi crept silently down a narrow hallway when he heard footsteps approaching from behind. He hurried his pace to avoid detection, but it soon became evident the hallway continued straight ahead. There were no turns, bends, or doorways to duck into.

He would be seen if he didn't do something quickly.

Toshibi smiled. The hallway was indeed narrow. He stood in the center and stretched out his arms. He could easily touch both sides. Yes, it would be perfect.

Using both his arms and legs to brace himself on either side, he kept his body rigid to support his weight, and shimmied up the walls until he reached the ceiling. He then flattened himself out so his back was touching the ceiling and he was looking down.

Although Toshibi used the shadows to mask his presence, he knew all it would take was a quick glance up from the monk, to be revealed. He remained calm however. People rarely looked up. So there he stayed, poised like a spider waiting for a fly to happen along.

"There are those who say the war is over. They say it raged for hundreds of years, from the first century during the Kofun through the seventh century Asuka periods. They claim it finally ended in the Nara period soon after the moving of the capital in the early eighth century. Do not believe this line of thought! The struggle between darkness and light is eternal. Only the nature of the war has changed. Now it is fought in secret, behind the scenes, and in the shadows. In the early days, the struggle was out in the open and fought with sorcery as much as with steel. We battled for control of certain items of great power then. Possession of such an object was a tremendous advantage in battle, and often ensured victory. At first, we sought to destroy these objects, for we believed them to be the cause of much suffering and death. Eventually we destroyed almost all of them. Later, we came to realize they were but tools. Mighty and powerful tools, but tools none the less. As with any tool, the one wielding it is good or evil, not the tool itself. It was because of that realization we are now in possession of the Horn of Ryujin."

There was a collective gasp from the novices. Ueda smiled at their surprise. It was good there was still reverence for the legends of old.

"Aahhh, I see you have heard of the dragon god's Horn."

Chapter 26

The Prophecy

The monk ambled by, lost in his thoughts. He was caught entirely unaware when Toshibi dropped upon him from above. The wind was completely knocked from him, so he did not cry out in surprise as he was forced to the ground.

He tried to yell for help as his head was roughly torqued backwards by Toshibi, exposing his neck. The sound came out as little more than a weak gurgling as the ninja's tanto knife sliced from left to right, through both his carotid arteries and his jugular.

Blood spewed forth from his neck and open mouth. The monk's last living sight was the ninja, casually strolling down the hall at an unhurried pace as if nothing had happened.

Toshibi slowed for an instant, and whipped out his arm, flicking the monk's life blood from his blade. He then re-sheathed the weapon, and continued on his way.

There is no place to hide the body here. He thought. *There is no need for subtlety.*

"Yes, young ones. The mystical Horn of the mighty dragon Ryujin, god of the sea, and guardian of Japan, has been entrusted to our care. It is the very tool Ryujin used to harness the awesome power of the ocean. From Ryugu-jo, his palace of red and white coral down in the deep, the dragon god would play his haunting music, and the sea would dance. The tides would ebb or flow, and the waters would rise or fall, all depending on the tune he played on his jewel-encrusted horn. It is a thing of great beauty, but that beauty belies its terrible power. Ryujin used it to slay hundreds of thousands with his devastating kamikazes. These storms, although terrible, saved Japan from invasion by the Mongol hordes and their massive fleets, not once, but twice. Thus, their name; the divine winds. Although I think if you were to ask the hundreds of thousands of slain Mongols, they would use different words to describe them. The divine winds were no ordinary typhoons. They were destruction incarnate. This beautiful horn can become a weapon of terrible power. It is our sacred duty to ensure it never falls into the wrong hands..."

Ueda paused, his words trailing off. To a casual observer, it would have appeared to be for dramatic effect, as the boys leaned forward, hanging on his every word. But the master carefully studied the faces of his young disciples, and read them like a veteran poker player. There was some skepticism, yes, but also excitement, and even some hope. Then, slowly, realization set in, and finally resolve and determination.

Yes, Ueda thought, *they are ready.* "Listen closely young ones to the words of the prophecy."

The hallway turned to the right, and came to another 'T' intersection, where it branched off. To the left, the hallway remained narrow, and was dotted with several doors at regular intervals.

Toshibi paused for a moment, then decided against going left, as they were most likely living chambers. Just as he was about to turn right, one of the doors opened, and its occupant slowly crept outside. Toshibi instantly crouched down low, below the normal line of sight, as he reached inside of his jacket. He produced several shuriken, or 'throwing stars'; small, circular, bladed weapons.

Toshibi relaxed and returned to a standing position as he recognized the occupant to be one of his brother ninja, sword crimson with fresh blood.

So these *were* living chambers, and his brother had been quietly dispatching the unsuspecting monks in their sleep.

The pair nodded to each other in brief salutation, and went their separate ways.

To the right, the hallway widened, and the throaty sounds of chanting could be heard. On the left side of the hallway were several ornately painted shoji screen doors, depicting cherry blossom trees, or seascapes with crashing waves.

The chanting came from behind the frail doors. From the sound of it, there were dozens of monks deeply engrossed in prayer inside.

Toshibi produced a leather sack from which he sprinkled numerous makibishi, wicked looking barbed caltrops, onto the floor as he passed by. When the monks emerged barefoot from their prayers, they were in for a nasty surprise.

"When the Horn first came into our possession, soon after the second attempted invasion by the Mongol hordes in 1281, his holiness Grand Master Iwasaki had a vision that was later to become known as *the prophecy*. It has puzzled many a scholar in the centuries since."

Ueda produced a scroll from within the folds of his robes. "I will read it to you now."

"There will come an age when man will shun both magic and the gods. For so great will become his might, by his own design, he will speed across the land faster than any team of horses, soar the heavens like eagles, and swim the murky depths like fish. In that age, in a far-off land across the sea, there will arise a swordless samurai; a man not born to Bushido, yet one who walks the path. He will bear the mark of the eagle and the dragon. That man will save the Horn of Ryujin from the hands of evil, and thus the world from great suffering."

Ueda saw the incredulous looks upon the faces of the novices. "Yes young ones, I understand. If these had not been the words of Iwasaki himself, I too would have discounted them as the ramblings of a mad man. Yet, only two years ago, before the Americans sailed into Yokohama Harbor with their mighty warships, we did not believe there were guns capable of such range and destruction. Had you spoken of these weapons and their ships with no sails, or that we would do business with these foreigners, these gaijin, people would have thought you mad. But now Japan's isolation has ended. Believe me young ones, the Tokugawa Shogunate did not open Japan to trade with the Americans out of the kindness of their hearts. They both fear and *covet* the mighty American guns. In time, I believe we too will possess the knowledge to construct steam ships and mighty cannons. Times do change. Who knows what other things will be available to us in the distant future? Perhaps this age of which Grand

Master Iwasaki spoke, is simply the distant future, in a time when things of wonder are common place."

Ueda smiled as he saw the novices struggling to come to terms with this possibility. "Remember young ones, always endeavor to keep an open mind in your quest for knowledge."

Chapter 27

Ignite

As Toshibi continued deeper into the monastery, he heard the distinctive sound of wood striking wood. It was not a steady sound with any cadence or rhythm, but rather erratic and chaotic in nature. Toshibi instantly knew these were the sounds of combat.

Possibly bo, six-foot-long oaken staffs, or maybe yari, long bladed spears, or even naginata, glaive like weapons with curved blades at the end of a wooden staff. But all those weapons were rarely employed by ninja. Mainly because ninja preferred clandestine methods, thus weapons that were easy to conceal. Even their swords, the ninjato, were much shorter and straighter than the katana used by samurai.

Toshibi crept closer to the sounds of the fray, his curiosity piqued. The hallway led to an expansive circular chamber that had several other hallways branching from it. There were massive wooden pillars covered with ornate carvings supporting the high vaulted ceiling, they must have been colossal trees before they were felled.

The walls of the chamber were adorned with hanging tapestries, and were lined with several shallow recesses, where statues of former masters were on display. Brightly burning candles sat lit at their bases. Several decorative censers, crafted to look like dragons, hung from the rafters. Burning incense wafted out through their gaping maws, giving the illusion that they breathed fire.

The dominant feature of the chamber however, was an immense statue of the Buddha, back-lit by hundreds of candles. Flanked on its left by a large bronze gong, and by a large ornate censer, resplendent with black onyx stones on its right.

In the center of the chamber was one of his brother ninja, wielding a bo, and embattled with three monks who wielded long oaken staffs. A fourth monk lay dead on the floor. A ninjato protruded from his lifeless body. When the sword became lodged in bone, the ninja picked up the weapon of his fallen foe to defend himself.

Crack!

The ninja blocked a blow aimed at his head.

Crack! Crack! Crack!

He fended off two more attacks, and countered with a strike of his own in rapid succession.

The ninja staggered backwards from a blow that got through his defenses. He managed to block a follow up strike, but winced and staggered back again as a blow from the opposite direction landed. Outnumbered, he was slowly overwhelmed.

Cloaked in shadows, Toshibi silently circled behind the monks to aid his comrade. The monks were too focused on their foe to notice him. They attacked in unison, one monk in front to press the attack, while the other two harried the ninja from either side. They took windows of opportunity when the ninja was busy defending or countering one of the other monks.

The tactic was working. Although the ninja could block most of the attacks, blow after blow still made it through his defenses.

After fending off a strike aimed at his head from the monk in front, and a quick follow up attack from the monk on his left, the ninja doubled over as the monk to his right landed a strike to his solar plexus.

The monk in front sensed an opportunity and rushed in. Just before he could land a deciding blow however, Toshibi threw a shuriken. It severed the chain suspending one of the dragon censers, and sent glowing embers cascading down onto the monk's bald head.

As the monk reeled in pain and surprise, the ninja with the bo staff seized the opportunity. Utilizing the long staff, he swept the monk's feet out from under him, and followed up with a vicious blow to his face that shattered his nose.

The other two monks were already in motion however. The first used a thrusting strike that landed at the base of the ninja's spine. His back arched and he spasmed forward, directly into the oncoming attack of his comrade. A powerful blow, with more than enough momentum to crush the larynx, landed against the ninja's throat. The ninja collapsed to the floor. He clutched his throat and convulsed grotesquely as he died, suffocating like a fish out of water.

Toshibi drew his ninjato, and entered the fray.

The monk with the broken nose regained his feet, and Toshibi was immediately upon him. He slashed with a horizontal attack that eviscerated the monk. The wounded monk staggered off. He clutched his bloody midsection, as entrails slipped between his fingers.

The other two monks launched a counter offensive, one thrust high at Toshibi's head, while the other attacked low, and slashed at his feet.

Toshibi parried the blow aimed at his head, and leaped over the strike aimed at his feet. The momentum of the jump carried him inside the striking range of his opponent. The monk with the long staff could no longer strike at him effectively without backing up.

Toshibi however, was at the perfect distance to attack with his much shorter sword.

The monk attempted to block a feigning stab, but Toshibi changed the angle of attack at the last second. The stab transformed into a chop attack that severed four of the monk's fingers.

The monk howled in pain, dropped his staff, and clutched his mangled hand. Toshibi tried to follow up with a killing blow, but had to contend with a flurry of attacks from the other bo staff wielding monk.

The attacks continued without pause. The monk expertly employed the superior reach of his weapon to keep Toshibi at a distance where he could not counter attack with his much shorter ninjato.

Meanwhile, the monk with the abdominal wound slowly made his way, unnoticed, toward the large gong in front of the Buddha. He struggled to keep his feet, and tried hard not to think about the gore that spilled from his hands.

Slipping dangerously in his own blood, the monk shambled forward, wobbling and tottering in a drunken, zig-zag pattern. The monk pressed on, determined to reach the gong. If he was to die, he would do so valiantly! He must sound the alarm, and warn his brothers.

As he attempted to hone in on the gong, the monk's vision blurred. He careened sharply off course, delirious with pain and loss of blood.

He crashed spectacularly into the large decorative censer. Hot coals scattered everywhere, and knocked over several dozen candles.

The flames spread like a cancer, leaping hungrily to one of the old, brittle tapestries.

Chapter 28

The Grandmaster

Master Ueda smiled as he answered question after question from the novices. Hiro listened, thoroughly spellbound.

"Master, how could a man fly?"

"Master, the one in the prophecy is said to walk the path of Bushido even though he is not from Japan. Do they practice Bushido outside of Japan?"

"Master how can there be a swordless samurai? All Samurai carry swords. They are never without them."

The master beamed. It was good to see the young ones so eager to learn. "It has helped me, young ones, to think of the prophecy as a riddle. Think of Master Iwasaki's words as cryptic clues. Perhaps if you…" Master Ueda stopped mid-sentence. The smile on his face vanished. His head snapped up from the novices, his gaze falling intently upon the shoji screen door.

The novice's questions trailed off as one by one they stopped to follow Master Ueda's gaze. They saw nothing.

"Master, what is it?"

Ueda continued to stare at the door. Suddenly he sprung to his feet. "Get behind me children."

The confused boys were slow to comply. "What is it Master? We see nothing."

"NOW!" Ueda cried.

The novices quickly flocked behind him, all eyes upon the shoji screen door.

Ueda might as well have become a statue. He stood like a stone sentinel, motionless and silent, as he gathered his Qi.

The tension in the room was palatable as everyone stared at the sliding shoji screen door.

Time seemed to slow, and several seconds crawled by with nothing happening. It seemed like an eternity to the children.

Hiro watched as Master Ueda bent his knees ever so slightly, and shifted his feet so they were in the fighting stance the novices had been taught. The master's hands were no longer at his sides, but in front of him, ready to fend off blows.

But no one was there.

As if on cue, the doors slid open ominously. In crept five ninja, clad in material that might as well have been made of the very shadows that surrounded them. Their crimson-streaked swords were drawn as they moved in, silently and gracefully as cats. They made no sound.

Hiro had no idea how Master Ueda could have possibly known they were there.

The ninja advanced forward menacingly, hatred blazing in their eyes.

Master Ueda stood his ground while the ninja formed a semi-circle and converged upon him.

Then, something changed in Master Ueda's posture. He leaned forward ever so slightly. His taut expression and body language seemed to be daring the ninja to attack.

There was a blur of motion, far too fast for Hiro to follow. One of the ninja swung at Master Ueda with his sword, but it seemed Master Ueda moved first, anticipating the attack. Before the ninja realized he had missed, Ueda moved towards his assailant, and was inside of the deadly arc of the weapon. The ninja was struck with a flurry of blows. To Hiro, none of the blows seemed very powerful, but the ninja collapsed to the floor, convulsing.

It suddenly dawned on Hiro, he was witnessing Kyusho Jitsu. The novices had been told of this secret art, where precise strikes against certain nerve clusters on the body could cause paralysis, or even death.

Another ninja stabbed at Master Ueda, but again, he moved towards his attacker at a very slight angle, and batted the blade away with palm of his hand.

Then, when he was up close, he snapped the ninja's arm.

Still, he maintained hold of his opponent, and moved the ninja into the path of an incoming assault, where the would-be attacker was skewered by one of his fellow ninja's swords.

Hiro stared, mouth open in utter amazement. There was Master Ueda, an old man, leaping about, dodging, bobbing and weaving. He was evading every attack that the ninja threw at him, contorting his body in seemingly impossible ways.

For the second time that day, Master Ueda's words echoed in Hiro's mind. *These vessels, our bodies, are capable of much more than we ask of them. Through discipline and training, you will find the supposedly impossible is indeed attainable more often than not.*

Master Ueda weaved his way through the slashing swords in a mesmerizing display of grace, agility, and skill. Ueda slowly worked his way closer to one of the ninja. Suddenly, he sprung forward, and covered a distance Hiro doubted most young men could manage. The leap landed him within striking range.

Once again, Master Ueda was a blur. He delivered four blows in the time most men could only manage one quick jab. The stricken ninja froze in place like a statue unable to move. Suddenly, he let out a spinetingling scream, clearly in terrible agony. Blood poured from the ninja's tear ducts before he collapsed in a lifeless heap upon the floor.

The remaining two ninja slowly backed away from Ueda, very much aware he had disposed of three of their brethren in very short order. Then, as if they finally reached a previously agreed upon safe distance, they stopped. In perfect unison, the ninja reached into their jackets and hurled shuriken at Ueda.

His concentration unbroken, Ueda swept the cape from his shoulders, twirled, and deflected the deadly blades. The ninja lost heart and turned to flee, though only one made his escape. Again, using his cape, Master Ueda snapped it like a whip, to entangle one of the retreating ninja. The cape wrapped around his neck. Ueda yanked it back roughly, and toppled the ninja to the ground.

The ninja landed well. He tucked into a ball, and rolled back to his feet, while simultaneously using his sword to cut himself free of Ueda's cape. By the time he had done so however, Master Ueda was upon him. None could track the flurry of his lightning fast Kyusho strikes.

The ninja didn't even have time to register what happened, let alone attempt any blocks or counters. In a flash of pain and surprise, he found himself on the floor. His body convulsed uncontrollably as his internal organs ruptured and burst.

Chapter 29

Smoke and Flame

The fire quickly spread from the tapestries to the wooden pillars, and up into the rafters.

Deep orange and sunset red flames were everywhere. Thick, black smoke produced soot. It was so difficult to breathe. Yet Toshibi and the monk battled on, heedless to their hazardous surroundings.

The monk used his much longer weapon to good effect, though he was unable to land any blows. Toshibi was too good a swordsman, and easily parried incoming attacks. Conversely, he kept Toshibi too far back to pose any actual threat with his much shorter sword.

After he recognized the futility in the battle, Toshibi disengaged. He stepped back, out of range of the staff, and threw shuriken at the monk. The dangerous blades shot in faster than the monk could defend against, inflicting wound after painful wound.

Shuriken protruded from his forearms, chest, and abdomen. The monk backpedaled away from Toshibi's continuous onslaught. He backed right into the hungry tendrils of the raging fire and was immediately engulfed in flame.

Toshibi surveyed his surroundings. Only two exits remained that were not blocked by fire. He chose one at random and hastened down the hallway.

Master Ueda called over his shoulder as he made for the door. "Quickly young ones, follow me. It is not safe to remain here."

As if to accentuate Ueda's point, the ninja he had just dispatched, twisted in the throes of a final death spasm. Ueda paused mid step and turned to survey the boys. Most were following, eyes wide with fear. Some remained rooted in place, as if stupefied by what they had just witnessed.

"FOCUS!" Ueda bellowed. "You are novices of the Hikari! Not timid milkmaids! Fear is a natural response to danger. It can be an excellent servant, but it was never meant to rule. YOU are masters of your emotions. Do not allow it to be the other way around. It appears you are all to be tested on this day. Much sooner and harsher than any of your teachers would have cared for, but life is not always a tranquil pool. Sometimes life is a stormy and treacherous sea. In such times you must FOCUS! Focus on your training, for it will serve you well. Focus, and do not give into despair."

"Yes Master," the boys shouted in unison. Emboldened by their teacher's words, they were as loud as soldiers, eager for battle.

Ueda beamed with pride. "Good then, let us act as true Hikari. We are Warriors of the Light!"

Ueda stood by the shoji screen door as he ushered the novices into the corridor. Hiro was the last one out of the room. A hazy fog of smoke hung thick in the air. The boys immediately started coughing. Hiro could taste the sooty cloud in the back of his throat, and he marveled at Ueda, who seemed immune, and totally unaffected.

Hiro forced himself to take controlled breaths through his nose, rather than panicked gasps through his open mouth. *FOCUS...* Although it was still unpleasant to breathe the smoky air, his coughing fit abated. Hiro beamed as he noticed Master Ueda give him a slight nod of approval.

"To the left young ones. We will make for the western gate into the gardens."

Focus, remember your training, focus, remember your training... Hiro repeated the mantra to himself over and over as he strove to shut out the horrors all around him. To Hiro, it was truly the stuff of nightmares.

The flames were everywhere! Everything was bathed in an eerie, undulating, blood-red blush as the blaze greedily devoured the once beautiful temple.

Battle cries mingled with screams of agony, as the combat between the monks and ninja raged all around them. The surreal, wavy, mirage-like effect caused by the extreme heat, coupled with the smoky haze, made it seem to Hiro he had stumbled upon the place where souls were tortured in Hell.

Chapter 30

The Wolf and the Ram

They hurried down the hall. Ahead, silhouetted figures could be seen behind the shoji screens, battling back and forth, larger than life. The terrifying visual was accompanied by the unmistakable ring of steel striking steel.

Suddenly, there was a crimson splash of blood upon the white rice paper, and one of the figures dropped from sight. After another moment, the shoji screen slid open and Toshibi strode out boldly to block their path. His fallen foe's life blood dripped menacingly from his blade.

"*The Horn,* old one. Tell me where it is hidden, or you and the young ones will not live to see another day."

Ueda calmly stepped forward to face Toshibi. "You will find no Horn here Shinobi, only a slow and fiery death. If you continue to bar my way, a faster, yet equally painful one awaits you at my hands."

"You may have been a ram among sheep, old one, but you are long past your prime. The time has come for the wolves to cull you from the flock."

Toshibi charged forward, his sword a blur of motion before him, far too fast for Hiro to follow. Yet Master Ueda evaded every strike. As Hiro watched, the two fought back and forth, neither one landing any blows.

The ninja came in with a flurry of attacks Master Ueda narrowly avoided. Before he could counter, the ninja would leap back out of range. This cycle repeated over, and over again. It seemed the two would be locked in combat for all eternity, neither one to emerge victorious.

As Hiro continued to watch, fear slowly crept in along with the encroaching flames. This ninja was clearly better than the others. He had survived much longer alone, then the others who faced Master Ueda en masse. He was armed, and Master Ueda was not. What if that was the difference that tipped the scales? Master Ueda was old after all. What if he could not keep that pace? What if the ninja wore him down and he could longer evade a swipe from the sword? What if one of the attacks managed to strike home?

As if he could read Hiro's mind, Toshibi spoke. "You will not be able to maintain this pace much longer, old one."

"Strength and speed are youth's substitutes for knowledge and skill. You will soon realize they are poor substitutes."

Toshibi was pleased with the current turn of events. *It is as I had hoped. This one is clearly a Master. He is better than the others. He knows to keep his distance. With this fire, I do not have the luxury to play with him all day. Thanks to my proclamation, he will fear for the safety of the Horn. With any luck, he will lead me right to it. Now, to give him the right opening, without making it obvious.*

As Hiro watched, the nature of the duel changed. It transformed from the ninja leaping in with a series of lightning fast attacks, and then leaping back out again, to Master Ueda as the aggressor.

Ueda relentlessly pursued the ninja, while his quarry hacked fanatically at the air in front of him, creating a blurred barrier that prevented the Master from getting too close.

Master Ueda sprung forward.

As Toshibi leapt backwards to keep Ueda out of the effective range of his sword, he swept upwards, the swordplay equivalent of an upper cut.

The swipe was so close, it sliced open Ueda's robes. He was unfazed, and pressed forward to close the distance.

Toshibi slashed downward diagonally. Ueda ducked and narrowly avoided the blow. In fact, if Ueda didn't have a shaved head, as the precept of his order demanded, the attack would have parted him from some hair.

The missed strike provided an opening for the Master. He rushed in, and was upon Toshibi in an instant.

Toshibi was ready though, and blended with his attacker's energy. Trying to parry incoming blows with his sword would be ineffective at close range.

Toshibi dropped the weapon, and let Ueda's rush knock him backwards. He rode the energy of the attack like a surfer on an incoming wave. As he kept a firm hold on Ueda, Toshibi tucked into a backwards summersault. At the last instant, he employed a technique called Tomoe Nage. Ueda was launched like a boulder out of a catapult as he pushed out with his legs.

Hiro gasped as he saw his master sail through the air at considerable height, certain the older man would crash painfully in a crumpled heap upon the floor.

But Ueda, dexterous as an acrobat, tucked into a forward summersault, and landed nimbly on his feet.

For one of the few times in his life, Toshibi became nervous. The old man's skills rivaled that of Grand Master Kubota, Head of the Kagé! Toshibi was a Master in his own right, as Kubota's protégée and heir apparent. Outside of his teacher, he'd never faced an opponent who rivaled his prowess in combat. He was definitely not one to be easily intimidated, yet Ueda gave him pause. There were probably only a handful of people in the world who could even discern the difference in skill levels between the two combatants. Toshibi wisely recognized that Ueda's skills eclipsed his own.

As Grand Master Kubota had taught him, a clash between true warriors was not a mindless contest of physical prowess, but more akin to a game of Go, or its western equivalent, chess. The sharper mind, the superior strategist, would be the victor.

Toshibi's goal was not to win the confrontation, but to feign defeat, and later follow Ueda to the Horn. The ruse would be no easy thing. To convincingly deceive Ueda into believing he had defeated the ninja, was only part of the equation. The truly important thing was to do so while avoiding serious injury, or worse.

Toshibi smiled beneath his mask. He had the answer. A simple feint would never work. It was a gamble, but he would have to commit to an all-out attack that he was sure would succeed. He had faith a master of Ueda's caliber would have a counter. He just had to stack the deck in his favor, and launch an attack that had very few lethal counter options.

The pair slowly circled each other, as they searched for some minute flaw in the other's defenses.

Then, Toshibi rushed forward. Seemingly from nowhere, he produced kunai, a type of throwing knife, and flung the deadly missiles at Master Ueda's head.

The attack forced Ueda to crouch down, in order to avoid impalement by the deadly implements. But it also unwittingly placed him right in the path of a vicious double front kick, the kick equivalent of a quick left-right punch combination. Toshibi launched the attack simultaneously, as he knew in advance how Ueda would react to the knives.

Most men wouldn't have been able to react fast enough to avoid the throwing knives, let alone evade a follow up attack such as a kick. Certainly not two lightning fast kicks in rapid succession.

But Grand Master Ueda, head of the Hikari, was no ordinary man.

As Ueda crouched down to avoid the kunai, he drew his arms in front of him, fists clenched, forearms parallel to each other, elbows pointing down. It resembled a western boxer's defensive position. As the kicks came in, he flung his arms the sides, while he rotated his palms from facing towards him, to facing *away* from him. The move not only warded off the kicks, but effectively spread-eagled the ninja, who was now wide open for Ueda's counter.

Ueda leapt back up from his crouched position. Like a spring uncoiled, he used his legs for substantial power. Ueda delivered a devastating head-butt that landed just under Toshibi's chin.

The spectacular blow sent the ninja flying into the air. He crashed through a wall enveloped in flames.

Chapter 31

Another Route

Ueda did not pause to see how his enemy fared. He turned back to the novices. "Quickly, this way, we have no time to lose! Hurry!"

The children raced down the hallway. The monastery was quickly becoming an inferno. The heat was intense and as they raced along, Hiro could barely recognize anything. It seemed as if they were running headlong into a kiln.

"Remember, your training, remember your training," Hiro repeated aloud. He struggled not to give into panic. He had gone to the gardens that way a thousand times before. True, the hallway had never before been wreathed in flame, but that did not change the fact that it was still the way out.

Then Hiro saw them, up ahead through the haze of smoke and the bobbing heads of the children running in front of him. He saw the double doors that lead to the gardens and safety.

The already massive amounts of adrenaline that coursed through Hiro's veins spiked even higher. Time slowed down for him, and his entire world suddenly adopted a surreal quality, as if it were a dream.

The children in the hallway bottlenecked as the ones in front paused to open the doors. Hiro could feel his heartbeat within his chest. It seemed it would explode, it pounded so hard and fast.

Suddenly, threatening groans and rumbles resounded over the crackling of the flames. The noise came from somewhere above, in the ceiling. Hiro looked up but could see nothing. All was obscured by a thick, billowing cloud of sooty, black smoke.

Finally, the doors opened, but to Hiro, it seemed the children ahead of him moved painfully slow. Again, he heard the ominous sound from above. Panic overtook him. For some inexplicable reason, he feared there was some shadowy creature lurking in the shadows. Hidden by the smoke and flames, a foul demon from the depths of hell was ready to drag the young novice into the fiery abyss. He had to get out! Why were the children ahead of him moving so slowly? Hiro tried to push his way through the dense wall of bodies that barred his way, but he could not.

Again, the sound from above, only much louder.

Finally, there were only two children standing between Hiro and the door, but the sound had become continuous, and hot embers rained down. They stung like fire ants.

Just one child! One child left between Hiro and the door to safety. The noise had become so loud that it drowned out everything else, but Hiro ignored it, for finally there were no children standing between him and his freedom.

Someone, or something grabbed Hiro by the scruff of the collar and yanked him backwards as the roof collapsed in a fiery avalanche of timbers and shingles, right where he stood an instant earlier. Hiro was oblivious to the fact he had narrowly escaped death. All he could focus on was the fiery mass that barred his way out into the gardens.

"No!!!" Hiro cried out as he franticly struggled to break away from whatever held him. His only instinct was to get lose and burrow his way through the flaming barricade that separated him from the safety of the garden. He had to get out. He couldn't meet his end in that hellish nightmare! He had to escape!

"Stop young one," Ueda said. "We can no longer continue that way!"

Hiro continued to struggle, heedless of Ueda's words.

"STOP!" Ueda finally bellowed.

Hiro finally snapped out of his hysteria and stopped his fight. Ueda recognized the look upon the boy's face, eyes wide like an animal caught in a trap, almost beyond reason. He was clearly in survival mode. Everything had been narrowed down to fight or flight.

He had to bring the boy back.

"What is your name, young one?"

Hiro did not answer at first, but Ueda persisted.

"Tell me your name. What is your name?"

"H-Hiro, my name is Hiro, Master."

Ueda smiled reassuringly at the boy. "Do not despair Hiro. We will leave by another route. Follow me."

Together, Ueda and Hiro sped off down a corridor to the left, neither aware they were followed.

Chapter 32

Uninvited Guests

As they continued to wind their way through the twisting passageways, deeper into the heart of the monastery, they came to an area that was off limits to the novices.

Hiro halted out of habit.

"Come Hiro, we will make an exception today. You may enter the inner sanctum."

The pair came to a narrow archway. Beaded curtains obscured what lay beyond. As they parted the hanging barrier and entered, the space ahead was nearly pitch black. The only illumination Hiro could make out was what feeble light managed to filter through a second beaded curtain at the opposite end of the room. It was not nearly enough to light the area, and did nothing more than show where the exit was.

Ueda and Hiro headed towards the light, flanked on all sides by the sound of melodious chimes, for as they continued forward, they inadvertently brushed past dozens of wind chimes that hung down at varying heights. Some as low as Hiro's ankles, they were impossible to see in the dark, thus impossible to avoid.

How very odd, thought Hiro.

Hiro's confusion was apparent. Master Ueda spoke, his tone hushed. "A way to announce uninvited guests."

As Master and pupil emerged to the other side through the second beaded curtain, they were met by eight guards brandishing Yari, wicked looking spears.

Two guards stood on either side of the archway, and six more stood in front of large oaken double doors.

The two guards on either side of the archway were positioned to ambush anyone emerging through the beaded curtains. Spears at the ready, they stood poised to strike. They relaxed upon seeing Master Ueda, however.

"The Kagé are here. They have set fire to the temple. I must remove the Horn and take it to safety."

The guard's eyes narrowed at the news. They collectively paused for the briefest of moments, as if steeling themselves for battle. They snapped to attention, and the ones at the doors stood aside for Ueda to enter.

As Ueda reached for the brass ring that would open the oaken door, chimes could be heard from behind the beaded curtain. It was a gentle melodious sound, but the monks in the room reacted as if it was the low, rumbling growl of a ravenous tiger.

Ueda turned and bowed to the guards. "You know your duty." Then he turned to Hiro. "Come Hiro, your destiny lies along a different path."

Hiro followed Master Ueda through the oaken doors. The room that lay beyond was a wonder to behold. Ahead was a massive shrine made of polished black marble. It was covered in carvings of majestic dragons, overlaid with silver, and accented by a matching altar, which was draped with a fine satin altar cloth, white as new fallen snow.

Atop the altar, contrasting starkly with the dark marble yet complementing it, were silver candelabras bearing white candles. The candles were surrounded by burning incense, and ornate vases full of hyacinth and wisteria, the fragrant white flowers from the gardens.

Hiro silently took in the awesome setting before him.

Master Ueda bowed before the altar. Then he knelt at its base, and depressed one of the silver dragons. There was a click, followed by the sound of stone scraping stone.

A section of the shrine swung in on itself, to reveal a hidden compartment approximately the size of a baby's cradle. The compartment was lined with quilted, white silk padding. Nestled inside, was a large velvet bag, cinched shut at top with a drawstring.

As Ueda peered inside the compartment, he spoke. "Although the Hikari are the ones entrusted with guarding the Horn, we are not the only ones who know of its existence. I do not speak of the Kagé, but rather others who travel the path to enlightenment, such as ourselves. There is an order of Zen Buddhists who are making preparations to build a temple in America, to minister to the ever-increasing numbers of Chinese immigrants who flock there in droves. They go in search of the gold that has been found there. They go with dreams of riches, and hopes of making new beginnings. Unfortunately, the majority have found a life of back-breaking toil building the railroads instead. They lose hope, and turn to opium to drown their sorrows. So our brothers go to bring them the light of the Buddha. The temple is to be in a city named San Francisco. We will take the Horn there."

Master Ueda reached inside, and lifted the bag as gently as if it were more fragile and delicate than a butterfly's wings. Cradled in his arms he whispered to it like a newborn. "It is time we find you a new home."

From outside, the harsh sounds of battle intruded upon the scene. The violence simultaneously ended the reverent moment, and validated Ueda's words.

Chapter 33

Deadly Sting

Fifteen had answered his call.

More than enough to overcome the old man and the boy, Toshibi thought.

Their number was reduced almost immediately. Two of his brothers abandoned subtlety after they triggered the chimes, and rushed headlong through the curtains, only to be skewered immediately by the spear-wielding guards who waited on the other side.

Toshibi and the others fared better.

After seeing the fate of the first two, they were better prepared to deflect the incoming thrusts. Even so, the ninja's situation proved dire. With the exception of Ueda, the final eight monks were obviously more skilled than any of the others they faced. They fought well, but more importantly, they fought in unison.

It was very apparent they were a cohesive unit, who had trained together. The ninja, although highly skilled, fought as individuals.

The difference was telling, for soon the monks had killed seven more ninja, and wounded another six.

"Idiots," Toshibi cried, "Remember your training!"

Ninja may not have included group tactics among their specialties, but they were masters of the unconventional.

Ninja were not mired down by the restrictive code of Bushido. Part of what made them so deadly, was that they did not adhere to the expected.

Toshibi broke off from the melee, and quickly produced several happo; small, hollowed out eggshells, filled with a blinding powder. He hurled the small grenades in the monk's faces. Even though several monks managed to block the grenades with the shaft of their spears, the fragile eggshell still shattered and released a cloud of blinding powder, to the same effect.

The ninja made short work of the blinded monks, and rammed through the oaken doors into the room beyond. All of the ninja carried on, except Toshibi. He stayed behind and rummaged through his gear. He procured a blowgun, a handful of darts, and a small vial.

He dipped the tip of one of the darts into the vial, loaded the blowgun, and slowly crept to a position to fire from.

Ueda handed the bag with the Horn to Hiro. He then grabbed a vase full of flowers from the altar, and hurled it at an approaching ninja's head. The ninja blocked the incoming missile with his sword, shattering the vase, but was unable to evade the vicious follow up kick that Ueda delivered to the ninja's groin. The ninja doubled over in agony as his testicles ruptured, but Ueda quickly ended his suffering by snapping his neck.

Ueda ducked under a swipe from another sword, and dodged to the side, narrowly avoiding a stab from another.

His back to the altar, he quickly snatched up one of the candelabras and used it to parry an incoming slash from a sword. He used the improvised weapon to entangle the sword with a quick follow up thrust. The Master gave the candelabra a sudden twist, and snapped the blade in two.

Before the ninja could disengage, Ueda was upon him. Moving faster than a striking cobra, Ueda attacked the ninja's face, savagely plucking an eyeball right from its socket.

The ninja shrieked in dreadful agony as he covered his ruined face. He never saw Ueda free his broken sword from the candelabra and use it to disembowel him.

Ueda then turned to face the remaining four ninja, who reacted as if he brandished a flaming great sword, and not a broken ninjato.

The ninja warily fanned out and encircled Ueda who calmly stood still, eyes taking in everything.

The ninja continued to circle like black sharks, waiting for the right moment to strike. Then suddenly, they attacked en masse. Ueda singled one ninja out and rushed to meet him, ignoring the others.

Broken ninjato in his left hand, Ueda redirected the incoming sword just enough to allow him to step in close, and grab the ninja's sword arm with his right hand. Close to the ninja, in the 'eye of the storm', Ueda used his momentum to whirl him into his comrade's sword blades, where he was mercilessly impaled.

As he faced the remaining three ninja, Ueda's back was turned to Toshibi. It was precisely the opening Toshibi needed.

The blowgun already to his lips, Toshibi gave it an explosive burst of air that sent the poisoned dart sailing. His aim was true and the dart buried itself in the back of Ueda's neck.

Ueda grimaced as he reached back and plucked out the dart. His face betrayed his irritation at the small projectile in his hand. A sickly green ichor mingled with his blood on the tip.

Poison! The cowardly snakes! Ueda whirled to face Toshibi, but the other three ninja, like sharks smelling blood in the water, rushed in for the feeding frenzy.

Ueda however, was no wounded seal.

As the ninja rushed towards him, the Master leaped towards them. He covered the gap in an instant, and met them more than halfway. He first collided with the ninja in the center, who had his sword raised above his head with both hands in the process of delivering a devastating downward strike, but Ueda interrupted the ninja's timing, and therefore the attack.

Suddenly, Ueda had both of his hands on the handle of the ninja's sword as well. Instead of trying to wrestle the sword from the ninja's grasp, he merely kept hold of it, redirecting the attack, while simultaneously pivoting his hips. Thus, he leveraged the ninja into a throw.

The ninja had to release his hold on the sword in order to break his fall, and roll out of it unharmed. The choice left Ueda with the sword, which he used to good effect. He parried incoming strikes from the other two ninja, and quickly countered. One of the ninja's lost an ear, the other was left with a wicked gash down his arms.

Suddenly, Ueda felt a sting. A second dart protruded from the side of his neck.

This time, Ueda did not pause to pluck out the dart. Instead, he spun around and hurled the sword at Toshibi's head. The ninjato struck the blowgun, split it in two, and continued onward. It tore through Toshibi's left cheek from the corner of his mouth to the bottom of his earlobe.

Toshibi staggered backwards. Pressing his hand to the side of his bloody face, he felt the dangling flap of skin that used to be his cheek.

Ueda started towards Toshibi, but the other ninja moved in for the kill, as Ueda was weaponless, or so they thought. As it turned out, Ueda wasn't completely without weapons.

As the ninja moved in, Ueda removed the dart from his neck, and plunged it into the eye of one of the attackers. Terrible agony filled his wail as the ninja dropped his sword.

Before another ninja could move in, Ueda snatched up the ninjato, and in one fluid motion, beheaded the wounded man.

The other ninja stopped short, obviously not overly eager to engage Ueda in swordplay. Slowly, they backed away from Ueda, and towards Toshibi.

Ueda made no move to follow.

Chapter 34

Warrior of the Light

Already, Ueda could feel the effects of the poison. He began to sweat profusely as a burning sensation coursed through his body. His stomach and limbs were suddenly racked with terrible cramps, and his vision became blurred.

Ueda somehow managed to keep his feet, but he started to visibly sway.

"Strike now you fools, he is poisoned," Toshibi shrieked. The words sounded unnatural as the bloody gash in his face hampered his ability to speak.

The ninja rushed in. One came in on Ueda's right, attacking high, and the other on his left, attacking low. If Ueda ducked or jumped to avoid either attack, he would run into the other.

Ueda avoiding both attacks, by the narrowest of margins, executing a forward dive roll.

Having practiced the move thousands of times over the years in his training, Ueda came out of the roll on his feet out of pure reflex, but the poison took its toll. He was losing his peripheral vision, and he could tell that his reflexes were slowed. The pain caused by the cramping, especially in his stomach, was excruciating.

Ueda knew he would not be able to avoid a lightning fast swipe from a sword in his condition. He had to close the distance.

The master staggered forward, and one of the ninja charged in to meet him, bellowing a battle cry.

Knowing that his vision was impaired, Ueda kept his focus on his opponent's torso, and used his enemy's posture as an indicator where the incoming attack would most likely be coming from. He had no choice but to trust that he had chosen the correct course of action, even though he could not see the incoming attack.

The ploy worked, and Ueda was able to block the downward strike aimed at his head, and counter with a horizontal slash of his own, that cut off the bottom half of the ninja's nose. It was not a lethal blow, but a painful one nonetheless.

The move was also a distraction. The ninja was so preoccupied with the loss of his proboscis, he could not adequately deal with the follow up thrust that punctured his trachea.

Toshibi watched in amazement.

The amount of poison delivered into the bloodstream from just one dart, should have produced almost instant excruciating pain, and debilitating cramps in all limbs, especially the abdomen. Within five seconds the victim should have been writhing on the floor in terrible agony. He should have suffered the loss of his eyesight within ten seconds, and in twenty seconds, he should have been vomiting uncontrollably.

In just fifty seconds he should have been dead.

That would have been from just one dart, and he had stricken Ueda with two. Yet, not only had the man refused to succumb to the poison, he continued to battle two highly skilled ninja, killing one.

Toshibi smiled, a grisly sight with his ruined cheek. The Hikari Master had only killed one ninja. Ueda apparently did not notice that the second ninja had circled around behind him. Perhaps he had lost his eyesight after all.

Hiro watched in horror as the ninja crept up behind Ueda, poised and ready to strike down his beloved mentor. Hiro heard the words of his Master once more, echoing in his mind. *To act as if there is no evil, to assume that evil will lie dormant if you are merely righteous enough, is not the path of the enlightened, but rather the path of the fool. There is evil in this world, and it must be actively opposed, not ignored.*

Without thinking, as the ninja slowly crept up behind Ueda, Hiro raced toward him as well. Hiro bent down and snatched up a fallen ninjato without breaking his stride. Hiro poured on the speed in a desperate effort to reach the ninja, before the assassin reached his Master.

Ueda slowed down his breathing, and forced himself to relax in spite of the excruciating pain. He used meditation techniques to dramatically slow down his heart rate, and therefore the delivery of the poison. Ueda focused, and channeled his Qi to his arms and legs to remain standing, and retain the grip on his sword despite the horrific cramps.

His eyesight was failing. He saw everything blurred and dimly, as if through a veil of murky water. But he did not need his eyes to recognize the man with the blowgun. His Qi was unmistakable. It was the same ninja he had fought in the hallway. He radiated supreme confidence, absolutely sure of victory.

Then he sensed it. *Ueda you old fool! No wonder he is so sure of his victory! You left an opponent at your back!* Ueda whirled around, and stood face to face with the other ninja. Mere inches separated the two of them. At that close distance, he was able to make out details, despite his impaired vision.

The ninja stood frozen, arms raised high above his head, ready to deliver a killing blow. Yet he remained rooted in place. Eyes wide with pain, he gazed down at a bloody sword blade protruding from his chest. Suddenly the blade was withdrawn, and the ninja instantly collapsed as if it was the sword that had been supporting his weight. Replacing his view of the ninja, was Hiro, in seigon no kamae, a middle guard stance, with the end of the sword pointed at his enemy's eyes.

Ueda beamed down at the boy. "A true Warrior of the Light. Go quickly, there is a passageway behind the altar that leads out of the temple. Hiro, you must take the Horn to the place I told you of. I will deal with this last ninja."

Ueda turned to face Toshibi.

Chapter 35

Clash of Masters

Eyes closed, Ueda slowed his breathing and heart rate further, while focusing and channeling his Qi to mitigate the effects of the poison as best he could. Although outwardly he appeared in a calm and meditative state, his mind raced. He had to defeat the final ninja very quickly if he was to stand a chance. He simply could not stave off the effects of the poison much longer. It would be no easy task against such a skilled opponent.

Toshibi strode forward, supremely confident. "A silent prayer before you meet your ancestors?" The words sounded odd through his wounded cheek, but they gave the Grand Master of the Hikari an idea. The Kagé were creatures of passion. Perhaps he could use that to his advantage. If he could sufficiently anger the ninja, maybe he would make a foolish mistake.

Ueda smiled mischievously. "No Shinobi, I am merely sparing myself the sight of your hideous face for a moment longer. I did not think my cut would leave you such an abomination."

Enraged, Toshibi charged forward with a downward diagonal strike, aimed at Ueda's head. Ueda parried and countered the blow with a thrust aimed at the ninja's throat.

Toshibi had developed too much forward momentum to stop himself short of the lunge. Instead, he had to veer off to the side at the last instant to avoid being impaled. He succeeded, but not fast enough to get by unscathed. Ueda's thrust still landed, and although not fatal, it did draw blood.

"Fret not Shinobi, the wound will only improve your voice."

Incensed, Toshibi charged in again, his sword a blur before him as he launched a flurry of attacks at Ueda, who parried and countered in kind.

The two men whirled about each other like blade wielding cyclones, relentlessly lashing out at one another again and again. The clang of steel striking steel echoed everywhere. Try as they might, neither combatant seemed to be able to gain the upper hand.

But Ueda struggled against two adversaries.

While Toshibi attacked with his sword, the poison attacked from within. The intensity and speed with which Toshibi attacked, was proving to be too much.

It wasn't fatigue setting in, but rather, as his heart pumped faster to deliver blood to his taxed muscles, it facilitated the spread of the poison as well.

The painful, debilitating cramps, and loss of vision returned.

Although Ueda was slowed only a fraction at first, it was enough for one of Toshibi's strikes to make it through his defenses; a graze across the back of his left hand. With each passing moment, the effects of the poison grew, and Ueda slowed more. Soon, there was another cut along his right forearm, and then another across his upper left thigh.

The wounds were superficial, and Ueda didn't even feel the cuts. Any pain caused by scratches was insignificant in comparison to the terrible agony he was enduring from the poison. Unfortunately, they were a tell-tale sign he could not keep the battle up much longer. That fact was not lost on Toshibi. Emboldened, the ninja upped the intensity of his attacks, quickly scoring a horizontal cut across Ueda's forehead that bled into his eyes, further impairing his vision. This impairment allowed yet another attack to strike home. The next attack left a diagonal gash from the corner of his left eye to his chin.

Ueda's counter was too slow, and Toshibi was able to parry. His riposte plunged deep into Ueda's shoulder.

Ueda staggered backwards, not from the stab wound, but from the horrendous cramps that mercilessly ravaged his body.

The master leaned heavily against a wall, allowing it, not his legs to take the majority of his weight, so as to remain standing.

Sweat, mixed with blood, poured profusely down his face.

Ueda tried to turn his dire predicament into an advantage. Perhaps he could play up the effects of the poison, and lure the ninja in for a final strike.

Suddenly his abdomen was wracked with searing pain, and he coughed up blood. Ueda smiled to himself. Perhaps he would not have to play up the effects of the poison after all.

Toshibi was impressed in spite of himself. It seemed the old man would finally succumb to the poison, but the length of time he had managed to endure, not to mention his ability to fight on, was truly extraordinary.

Ueda wasn't sure if he could stand much longer, even though he used the wall for support, and the ninja seemed content to watch him die from a distance. He had to try and goad him into another attack.

"Come, Shinobi. Why do you hesitate to cross blades with me again? It is unbecoming for a warrior to cower so. Will it help if I promise to kill you quickly?"

"You have spirit, old one. I suppose I could do you the honor of easing your passing."

Ueda stepped away from the wall, and staggered towards Toshibi.

Toshibi lunged forward to meet him, a stab aimed at Ueda's heart.

Ueda saw it come, but the poison was too much, his reaction too slow. The parry deflected the incoming blade downward, avoiding his heart, but Toshibi's blade still ran him through. It pierced his liver, and emerged out of Ueda's back.

It was the end, Ueda knew it. But the Grand Master of the Hikari would not go quietly into the night. Focusing all his Qi, he clamped down on the wrist of Toshibi's sword arm with his left hand.

Toshibi tried to withdraw his blade, but Ueda held him fast. Toshibi tried again with more effort, and again, could not escape. Panic struck hard. Toshibi bent his knees and used his legs to try and pull away, but was still unable to break Ueda's iron grip.

"Why are you in such a hurry, Shinobi? Come, join me in death."

Ueda stabbed desperately with his blade, but Toshibi batted it away so the thrust pierced his oblique muscles, instead of vital organs. Then he clamped down on the wrist of Ueda's sword arm, so he could not withdraw his blade.

The two struggled against each other, trying to break free of the other's grip so they could strike again, but neither was able to do so. As the stalemate continued, Ueda knew his strength would not last.

"So Shinobi, you won't follow me into the next world? Pity. Allow me a parting gift, then."

Ueda head-butted Toshibi in the face, shattering his nose. Adding insult to injury, he vomited blood and bile onto the ninja's face. Laughing maniacally, Ueda slid off Toshibi's blade, and dropped to the floor.

Disgusted, Toshibi wiped the vomit from his face. Ueda continued to laugh. "Still worried about your looks? With *that* face?" Ueda burst into mocking laughter again.

There was a brief pause, as his body seized up with terrible pain, and he vomited forth more bile and blood. "Don't look now Shinobi, but I believe I got some on your shoes that time." Ueda burst into another fit of laughter.

Furious, Toshibi stabbed Ueda in the chest.

After a brief wince, Ueda renewed his manic laugh once more, louder, as if a mere stab from a sword was a futile and ludicrous gesture, incapable of causing him any harm.

Toshibi stabbed Ueda again, twisting the blade back and forth. Thus passed Ueda, Grand Master of the Hikari, laughing in the face of death, and his enemies.

Chapter 36

Through Smoke and Flame

Infuriated, Toshibi plunged his sword into Ueda's chest again and again. The Grand Master's laughter rang in his ears, mocking him even in death.

The ninja vented his wrath upon Ueda's corpse. In a berserker rage, Toshibi beheaded his greatest enemy, then cut off both of his arms. He continually hacked at the upper torso until it was a grisly monstrosity.

Panting, Toshibi finally came to his senses. *Damned Hikari! Even in death he has managed to delay me.*

Wasting no more time, he sheathed his sword and ran after the child.

Hiro raced down the corridor, clutching the bag that held the Horn to his chest. There was thick smoke billowing down the corridor. The boy knew it wasn't just a foot race against the ninja, but against the quickly spreading fire as well.

Hiro glanced over his shoulder and saw the shadowy specter of the ninja through the haze of smoke. He was gaining on him, and moved impossibly fast.

Hiro careened around a corner. He tucked the Horn under one arm and poured on the speed, adrenaline and fear allowing him to pump his legs even faster than before.

The smoke was thicker, and there was a burning beam from where the ceiling had collapsed ahead. Lying at a forty five degree angle, it partially blocked his path. Hiro leaped over the flaming hurdle without pausing, graceful as a gazelle.

Toshibi pursued him like a ravenous lion. With each passing moment, he seemed to close the distance bit by bit. Both parties sensed it would soon be over. The smoke thickened as the pair turned another corner.

Hiro's heart sank. The corridor before him was barred by more burning debris, his escape completely blocked.

Desperately, Hiro looked for a way out. There was no gap large enough to crawl under or room above to leap over in the jumbled mass of burning wreckage. He was trapped.

Toshibi stood behind him, cutting off his escape. The ninja Master was a gruesome sight to behold. His ruined cheek dangled grotesquely, teeth visible through the wound. It seemed to give him an evil, lopsided, yet triumphant grin. He was covered in gore, and bathed in an eerie reddish glow from the flames.

To Hiro, it seemed the devil himself had trapped him. "It is over boy, give me the Horn."

An overwhelming sense of loss descended upon Hiro. He had lost his home and his family for the second time. First, his parents had been killed by pirates, and their little seaside cottage burnt to the ground. Now the benevolent monks who took him in, and their beautiful temple, would be stripped away from him as well. Why was it that everything he loved ended in ashes?

For some reason, a part of the burning pile of wreckage in front of Hiro caught his attention. There was a lovely garden scene, depicting birds and flowers in bloom, on a part of a broken shoji screen that had not yet burned away. It was one last tiny piece of beauty in the nightmarish, roiling hell that stood around him. This tiny piece stubbornly refused to succumb to the ravenous flames.

Toshibi's voice thundered forth, intruding upon Hiro's contemplation. "Give me the Horn boy, or your last moments in this world will be spent squirming at the end of my blade, like a worm on a hook."

As Toshibi issued his ominous threat, the beautiful little painting went up in a flash, and was suddenly gone. The once beautiful scene depicted on the rice paper, was now curled up into a black, shrilled husk; a dark and ominous parallel to the youth's tragic life.

Hiro remained, staring blankly at the dancing flames where the scene had been a moment before.

Just like his life. Everything gone in an instant.

Toshibi drew his sword and slowly walked down the corridor towards Hiro. "Very well little fool. I will take the Horn from you after I have spilled your entrails upon the floor."

Hiro stared at the flames, unmoved by Toshibi's threat, for Master Ueda's words echoed in his mind.

These vessels, our bodies, are capable of much more than we ask of them. Through discipline and training, you will find the supposedly impossible is indeed attainable more often than not.

Hiro looked over his shoulder, towards the slowly advancing ninja. To Toshibi's surprise it was not a mask of terror the boy wore upon his face. The boy's countenance had changed. There was no more fear in his eyes.

The Kagé Master and the Hikari acolyte locked gazes.

To Toshibi, the look on the boy's face was eerily reminiscent to that of Ueda, who had laughed in the face of death moments earlier.

"You will never lay your filthy hands upon the Horn! Instead you will burn in hell, Shinobi!" Hiro sprinted towards the burning wall of wreckage.

Toshibi gave chase, but only halfheartedly. There was no escape. Was the little fool trying to commit suicide?

It was the inferno before him that held Hiro's attention, not the ninja promising death behind. There was a small gap in the wreckage, a tiny window where the painted scene had once been. It was no more than thirteen inches across, but through the vacillating flames, he could see the corridor beyond.

Hiro continued to race forward, then, like a shot fired from a cannon, he leapt into the air.

He grasped the Horn tightly, his arms stretched before him like a diver about to plunge into water. He sailed through the air and through the little flaming portal in the wreckage, a gap too small for Toshibi to follow. He emerged slightly singed, but otherwise

unharmed on the other side. He heard Toshibi roaring impotently
behind him.

"You are as good as dead you little Hikari worm! Do you hear
me?! DEAD!!"

Hiro ignored the hollow threats. He would do as Master Ueda
instructed, and take the Horn to safety, far away from the reach of the
Kagé.

He would take the Horn to America, to the new temple that
would be built there, in the city of San Francisco.

Scroll III
The Eagle and the Dragon

Chapter 37

Hesitant Heroism

I ran with Hiro, matching his pace step for step, but then he pulled away from me. Rather, *I* began to drift away from *him*. I rose up to where my vision was obscured by smoke, and all was black.

I discovered that I was once again on the beach, looking at the temple perched high upon a cliff overlooking the sea. Only this time, it was engulfed in flames.

As I stared, the world began to spin. I lost my balance, stumbled, and stretched out my arms, readying myself for the plunge into the cold water. Instead, I staggered into Onosai, who caught me, and gently guided me back to the bed.

"Now you see what it is you face. Our struggle with them is nearly two thousand years old. It has taken the form of outright war, and it has been fought in secret on a smaller scale, but the conflict has never ceased. It has always been bloody. The Kagé will lie, cheat, steal, torture, and kill to get their hands on the Horn. They have even enlisted the very forces of Hell to that end. I have lost many friends, not just on this night. They will be mere drops in a sea of blood if the Kagé keep the Horn."

"Look Onosai, I was hired to find the Horn, but my client doesn't believe it has mystical powers to summon super death storms. They certainly don't want to get caught up in any ancient power struggle."

"Then why does your client seek it?"

"They believe it to be an archeological find, a piece of history to be displayed in a museum."

"Even if your client is ignorant to the Horn's great power, the Kagé are not. You know you must stop them."

"Why me? I just stumbled across this whole mess by accident."

"It is your destiny. You are the Chosen One."

"Hey man, I'm just a private investigator, not some supernatural spirit warrior."

"Yet your very name, *Gideon*, means mighty warrior."

"Look, that doesn't mean that I'm the Chosen One."

"You heard the prophecy. An age where man has shunned both magic, and the gods. An age where by his own design, man can travel faster than horses, and soar up into the heavens. Does that not sound like our modern times, with cars and commercial jet liners?"

"Well maybe, but I'm no samurai."

"Aren't you? The Samurai had a strong sense of duty, and honor. The very word 'samurai' means those who serve. As a private investigator, is that not what you do? Serve your clients?"

"Well yes, but…"

Onosai narrowed his eyes as he spoke. "It would take more than a retainer to make a man face death. Promised recompense for retrieving an artifact to be put on display in a museum is not reason enough to incur the wrath of a clan of assassins such as the Kagé. It is certainly not reason enough to face down a demon."

"I couldn't just stand by and do nothing, while good men died!"

"Exactly. You walk the path of Bushido, the way of the warrior."

"Just because I live my life by a code of honor, doesn't make me the Chosen One."

Onosai walked to where I sat on the bed, and parted my torn shirt sleeve. It had been ripped open when the demon threw me into the broken, jagged temple doors. The parted material revealed my tattoo of the Eagle and the Dragon.

"A man not born to Bushido, yet one who walks that path. He will have the mark of the eagle and the dragon. That man will save the Horn of Ryujin from the hands of evil, and thus the world, from great suffering."

Ok, maybe I could see why he thought I was the Chosen One, but I sure as hell didn't see myself as some mystical warrior. A bit of a badass maybe but not some supernatural spirit samurai. "Listen, Onosai, I just don't know about all this prophecy stuff."

"Whether you are ready to believe you are the one who the prophecy spoke of or not, is of little importance. I know it to be true, and you have shown me the kind of man you are. You would not let one hundred good men die at the hands of the Kagé and their demon. I do not believe you will sit idle, while the lives of hundreds of thousands more perish if the Kagé keep the Horn. Not if you could stop them."

Damn it, he was right about that. "But what can I do? I'm only one man. I don't even know where they took it."

Onosai handed me a business card. "Have faith."

I looked at the card in my hand. It read: Father Dominic Lane, Old Saint Mary's Cathedral. Old Saint Mary's was an historic landmark. The church was over a hundred years old, located at the intersection of Chinatown and the financial district, near downtown San Francisco.

"What's this? Are you saying I should go to church and pray? I'm catholic, but I'm not exactly your devout, never miss a Sunday service, church-going type. I believe in God and all, but-"

"The Hikari are not the only ones who struggle against the forces of darkness. Father Dominic is a member of the Order of Saint George, a secret sect within the Catholic Church. They fight the supernatural forces of darkness as well. They are an ally of ours in this fight."

"Ok, so why give me his card?"

"You need to go to confession."

"Go to confession? Why? Wait a minute, are you saying that I need get right with God, 'cause I'm going to die!?"

Onosai smiled. "No, it is only a means of contacting Father Dominic. You will have my help as well, but I think it best if we use all available resources at our disposal to find and take back the Horn. Father Dominic hears confession on Saturdays, between one and two."

"I'll go see him tomorrow afternoon, then."

"Time is of the essence. You should leave now."

"It's night, you said he hears confession between one and two."

"It is twelve-forty in the afternoon. You have been asleep for nearly fifteen hours."

"You'd think I'd feel better after that much rest."

"The wizard's lightning killed everyone else it struck, but I think you survived because you cut the blast short when you shot him in the groin." Onosai smiled a bit at that. "Nevertheless, the attack did take its toll on you."

"You're right on that one. I feel like hammered shi- I mean, I've felt better."

"I will have Brother Lin bring you a change of clothes. Then you must be off to see Father Dominic." Onosai bowed and left the room, and I sat staring at Father Dominic's business card.

Gideon, how do you get yourself into these messes? My thoughts drifted back to Dr. Nia Lockhart, and I couldn't help but smile. *Oh yeah, that's how.* Onosai was right. Regardless of prophesies about the Chosen One, I couldn't live with myself if people died because of my reluctance to get involved. Besides, I'd been hired to get that Horn, and when Gideon Jones takes a case, he sees it through to the end.

Chapter 38

Mend and Maneuver

Daraku sat cross-legged on the filthy warehouse floor, his back to a wall for support. He repeated the mantra over and over. The mantra was part of an ancient, nearly forgotten technique used to block out pain. The use of magic took great concentration, and was extremely fatiguing, both mentally and physically. Breaking through the defenses at the Tin Hau Temple, and battling the Hikari monks had left him exhausted. Then that damnable American shot him with rock salt!

Although his wounds were not fatal, they were *excruciating*. The healing arts were never his strong suit, and with his mana, or magical power reserves, completely depleted, he could not employ any spells to help alleviate his suffering. Instead, he was forced to resort to mental disciplines, like the mantra, to help keep the debilitating pain in check.

If he was well rested, Daraku could use the mantra to consciously suppress, or completely stop, the passage of impulses in a nerve, so pain essentially did not exist for him. In his weakened state, it was all he could do to remain conscious. He reached deep down, into his vast well of will power and resolve, to find the strength he needed.

He was a wizard of the first-order after all. To master the dark arts as he had, it was necessary to witness, endure, and *do* terrible things; things that would break and destroy most men. But that which did not kill him, had indeed made him stronger. He would not be stopped short, not when he was finally so close to his goal! Pain was merely a signal that the vessel he called his body was damaged, nothing more.

That simply meant he required some rest and recuperation. It would have to wait until he had the final preparations in place. Those preparations would require his full concentration, something the pain prevented.

He renewed his efforts, and the mantra increased slightly in volume. Deliberately, by intense concentration and sheer force of will, he began to replace the terrible pain that was now his reality, with the focus of the mantra. Very slowly, the pain began to slip away. It was a tedious and gradual thing, but Daraku knew from experience, that he could increase its momentum with concentration.

Just then, the door opened and in stepped Takeshi.

The fool's timing couldn't be worse, Daraku thought. "I said I was not to be disturbed, Shinobi!"

Takeshi did not retreat, but remained in the doorway, appraising the situation. The wizard was wounded, and appeared to be in great pain. Perhaps the time to rid the world of the vile sorcerer had come! Dare he try to destroy the abhorrent fiend who sacrificed children to demons?

He had, after all, fulfilled his function. He'd led them to and helped capture the Horn. But now that their job was done, what purpose did he serve? Why should the Kagé taint their reputation, and continue to associate with such a degenerate? To kill an enemy in battle was the way of the warrior, but to torture? To take perverse pleasure in the suffering of others? He knew nothing of honor! Whatever power he added to the clan with his sorcerer's ways, was eclipsed by that of the Horn.

"Why do we delay? We were to take the Horn back to lord Oh-maga immediately after its capture."

To Daraku, Takeshi seemed very much like a wolf who smelled blood. He must be careful to show no weakness. In his debilitated state, he was no match for the ninja.

"You insolent worm! How dare you question me!"

Takeshi knew he played a dangerous game. In the past, he had seen the wizard strike men dead, who dared challenged him. "I am merely asking a question Lord Daraku. Our orders were clear. Take the Horn back *immediately* upon capture."

Daraku's eyes widened with outrage. "What I do is necessary, and that is all you need to know. I will not explain myself to the likes of you!"

Despite Daraku's outburst, Takeshi remained in the doorway. *The wizard does not take insults lightly. If he is truly as offended as he appears, then why has he not thrown a spell? Perhaps it is because he is unable to do so.*

Emboldened, Takeshi took a step into the room.

Daraku was furious, he could see full well that his ruse had not worked. It was time to play his ace in the hole. "Takeru, would you be so kind as to take your men, and escort Takeshi out before I lose my patience? I would rather not explain to Oh-maga why I killed his favorite assassin."

All at once, several ninja materialized from the shadows, and began to slowly advance towards Takeshi, who immediately drew his sword. In response, the other ninja drew their weapons. Some of them carried swords, but the others carried kusarigama - a traditional

Japanese weapon that resembled a sickle, with a long, weighted chain attached to it. Attacking with the kusarigama usually involved swinging the weighted chain in a large circle over one's head, and then whipping it forward to strike with the weighted end of the chain while still outside the range of an opponent's hand weapon. One could also use the chain of the kusarigama to entangle an opponent's weapon or limbs, allowing the kusarigama user to rush in, and strike with the sickle.

Daraku smiled triumphantly. "You brought your strike team, Motobu brought his war band. Did you think I would not bring my own men? You have heard of my Kuari Senshi, have you not?"

Indeed, Takeshi had heard of the Kuari Senshi, as had all of the Kagé. They were Daraku's personal guard; ninja who had come to the wizard looking to enhance their abilities through the dark arts. Daraku had marked them with mystical tattoos that granted them either enhanced strength, speed, or agility. Some even had the ability to heal, depending upon which symbol they received. A few had more than one. The marks came at a great cost. The ninja were beholden to Daraku, and their lives were no longer their own.

Also, this magical branding caused great pain. Recipients were often driven mad. Some did not survive the process. It was whispered that the power of these marks were addictive, and that the Kuari Senshi became dependent upon them. It was also said the great powers were fleeting, and only temporary, they slowly faded with time. Each time a Kuari Senshi returned to Daraku to have the mark's power restored, it cost them another piece of their soul. Over time, they became less human and more like mindless zombies, until finally they were merely Daraku's puppets.

Takeshi quickly took stock of the situation. Perhaps he could defeat one of the Kuari Senshi, but not five. He made a show of sheathing his sword, and bowed his head in supplication. "Forgive me lord Daraku. You know best."

Maintaining a submissive posture, Takeshi backed out of the room. All the while, he thought, *this is not yet over, vile one.*

Chapter 39

Sacraments and Sandwiches

Old Saint Mary's was a sight to behold. It was the tallest building in all of California when it was built in 1853, but by 1985 its cross-topped, brick spire no longer dominated the skyline. In fact, it was dwarfed by modern towers of glass and steel. Yet it still had a certain stately quality to it, radiating a bit of old-world elegance alongside it's newer but soulless neighbors. It gave the old church its own unique brand of magnificence.

Inside the church, there were great vaulted ceilings, and radiant stained-glass windows. Behind a beautiful white altar, there were three, giant, breathtaking murals. The ones in the center and on the right were of the Virgin Mary. She was surrounded by angels of the long robed, rosy-cheeked baby/toddler variety. Cherubs, I think that's what they're called. The one on the left showed the Archangel Michael, triumphant over Satan in single combat.

It was to the left of this mural that I found the confessional - a small enclosed booth used for the sacrament of penance. The priest and the penitent are in separate compartments, and speak to each other through a grid, or lattice in hushed whispers, but cannot see one another. Being raised Catholic, I knew the drill. I used the padded kneeler provided, and made the sign of the cross. I said the requisite words.

"Bless me Father for I have sinned. It has been... it's been, well I'm not exactly sure how long Father, but it's been a while since my last confession."

"I see, and what are your sins my son?" The priest said with a pronounced Irish accent.

"Well, I have this weakness, more of an appreciation really, for the female form.

"Ah, and this temptation leads you to impure thoughts?"

"I guess you could say that."

"And what would *you* say?"

"I would say that women are among God's greatest gifts. I have no idea how you priests are able to stay celibate, or why you would *want* to."

"It is a sacrifice we make in order to be closer to God, but are you here to question the vows I have taken as a priest, or make a confession?"

"Neither, actually."

"Then why have you have come here my son?"

"Master Onosai of the Hikari said I should seek your help."

"Did he now?"

"Yeah."

"How long have you known Master Onosai?"

"I just met him last night."

"And why did he tell you to seek *my* help?"

"Well, I killed a demon, and now he thinks I'm the Chosen One."

"You did *WHAT?*"

"I killed a demon."

"And *HOW* did you kill a demon?"

"With a sawed-off shotgun and rock salt."

"I guess that would do it."

"Wait a minute, you don't think I'm crazy?"

"Son, we need to finish this conversation someplace else. Do you like steak sandwiches?"

"Yeah, I love a good steak sandwich."

"Then I know just the place."

Father Dominic took me to an old tavern down on O'Farrell Street. It was called the Mighty Mug. Outside the door, an old, painted sign of a frothy beer mug filled to overflowing hung precariously on old, rusted hooks. I call it a tavern, not a bar because it wasn't your run of the mill sports bar with guys shouting at TV screens, or some trendy place blaring new wave music. No, that joint looked like you'd just stepped back in time, all the way back to the turn of the century. It was done up in manly, dark-stained woods, complete with a huge polished wood bar, wood beams, and wood paneling. There was also a noticeable lack of neon signs and sports memorabilia.

The heavenly aroma of roasting meat hit me in the face like a good, stiff jab, as we stepped through the doorway. It was awesome. I started to salivate, I just couldn't help it. Master Onosai's tea was good, but I'm more of a meat and potatoes guy.

Father Dominic waved at the bartender. The priest looked like he might be a bit past his prime, maybe in his late forties. His light brown hair had streaks of grey, but his shoulders were broad, and his back straight. He still walked with a spring in his step. "Allan, let me have two pints of the good stuff, and a couple of steak and cheese sandwiches if you please."

Allan, the bartender, was a little bald guy, with a not so little stomach. I don't want to say that he was ugly, but it's a safe bet he wouldn't win any beauty contests.

"Coming right up, Father Dom."

Father Dominic turned to me. "Do you like mushrooms and onions?"

"Yeah."

"With mushrooms and onions, Allan."

"You bet, Father."

The good Father and Barkeep were obviously accustomed to that little rendezvous, but I was still at a loss as to why we were there.

My curiosity finally got the best of me. "What's going on Father?"

"Any man who kills a demon, deserves to be bought lunch, and a couple of beers."

"Oh, well I can certainly go along with that tradition."

Father Dominic led me to a booth at the back of the room, and took the seat that afforded him a view of the place, especially the door. I noted the way his eyes scanned everything, not with unease or apprehension, but rather the cool precision of someone making himself aware of his surroundings at all times.

I'd seen vets who'd returned from 'Nam with the same habit. It applied to anyone whose life had included its fair share of nasty surprises. Hell, I was going to take that seat for myself, if Father Dominic hadn't beaten me to it. I probably would've felt a bit uneasy it wasn't me who could keep a sharp eye out, but I could tell by his alertness and vigilance, that the good padre was no stranger to violence.

Father Dominic saw me watching him and smiled. "Where are my manners? Let me go fetch us a couple of pints."

He came back with two glasses filled with a dark brown, almost black, liquid.

"I thought you were going to get beer, not motor oil."

"Can it be that you've never had a stout?"

"A what?"

"A stout, lad! There are more kinds of beer than American lagers. There are ales, bocks, pilsners, porters, and *stouts!*"

"You sure do seem to know your brews, padre."

"Well, I'll quote one of the founding fathers of this great country; the renowned scientist, statesman, and diplomat Benjamin Franklin. 'Beer is proof that God loves us, and wants us to be happy'."

He raised his glass, and I did the same.

"I'll drink to that!" I took a pull from the glass. Mmmmm, stout was a good name for that beer. It had a big, bold flavor. It was definitely something I could get used to.

Father Dominic was smiling. "I can tell by the look on your face, that you like the brew, boyo."

"That I do padre, that I do."

"Well, it's not just good tasting, it's good for you. There are nearly as many, if not more, vitamins in this beer, as there are in the sandwiches we are about to enjoy."

As if on cue, Allan the bartender brought us our steak sandwiches.

To say that they were yummy, is to say The Grand Canyon is kinda' big. Mere words cannot convey how delicious they were. For the record, I'm heterosexual, about as heterosexual as they come. If Allan were had proposed marriage to me, right then and there, I would have given it some serious consideration. That's how frikkin' good that steak sandwich was!

I looked up, my mouth full, and stopped mid-chew. I realized Father Dominic hadn't touched his sandwich yet.

"Do you mind if I say grace, lad?"

Embarrassed, I swallowed so I could speak. "Sorry Father. Please, by all means, go ahead."

Father Dominic gave me a smile that seemed to say, *I forgive your barbaric lack of manners*, and then bowed his head.

"Bless us O Lord, and these, Thy gifts, which we are about to receive from thy bounty, through Christ our Lord, Amen."

"Amen," I echoed.

When we finished our sandwiches, Father Dominic bowed his head once more. "We give Thee thanks for all Thy benefits, O Almighty God, who livest and reignest, world without end, Amen. May the souls of the faithful departed, through the mercy of God, rest in peace. Amen." He paused, staring at me intently. "Now son, tell me about this encounter you had with the demon."

I did as I was asked. Not once did Father Dominic's facial expressions convey any sort of disbelief. In fact, he frequently stopped me, and asked questions about the demon and the sorcerer. He asked odd things, like: 'what color were the demon's eyes', and 'did the sorcerer employ any objects like a talisman, wand, or staff'. During certain parts of my tale, I noticed he would nod, as if in agreement with things I said.

When I was done, Father Dominic looked me square in the eye, clearly thinking. "I think I'll get ya another beer." He went over to the bar, and came back moments later with two more pints. He slid one over to me. "I know how you're feeling, son."

"With all due respect Father, I seriously doubt that."

Father Dominic smiled. "Ah, but I do, boyo. Ya' see, I've had scrapes with the monsters myself. Fair is fair. I heard your tale, now it's time ya' heard mine."

Chapter 40

Faith and Firearms

"You see, I wasn't always a man of the cloth, boyo. I was a member of the Provisional Irish Republican Army once. Oh, I didn't start out a gun wielding fanatic, but the troubles brought me there. You see, in the late 60's, I wasn't much younger than you. I was part of the nonviolent civil rights campaign in Northern Ireland. We protested the severe discrimination Catholics faced. You see, boyo, Catholics were less likely to be hired, especially for government jobs. Worse still was the discrimination in housing allocation. Unionist and Protestant controlled city councils allocated housing to Protestants ahead of Catholics. And boyo, that was doubly inexcusable, because in Northern Ireland, only property owners could vote in local elections. Catholics had less voting power, even where they were a majority. Police brutality was commonplace, because the police force was nearly 100% Protestant. The atrocities they committed under the Special Powers Act were inexcusable! The Special Powers Act allowed police to ban any assemblies, parades, or publications. The police could search without a warrant. They could arrest and imprison people without charge, or a fair trial. The Act was used exclusively on Catholic nationalists! In answer to our peaceful marches, the UVF, or Ulster Volunteer Force, a British backed paramilitary organization lead by a former British soldier, fire bombed several Catholic homes, schools, and businesses. They fatally shot several Catholic civilians."

Father Dominic's countenance changed as his memories brought him back, and raw emotion caught in his throat. "I was part of a four-day march from Belfast to Derry, in protest of those atrocities. The marches were peaceful, legal protests, but we were savagely attacked at Burntollet Bridge by a mob of over two hundred loyalists. The mob was comprised of mostly off duty police, armed with iron bars, in a pre-planned ambush. It wasn't just young men like me who were marching. There were women too, and they were beaten just the same. They chased us into the night through the streets of Bogside. A sympathetic Catholic Family gave some of us shelter. Their names were Sam and Rachel Daly."

Tears welled up in Father Dominic's eyes. "The police broke down the door. They took Sam and Rachel, and their two teenage daughters, Rebecca and Katie, who were just thirteen and fifteen, and beat them to death. I think I managed to kill at least two of the bastards, maybe three. God forgive me, I wish it was more. My friend, Ryan, probably took another three himself, but they killed him too. I lived, of course, but I had a fractured skull, broken jaw, broken nose, broken collar bone, broken forearm, and six broken ribs."

Father Dominic took a long swig from his beer. "When I'd finally recovered from my injuries, I joined the Provisional Irish Republican Army, and I took the fight to them."

Allan approached, carrying two more stouts.

"Ah, bless ya' Allan! Ya' read my mind, ya' did. Do ya' think you could bring us a couple more, along with two shots of Jameson perhaps?"

I butted in at that point. "Allan, make sure they go on my tab."

Allan gave me a slight nod of approval.

"Well, thank ya', boyo. All you've gone through, and you're buying me drinks?"

"Pardon my language Father, but it sounds like you've seen more than your fair share of shit. Therefore, you deserve a few rounds yourself."

"Oh, I've heard worse, lad. Believe me, you don't know the half of it!"

"Then please, do tell, Father."

"That I will, boyo. That I will. And it'll be a story a wee bit more pertinent to your situation."

Father Dominic took another long pull from his pint of stout, exhaled loudly, and settled back into his chair. His face bore the look of a man steeling himself against some unpleasant memories. "We had to smuggle in weapons. There were no factories to mass produce them, like in a conventional war. We chose a remote place the locals shunned to receive one of our shipments of AR15s from the states; the ruins of Saint Katherine's Abbey, a former Augustinian nunnery founded in the late thirteenth century, and abandoned in the mid sixteenth century. It was located in a valley, a few miles east of the tiny village of Shanagolden, in county Limerick. It was said the last abbess practiced witchcraft in a room now called 'The Black Hag's Cell', so the grounds were haunted. We figured *that* little rumor, combined the exchange taking place on Halloween, pretty much ensured our privacy."

Father Dominic shook his head. "Oh, but we were in for one hell of a surprise. In that part of Ireland, they don't call it Halloween. It's called *Oiche Shamhna*. That's Irish for *'night when the boundary between life and death vanishes'*. It turned out that we weren't the only group who had picked that locale and date expecting privacy. A coven of witches was summoning a demon forth into our realm. We interrupted the dark ritual before the binding they attempted to place on the creature was complete. The demon broke free!"

"The vile hell spawn literally tore most of the witches and my men to bloody shreds. It seemed bullets had no effect on it. I emptied two thirty round magazines into the thing, and when that didn't work, I threw a few pipe bombs at it for good measure. Just then, a strike team from the Order of Saint George showed up, barely in time to save me. You see, The Order of Saint George is a very ancient, secret sect of the Catholic Church, nearly as old as the church herself. Sometime in the early ninth century, it became known as the Order of Saint George but it existed long before that. Its purpose is to protect the laity from those who practice the dark arts, and the vile hell spawn they call into this realm."

"In Ephesians, chapter six, verse twelve, it tells us our struggle is not only with flesh and blood, but against principalities. We fight against the powers of this world of darkness, against the spirits of wickedness. You see Gideon, there is a vast array of evil and malicious spirits that wage war against the people of God. Now, that warfare is usually spiritual, but those spirits *can* take form. When they do boyo, it becomes *very* physical indeed."

"Make no mistake, demons are more powerful than any creature on earth, but they are not invincible. The Order has been sending them back to the abyss for nearly two thousand years now, and we've gotten increasingly efficient at it."

I was fascinated. "How?"

"Faith, boyo! Faith and superior firepower!"

I laughed. I just couldn't help it.

The padre's eyes narrowed. "I know you think I'm joking, but hear me out. You see, when demons take physical form, they make themselves subject to the laws of physics. For instance, the reason my AR15, or your .45, had little effect on them, is their skin is much harder than soft lead. If you use armor piercing rounds instead, say a beefy .30-06 caliber round with a steel core, fired from a BAR Browning Automatic Rifle! Well, boyo, you'll have very different results. I guarantee it!"

"So the answer is bigger and better guns, then?"

"Well, that's an over simplification, but yes. You need to be prepared with the right tools, if you want a decent chance at success. You accidentally found one of their weaknesses though. Salt! Did you know that salt is a component of holy water? Now we consecrate the salt, which in the case of demon fighting, makes it much more effective. But even unconsecrated salt, if ingested, or say delivered by shotgun shell to the face, can prove deadly to them."

"It's a good thing your first shot was to the demon's face by the way. It caused the beast to lose hold on its corporeal form. Had your first shot been to the torso, it would have burned the demon, but not eaten its way clear through the creature, like you described. You would have needed to hold *unconsecrated* salt directly against the demon's hide, and keep it there for several seconds to do real damage. In my experience, demons aren't usually that accommodating."

"Just lucky, I guess."

"Luck, boyo? Or providence? Which brings me to your greatest weapon: *faith*. Never underestimate the awesome power of divine care and intervention."

"So you're saying, just pray then?"

"Don't be a dolt, lad. One of the reasons the good Lord gave us free will, is so we could act! In James, chapter two, verse seventeen, it says that faith alone, if not accompanied by action, is dead. But don't go discounting faith either! It is the most powerful tool at your disposal. In the first book of John, chapter five, verse five, it reads, 'Who is it that overcomes the world? Only he who *believes...'.* It takes faith to fight the good fight. So fortify yourself with the word of God. In Joshua, chapter one, verse seven, it tells us to be strong and very courageous. We must be sure to do according to God's word and not turn from it. Just as the good men in the Order of Saint George took me, *a poor misguided wretch,* in, forgave me, and showed me a way I could use my particular talents to do some good for God's people. You did not stumble upon this mess by accident, Gideon. The Almighty, in his divine wisdom, knew that you could make a difference. I will prepare you with the proper tools for the task, but *you* Gideon, must shore up your faith, and couple your faith with action!"

Allen delivered the extra stouts, and shots of Jameson. Father Dominic took one of the shot glasses, and raised it high. "To recovering the Horn!"

"To recovering the Horn!" I echoed as I put the glass to my lips and tilted my head back. I relished the potent flavor of the amber liquid. Taking the time to enjoy the heat a good whiskey delivers, with its almost burning, yet somehow pleasant sensation? It's sadly almost a lost art. I noticed Father Dominic eyeing me with approval.

"Ah, aqua vitea. Water of vitality. It's good to see you appreciate it, lad."

"Father, I do believe we've gotten off on the right foot here."

"I agree, boyo, I agree. That's enough of the libations. Down to business, then. Let me give you some pointers on demon butt kicking!"

I leaned in close. *This was going to be good.*

"Demons loathe mankind with a great and terrible fury. All that hatred? It blinds them! You can use it against them in a fight. They're suckers for a hasty ambush. In a blind rage, they'll charge right into a trap, especially if there's bait. Also, you should know a thing or two about witches and wizards. It's usually those power-hungry fools who summon demons into our realm."

"The talents and capabilities of magic users vary greatly from minor parlor tricks, to mighty powers. The one you saw throw lightning was at the high end of the scale. That kind of power is very rare, but even so, has its limits. Just like a professional athlete may have far better endurance than your average Joe, it doesn't mean he is inexhaustible. He can still get tired, it just takes longer."

"A magic user's powers are not infinite. They can run out of gas so to speak, like you or I can run out of ammo. The more powerful a spell, the more energy it requires. Also, bear in mind, when a witch or wizard attempts a powerful spell, they are vulnerable. The concentration needed to manipulate such forces is intense. They will have to focus their entire attention on the spell, so they have nothing left for defense. It's the perfect time to strike."

Father Dominic was a wealth of information. I felt better prepared. Maybe, just maybe, ours wouldn't be a suicide mission after all.

Chapter 41

Tools of the Trade

After our talk, Father Dominic drove me to Tenderloin, a seedy part of town that got its name back in the 1930's. Back then, it was so dangerous, the police received hazard pay just for patrolling there. Some of them would joke that if you didn't patrol there, you could barely afford chuck steak, but after the hazard duty pay, you could afford the finer cuts of meat from the butcher. Soon, they took to calling it Tenderloin and the nickname stuck. Fifty years later, and not much had changed. It was still a real rough part of town, with a high crime rate. Not exactly the kind of place I would have thought the good padre would be headed to.

"Where are we going to, Father?"

"Oh, I have a little apartment down here."

"Don't you live at the church?"

"I'm not the pastor of Saint Mary's. I'm an assistant priest to Father Cassimere. *He* is the one who stays in the rectory. Besides, some of my duties are best conducted a safe distance away from the parish."

Father Dominic's little one bedroom apartment didn't look like the kind of place that would inspire theft, but it had a steel security door and bars over the window, something his neighbors lacked.

The place was tiny, and a bit cramped. Every inch of space seemed to be utilized for something, but it didn't have the feeling of being cluttered. In fact, it was the opposite. Father Dominic imposed his will upon the potentially chaotic environment, and thus his little domicile was very neat, tidy, and organized. His little living room had an old, but comfortable looking recliner, and a little couch. There was no TV or radio. Instead, every other bit of wall space was filled with bookshelves, or gun racks.

There was a small, but tidy kitchen, and a little area with a tiny, but sturdy looking table and two chairs. Off to one side, there were still more shelves, plus another gun rack. There were two closed doors I assumed lead to his bedroom and the bathroom, and both rooms probably held more books and firearms.

"Nice place you have here padre," I said, as I scanned the contents of one of the bookshelves. The books were a mix of spiritual writings and military manuals.

"Why thank you, lad. I know it's not much, but my treasures are stored up in heaven. This world is temporary, and I don't require much in the way of creature comforts. While I'm here though, there is work to be done. My calling happens to be protecting the children of God from those who would do them harm. Most threats God's people face are spiritual in nature, and so there are few who do what I do. Just because there are not many of us in the Order of Saint George, doesn't mean our work isn't of vital importance. It is a noble calling, if not a glamorous one. Often times, our intervention goes unnoticed. Accolades are not the reason we do this work. Our reward will be in the next life. In this life though, nos vero pugnabimus in illis bonam militiam! We shall fight the good fight."

There was steel in his voice, and though my instincts told me this was a good man, my gut also told me Father Dominic was very much a warrior, and not somebody you wanted to cross.

I was impressed. "I can see why Master Onosai sent me to see you Father Dominic."

"Forgive me, lad. Here I am prattling on about the Order of Saint George, when you have your own work to do." Father Dominic motioned for me to take a seat at the little dining room table, and stepped out of the room. I heard him rummaging around. When he returned, his arms were loaded with equipment.

He laid down a solid looking rifle, with an audible thunk onto the table.

"This, boyo, is the Browning Automatic Rifle, or BAR. It's tough, reliable, and well made. It offers an excellent combination of rapid fire and penetrating power. It is a seven point six two millimeter, or as you Yanks say, thirty ought six caliber. It has an overall length of forty seven point eight inches, twenty four of them barrel. It weighs nineteen point four pounds, has a twenty round magazine, and a muzzle velocity of over two thousand eight hundred and five feet per second. It can be fired single shot, or full automatic. This big beautiful darlin' will serve you well."

He then set a cardboard box down next to the big rifle, with another audible thunk. "Ah, but this here boyo, is the pièce de résistance."

I stared at the box, which had 'Armor Piercing' stamped on it in big, bold print.

"These are M2, thirty ought six caliber, military surplus, armor piercing rounds. They have a hardened steel core, instead of soft lead. At a range of two hundred yards, these babies can punch clean through a tree, fourteen inches of wood, four and a half inches of reinforced concrete, one inch of solid steel, *or* a demon's hide."

I whistled in appreciation. "Impressive, padre. Impressive."

"That they are, boyo. That they are. Unfortunately, a scrap with a demon can be in close quarters, and the BAR is more of a 'reach out and touch someone' weapon, not an 'up close and personal' one."

I thought back to my run in with the demon at the temple. "Right you are, padre, right you are."

"So at distances inside of fifty yards, I like this little beauty here." Father Dominic set down a rifle that looked like it came straight out of an old nineteen fifties, black and white western.

"Are you kidding? I'm not going to be fighting wild Injuns!"

"Now, even though a bolt action rifle may be a bit more accurate, and they can't quite match the rate of fire of a semi auto, don't you go discounting the lever action rifles, boyo."

I shook my head in disbelief.

"I can see you still need a bit of convincing, so allow me to enlighten you. This is not an 1860 Henry rifle, or a Winchester model 73, although both were fine rifles that won your American west. You are right, those two rifles are antiquated. This beauty here is a Marlin 1895! It's a modernized version of those older rifles. This one here has been slightly modified. It's been cut down to eighteen inches, so it's a handier brush gun. It has a six-shot magazine tube so with one in the chamber, it has a total capacity of seven. It is nicknamed the guide gun, because the power generated by the substantial .45/70 caliber cartridges this darling uses, offers peace of mind in bear country. I know more than a few big game guides in Alaska, and at least one in Africa, who rely on the prodigious power and rapid cycling of this here beauty to protect them from grizzlies and lions!

Unfortunately, we deal with even nastier beasts." Father Dominic walked out of the small dining room and motioned for me to follow.

"Lions and grizzly bears are big and dangerous to be sure, but they still aren't as big as some demons, and their hide is not nearly as tough. So, we in the Order of Saint George have made some modifications to the ammunition the Marlin 1895 uses."

Father Dominic stuck his head out of his bedroom, and waved for me to follow. "Come in boyo, come in."

Inside was a little single bed, neatly made with hospital corners that would have passed military inspection. On the wall above the headboard, was a crucifix, and below that, a pump action twelve gauge shotgun. There was a little nightstand with a lamp, a bible, and a Webley revolver. Next to the door, was a rifle rack, and opposite his bed, were bookshelves.

The wall nearest the foot of his bed, where one might have expected to see a desk, was a workbench.

The bench had a reloading press, powder dispenser, reloading dies, case cleaner, scale, case trimmer, and calipers. In other words, it had everything you would need to make your own ammunition, or technically assemble the individual components: case, primer, powder, and bullet, rather than purchasing completely assembled factory loaded ammunition. I had a similar set up in my garage. As often as I went to the range, which was three or four times a week, sometimes more if business was slow, the cost of ammunition became prohibitive. It was a lot less expensive for me to do my own reloads.

Father Dominic was talking about something else though, custom hand loads! A completely different animal. Custom hand loaded ammunition was done because you wanted to enhance the *performance* of factory ammunition. Increased range, velocity, penetration and stopping power could all be achieved, but it was tricky and potentially dangerous stuff best left to the professionals.

"Now the .45/70, the .450, and the .444 are all fine rounds to be sure, but we in the Order of Saint George have been able to give them a wee bit more oomph. You see, the unmodified rounds pack enough gun powder to punch a hole clean through a grizzly, but it still has a soft lead core, not hard enough to penetrate the much tougher hide of a demon. So we greatly improved the penetrating power by inserting and gluing sections of 7/32 inch hex key hardened steel into the hollow points of the ammunition! That particular grade of steel is even harder than what's used in drill bits."

Father Dominic's eyes were gleaming with pride, his enthusiasm was contagious and I no longer felt helpless. In fact, I was beginning to think that there was a real possibility of pulling it off. As I listened, I felt the warmth of a fierce grin spreading across my face. I was no longer a lamb being led to slaughter. I had transitioned into more of a scrappy, underdog role. I was still a long shot, but now I had a fighting chance.

"Presto! Now you have demon killers," I said.

Father Dominic matched my grin with one of his own. "That you do boyo, that you do. In addition to powerful firearms and armor piercing ammunition, you have other weapons at your disposal. For one, holy water is like acid to demons. There are also holy relics, or items imbued with fantastic powers that can be mighty weapons, or potent means of defense. To utilize these however, you must employ faith. Always remember Gideon, there is great power in the name of Jesus. By evoking the name of our Savior with authority, and with faith, you can activate these holy relics. I have seen a crucifix repel both demons and vampires. It wasn't just the holy item itself, it was the faith of the one wielding it. I just so happen to have such an item."

Father Dominic produced a small silver Roman Catholic devotional medal. "It's Saint Jude, the patron saint of desperate causes. I have found when I wear it, miraculous good fortune seems to happen just when I need it most. I want you to wear it boyo, and remember to have faith. The good Lord will not put you in a hopeless situation. Even when things seem impossible, he will provide a way. In Romans, chapter 8, verse 37, it says, 'Nay, in all things, we are more than conquerors through him that loved us'."

Father Dominic placed the medal around my neck. I had to bow my head in order for the good padre to do so, and I figured that was as good a time as any to pray.

Now I was raised Roman Catholic. My family went to church on Sundays, the whole nine yards. Since the days of my youth I'd experienced enough unanswered prayers, and seen enough bad stuff happen that I'd eventually put prayer on the back shelf, and decided to take a more hands-on approach.

I got into my line of work to do some good, and to help people, but in doing so, I got my hands dirty. I found the law designed to protect the innocent had been twisted to shelter the wicked. In order to help people, I found myself bending and sometimes breaking rules. Somewhere along the way, I'd strayed off the straight and narrow. My world of black and white had become grey. Now, I'm still one of the good guys, and I feel confident if you asked around about me, that is what you'd hear. Gideon Jones is one of the good guys, but word on the street wouldn't say I was a very pious, church going individual.

It had been a while since I'd had a heart to heart with the man upstairs. I felt a bit rusty, and bit unworthy. From where I was standing though, the situation definitely qualified as a good time to ask for a little divine intervention. So, I closed my eyes, and gave it a shot. Father Dominic noticed my head remained bowed, and my eyes were closed, so he remained respectfully silent.

A bit nervous, I proceeded on with my first prayer in quite a while.

"Um, Jesus, I know it's been a while since I've prayed Lord, and I know I haven't exactly been a model Christian. Lord, there are a lot of lives on the line here, and I feel overwhelmed. I'm in way over my head here. I definitely need your help to pull this off. Jesus please, help me. Amen."

"Amen," Father Dominic echoed. As soon as he did, my pager went off.

It was Jimmy Chen.

Chapter 42

Deviants and Devious Plans

I went back to my place and called Jimmy. "Jimmy, I got your page. What's up?"

"Remember when you asked me to keep an eye out for anything that might look like the Yakuza trying to muscle in on the Triads?"

"Yeah, you hear something?"

"Well, it might be a bit of a stretch, but yeah, maybe."

"Lay it on me."

"I got word from two different sources about suspicious activity down in Dogpatch."

"Define 'suspicious'."

"Well, one source told me some Japanese rented an old dilapidated warehouse down by the water."

"Why did that ping your radar?"

"My source said they fit the Yakuza stereotype. They looked more like hard cases than businessmen, and he said they acted shady. They wanted the deal kept quiet, and off the books. He also said they over-paid, and did so in cash."

"Hmmm. It's a bit thin. Did you hear anything else?"

"Well, yeah, but I don't trust my second source as much as my first."

"Why?"

"It's Strapon."

Strapon was a sleazy informant, or "rat". In his case I prefer the latter term. His real name was Sean McGuiness, but people rarely used it. Everyone called him Strapon because of an infamous incident with a very kinky gal named Vickie. As you might have guessed by his nickname, Strapon was a real low life. He'd stab you in the back in half a heartbeat if he thought it would earn him an easy buck, and he wouldn't lose a wink of sleep over it. If you had the cash, he'd rat on anybody, even his own mother. So the mafia, the Triads, and even the cops occasionally used Strapon as an informant.

"Jeez Jimmy, anything you hear from that creep is suspect, to say the least."

"I know. That's why I didn't give him any cash up front. More importantly, I didn't give him any specifics. But Strapon gave me the exact same locale as my other source."

"Hell Jimmy, he probably just overheard your other source."

"Not a chance. My other source only speaks Chinese, and Strapon barely speaks English!"

Jimmy was referring to an idiosyncrasy of Sean's. He carried a pocket thesaurus around with him. In an attempt to sound intelligent, Sean would try to incorporate new words into his vocabulary. It was a seemingly worthwhile endeavor, except Sean often mispronouncing the words, or was just a little off in his attempt to use them. For example, instead of saying something like 'the citrus trees were heavily laden with fruit', he would make an odd comment, like, 'the pecan trees were weighty'. My favorite was when Sean got called out on it, and he replied, "You're just jealous of my ability to photosynthesize!"

"So Strapon saw Yakuza types in the same part of Dogpatch."

"Well, not exactly."

"What do you mean?"

"Strapon didn't say that he saw Yakuza.

"What did he say then?"

"Strapon said he saw *ninja*."

"Ninja!?"

"Yeah, I know we can just ignore what Strapon said."

"No! Aside from being a poster child for birth control, I think for once in his life, Strapon might have actually been good for something! Jimmy, I need the address of that warehouse."

I scribbled it down as Jimmy rattled it off. That was Dogpatch all right. Near the water too. It made perfect sense.

Dogpatch is a gritty, working-class neighborhood on the east side, adjacent to the waterfront. Back in the day, it had a healthy waterfront-oriented industry, including shipbuilding, drydocks, and warehouses. Even today, it's much more industrial than residential. After World War II things started to decline, and now it's a real rough part of town. Definitely not the kind of place you want to hang around after dark. That, coupled with its access to the water, made it a good base of operations for the ninja.

"Ok Jimmy. I need you to get a hold of Tommy Wang and Johnny Tao."

"The knockoff artist and the demolitions expert?"

"Yep, those two."

"Gideon what is going on?"

I looked down at the medal of Saint Jude Father Dominic had given me and heard his words echo in my mind. "Have faith. The good Lord will not put you in a hopeless situation. Even when things seem impossible, he will provide a way."

I felt the corners of my mouth turn up into a devious grin as I replied. "A plan Jimmy! A masterful plan!"

Chapter 43

Knock-Knock

After I'd finished working out the details with Jimmy, I called Father Dominic and Master Onosai and filled them in.

Just as I hung up the phone, there was a knock at my front door; if you could classify a knock as someone pounding franticly.

It didn't seem like a ninja ambush, but you never know with those sneaky bastards. After my recent run in with them, as far as I was concerned, there was no such thing as too careful. I had my Colt .45 pistol out and ready. "Who is it?"

"Gideon, it's me. Please let me in! Hurry!" It was Doctor Nia Lockhart. I opened the door and she stumbled inside, disheveled and panicked.

"What's wrong, Nia?"

"It's the Japanese research team! One of them tried to kill me!"

I noticed a nasty bruise on her right cheek. I know it's old-fashioned, but in my book, you don't hit women. I began to see red, but I forced my voice to remain calm.

"Tell me what happened."

"I was starved, so I grabbed a bite to eat at a little coffee shop near the Embarcadero Center. While I was eating, I saw one of the men from the team come in. I immediately left, and made a beeline for my car. He spotted me and gave chase. I made it to my car, but he caught me before I could get in. He dragged me out, and demanded the diary. When I refused, he hit me. I tried to fight back, but I was no match. I didn't know what else to do, so I started yelling for help as loud as I could. A man came to my aid, and tried to help me." Her voice caught in her throat and her eyes welled up with tears.

I was afraid to ask, but did so anyway. "Then what," I gently prodded.

"He killed him! He took out a knife, and stabbed him. Over and over! I panicked, and ran screaming, back inside. A crowd gathered. That must have spooked him, because he ran off. I didn't know what to do, so I came here. Gideon, the blood! There was so much blood! It was everywhere. I can't get it out of my head!" She lost it and started sobbing.

Now go ahead and call me a softy, but I get all mushy when I see a lady cry. I can't just stand there and do nothing. I have to try and help somehow. I took Nia gently in my arms and held her close. "Ssshhh. It's all right. You're safe now. No one is going to hurt you. I've got you." I rocked her gently back and forth like a small child who'd just woken from a nightmare. "It's ok baby, I've got you. You're safe now. I've got you."

I don't know how much the good doctor spent on shampoo and conditioner. Whatever the amount, it was money well spent. Her hair smelled like fresh-cut flowers. All of a sudden, something changed. I don't know what trigged it. Maybe it had just been too damn long since I'd held a woman. One moment I was comforting her, my intentions pure and noble, the next moment I was suddenly and acutely aware of her body pressed close to mine.

I wanted her. Hell, my body *ached* with need. Our eyes met. As we locked gazes, I gently cupped her face in my hands, taking care to be especially gentle with the bruise on her cheek, and drew her in for a kiss. It was slow and sensual at first, but grew in intensity until I practically devoured her with my mouth.

As she clung to me, I kissed her desperately, as if she was a mirage that might disappear. My brain was in a fog of lust, but I distinctly heard the rasp of a zipper. Then she tugged my jeans down…

"Go on. Then what happened?"

"Hey Mac, that's not something your readers need to know. Besides, a gentleman doesn't kiss and tell."

"Aw, come on! Tt was just getting good!"

"Believe me Mac, good doesn't even *begin* to do it justice."

"So share a little, off the record."

"Are you a virgin, Mac?"

"No!"

"Then you pretty much know what happened next."

"Ok, smartass."

"Well, that's the truth. Except…"

"Except, what?"

"Well, I've pretty much always put sex in the 'good' category. I know people say there is good sex and not so good sex, and I get where they're coming from. All women are not created equal, and some experiences have stood out more than others, but it's not like I've ever had a *bad* orgasm."

"Where are you going with this, Gideon?"

"Nia is so much more than just good, or even great. She's in a completely different league. That woman is more intoxicating and addictive than any drug or elixir!"

"Don't rub it in, man."

"Sorry Mac, I don't mean to brag, but you can't blame me for reminiscing. Not when it comes to Nia. That woman, she makes life worthwhile!"

"All right! All right! Moving on!"

"Yes, yes. Where was I?"

"She was taking off your pants."

"Oh yeah. Well, let's fast forward a bit."

"If you must."

I ignored Mac's comment and picked up the story just after the real steamy part.

"She took her time putting her clothes back on, and I must say I truly appreciated the show."

"Gideon, you're killing me!"

"Quit interrupting, Mac."

"Then fast forward a bit further."

"Ok, ok. Don't get your panties in a bunch."

Mac flipped me the bird, but didn't say anything, so I continued.

I put a fresh pot of coffee on, and over a steaming cup of joe, filled Nia in on what had transpired since we last parted company. She appeared to be a tad bit skeptical.

"You're serious," she asked incredulously.

"As a heart attack."

"So let me get this straight. You battled ninja, then a demon ripped some Shaolin monks apart, but you stopped it with rock salt. Then, a wizard zapped you with lightning and took the Horn. Now, with the help of a heavily armed Catholic priest, you and the remaining monks are going to Dogpatch to get it back."

"Yup."

"Gideon, I think you hit your head."

"Now that's a bit harsh."

"I'm sorry Gideon, but that's an awful lot to swallow."

I could have made a lewd comment but I bit my tongue. "I know it sounds crazy, but that's the honest to God truth!"

"Do you even hear yourself? How in the world do you expect me to believe something like that?"

I sighed. She had a point. Tt sounded bat-shit crazy. "I know, I know. I don't blame you. If I hadn't *lived* it, I wouldn't believe it either! Let's just stick to what we both agree on. Ninja or not, the Japanese research team is dangerous, and willing to kill. You saw that firsthand."

Nia shuttered visibly. "Yes."

"Well, they have the Horn, but I know where they are. I'm going to get it back!"

Nia reached out and touched my hand. Her next words were in a much gentler tone. "Gideon, this isn't worth dying over."

"Look, I understand from where you're sitting, this is crazy. I honestly believe that lives are at stake here. I just can't sit idly by and let innocent people come to harm. Not if there's something I can do to prevent it. Besides, at the very least, those assholes have no more right to the Horn than you do, and you've hired me to find it. Once Gideon Jones takes a case he sees it through to the end."

Nia shook her head, but she was grinning. "You know how corny that sounds?"

"Yeah, I'm old school, and some of my ideals are definitely no longer en vogue. But damn it, some things should never go out of style! Things like honor. Sometimes, even in this modern world we live in, there is need of a knight. Nia, you hired the White Knight Detective Agency!"

She was still shaking her head, but her grin had grown into a full-fledged smile. "I guess I did, didn't I?" She leaned in for another kiss.

It was a good one. So good, I didn't want it to ever end.

I started to think the ninja could keep the damn Horn, but then I remembered all the lives at stake. Stupid, inconvenient honor.

"Darling, I have to go. You should be safe here, but…" I took out my .45 pistol and laid it on the table. "Keep this, just in case."

I indulged in one last goodbye kiss, and headed out the door.

From the shadows, Takeru watched Gideon leave. He reported in on his walkie-talkie. "Lord Daraku, he has left. Shall I follow?"

"No. Stick to the plan. Bring me the woman."

"Yes, my lord."

Chapter 44

The Terrible Ten

It was no big surprise the ninja chose the docks of Dogpatch as a base of operations. San Francisco supports an enormous amount of shipping traffic from around the world, and offloads cargo to be transferred to railroads and trucking companies for delivery throughout the United States. Such ships remain one of the best means for moving illegal goods without being discovered.

There are plenty of storage buildings down by the docks, and the ninja were at one of the seedier, run-down warehouses on the waterfront. There wasn't much to see. The warehouse had a single door that probably lead to a front office, and several large steel doors that would roll up to allow crates and shipping containers to be brought inside. They were all closed. A single guard patrolled outside of the building.

I looked to Father Dominic. He had the Browning Automatic Rifle at the ready. "Do you think you could take out the sentry?"

"Gideon, I know these ninja are a bad sort, boyo, but I am a priest. I can't go around killing people, even bad ones. I am here mainly as a counter measure, in case any demons should show their ugly faces." The priest found a spot with a good view of the warehouse, but where he couldn't be easily seen. He got into the prone position, set up the tripod, and put the scope to his eye with the crisp, fluid movements of one who had done that sort of thing many times before. "Don't you worry, boyo. I still have your back. Although the bible is very clear on the whole 'thou shalt not kill' commandment, there are a lot of grey areas. Kneecapping, wounding, maiming? It's a great deal hazier there." His grin was fiercely contagious.

"You da' man, padre."

"That I am boyo. That I am."

I turned to Master Onosai. He brought along the remaining seven monks who were still fit for action. His eight, plus me and Father Dominic made ten. I would've preferred a couple more on our strike team. Hey, it worked in the movies for the Dirty Dozen. Maybe we could call ourselves the terrible ten? "Looks like we're up, Master Onosai. Let's move in real quiet like, and see if we can't take out that sentry without alerting anyone inside."

He nodded in agreement. "Brother Lin, you and three others will go with the Chosen One. I shall take the remaining three."

I nodded in greeting to Brother Lin. Using hand gestures, I motioned for him to follow me left, and for Master Onosai and his group to go right.

I produced the Marlin Guide Gun from under the folds of my long trench coat.

Lever action Marlin 1895 close to my chest, I moved out, followed closely by Brother Lin and the other monks.

When we got close, I motioned for him to stay put, while I slipped in a bit closer. I stayed where it was dark, using the shadows to hide my approach. In a particularly deep patch of darkness, I waited.

It wasn't long before the sentry walked in front of me. As he passed by, unaware of my presence, I chose my target.

There is a spot on the back of the head, just beneath the base of the skull, where if you get hit, it's lights out. It doesn't take much force to knock a man out cold if you hit the right spot, either. In fact, if you hit it hard enough, you could kill a man. I know exactly where it is. I've trained at the dojo hundreds of times to get it just right.

I've actually knocked out a few bad guys on the mean streets, and one training partner at the dojo with that shot. Of course, I apologized to my training partner profusely.

It's usually done with a hammer fist, which is made the same way a western boxer makes a fist. Instead of striking horizontal with the knuckles, you strike vertically, with the bottom part of the hand, in a chop, or hammer motion.

On that night however, I used the butt of my rifle instead, for a much harder blow. Of course, I ran the risk of killing him, but I also knew those guys were stone cold killers themselves. We were playing for keeps. So I hit him hard, holding absolutely nothing back. Instead of collapsing to the ground in a crumpled heap, the ninja staggered forward a step, quickly recovered his balance, and spun to face me. He drew his sword.

I didn't hesitate. I rushed forward, ramming the butt of the rifle into his face. The ninja's head snapped back, and I heard his nose break with an audible crunch. To my astonishment, he still didn't go down. In fact, he recovered even more quickly, and I barely had time to block a swipe of his sword with my rifle.

Things were starting to look bad. The Marlin was a lever action rifle, not a mêlée weapon. I didn't even have a bayonet attached to the damn thing. Even if it did, I still wouldn't want to take on a sword wielding ninja with it.

My main concern was, how the hell was he still standing, let alone fighting!?

Oh well. I figured I'd just have to hit him harder.

I brought the butt of my rifle up, lightning fast, with everything I had, and caught him right under the chin.

The blow lifted the ninja clean off his feet. He went down, but didn't stay there. He did a back roll, and was on his feet again in an instant. It was crazy! I began to wonder if he was even human! He hadn't even dropped his sword for crying out loud! *Shit! There goes the element of surprise,* I thought, as I brought the stalk of the rifle back to my shoulder. I put my finger in the trigger well, and prepared to squeeze off a shot before the ninja could cut me down with his sword.

Brother Lin joined the fray, and blindsided the ninja. He thrust his spear right through the ninja's neck. In through the right side, and back out through the left. The sentry tried to cry out and sound the alarm, but Brother Lin's spear head must have severed his vocal chords. Only blood spewed forth from his open mouth.

Incredibly, the ninja grabbed the haft of Brother Lin's spear, and began to pull it out, despite the fact the monk did his best to keep him from doing so, using two hands.

I was flabbergasted! *What the hell! How is this guy still alive, let alone overpowering Brother Lin!?!*

The other three monks in our group rushed forward, skewered the ninja on their spears, and drove him to the ground, pinning him there.

Astonishingly, the ninja *still* wasn't dead. One spear through the neck, three spears through the chest, but still, he wasn't dead!

He thrashed about like an insect held fast by a straight pin, but he was still very much alive.

Master Onosai arrived at that point. He stepped past the other monks, and stabbed the ninja through the head with his sword. He twisted the blade back and forth a few times for good measure.

Finally, the ninja died. Fortunately, it all happened quickly, and without much sound. We hadn't given ourselves away.

"What the hell was that? It couldn't be human," I whispered.

"It was one of the Kuari Senshi, dark warriors. They are demon possessed, and have traded their immortal souls for supernatural powers. They have either great strength or speed, and are not easily slain, but they are still mortal."

"That's great! Just great."

"Fear not Chosen One, you are destined to save the Horn."

"Does the prophesy say anything about me coming through this unscathed?"

"No, it does not. You may die, but you will not fail. Even if you die, you will do so saving the Horn."

"Oh, that's very comforting, Onosai."

"Yes, I know, but we should not dally. Time is of the essence." Onosai grabbed the dead ninja, and dragged the body off into the shadows so that it would not be easily discovered.

"Somebody needs to explain the concept of sarcasm to him."

"What is sarcasm," Brother Lin asked, in his heavily accented English.

"Never mind," I said, shaking my head. "Just… never mind."

Cloaked in shadow, we made our way as quietly as possible to the front door. I took the lead, lifting the Marlin 1895 up to my shoulder. If we ran into any more of those Kuari Senshi guys, I wouldn't pull any punches.

We made it undetected, and fanned out on either side of the doorway. I kept the Marlin cradled in my right shoulder as best as I could. With a finger readied in the trigger well, I gingerly tested the doorknob with my left hand. It turned freely. Whoever was inside had relied on the sentry to keep intruders out.

I paused for a moment, imaging more of the Kuari Senshi, or that dark wizard waiting to ambush us on the other side.

I noticed the monks looking anxiously at me. All clearly took their lead from the Chosen One.

Great! No pressure, I thought. *Screw it! I can't just stand here all night.*

I turned the doorknob slowly, keeping my body as far to one side as possible.

Then I pushed in gently and prayed the hinges were well oiled.

Chapter 45

The Element of Surprise

The door swung open by an inch or two making no sound.

I waited a moment, but nothing burst through to attack us. No alarms blared, so I eased up next to it and peeked into the building. I realized I'd been holding my breath. I slowly exhaled, nudged the door open a few more inches, and slid into the warehouse. Rifle at the ready, I moved as quickly and silently as possible.

Inside, it was dimly lit, but I could make out rows of shelving more than twenty feet high, stacked with boxes, crates and pallets along with the occasional barrel. At the end of one the rows of shelving there were three ninja, loading crates into a large metal shipping container nearly the size of a railroad car. It was a common sight on cargo ships. In fact, some of the larger vessels could carry hundreds of the metal boxes.

That's when I started shaking in my boots.

Why was watching ninja load crates into a shipping container so unnerving you ask? Well, those crates were perfect cubes: about five feet high, and five feet wide, by five feet long. Unless they were filled with just Styrofoam packing peanuts, they had to weigh close to a thousand pounds each. The ninja weren't using a forklift to move them. Nope! They moved them by hand, pretty as you please, just like you or I might grab a laundry basket full of dirty clothes.

If that wasn't bad enough, the wizard that zapped people with lightning showed up, and started barking orders in Japanese. I swear to you, those super ninja, who seemed strong enough to shot-put a

Volkswagen, got all jumpy. Their body language went from comfortable and confident, to submissive and nervous. If those guys were afraid, it made good sense that I was too.

Once again, the monks looked expectantly to me for guidance. Being the Chosen One and all, I had to put on a brave face for those guys. Oh well, that time I wasn't packing rock salt! I was loaded with Father Dominick's demon killers, which should have evened the playing field a bit. Also, we still had the element of surprise, and we outnumbered them by more than two to one. I figured that should count for something.

I took a moment to channel my inner Special Forces operator. In a hushed, but still manly whisper, I laid out a plan of attack. "Ok men, let's flank these guys while they're occupied. Brother Lin, you come with me to the left. Master Onosai, you take your men and strike from the right."

Crouched low, concealed behind the assorted boxes, we quickly made our way along the outermost row of shelves, towards the ninja and the wizard.

We got into position undetected, and our timing couldn't have been any better. The wizard produced the Horn of Ryujin, and said something to the closest ninja in Japanese. The ninja set down his crate, and opened it up. The wizard handed the Horn to him, I assumed to place it inside one of the crates, but I'll never know for sure.

Master Onosai took that moment as a cue to throw a spear into the ninja's face.

All hell broke loose.

The monks, bellowing war cries, swarmed the Kuari Senshi. Chaos ensued as they hacked and stabbed wildly.

I focused on the ninja who had the Horn. Despite the fact that he had a spear lodged in his face, he still hadn't dropped the damn thing.

I snuggled my rifle in close and tight, took a deep breath in, held it for half a heartbeat, and exhaled slowly as I smoothly squeezed the weapon's trigger. There was a flash and a thunderous boom, as the rapport of the Marlin 1895 echoed inside the warehouse, and ninja's head exploded into a cloud of scarlet gore, the consistency of mucus.

Both the spear and the Horn fell to the ground.

I rushed in to scoop up the Horn, but as my left hand closed on the large, jewel encrusted conch shell, so did another.

I looked up, and locked gazes with the wizard.

His lips curled back in a bestial snarl, and his eyes widened into a gaze that could only be interpreted as murderous. I couldn't come up with a smart-ass comment on the fly, so I head butted him in the nose. His head snapped back, and blood began to gush from his broken schnoz, but he didn't relinquish his grip on the Horn. I was too close to effectively use my rifle to club him. I didn't want to drop the Marlin, or let go of the Horn, so I settled for kneeing him in the groin.

I knew it must have hurt. The wizard made a satisfying groan of pain, but the S.O.B still had a death grip on the Horn.

In a close quarters fight like that, with both your hands full, your options are pretty limited. That certainly wasn't my first rodeo.

I still had a nasty surprise in my bag of tricks. I stomped down hard with my heel onto the top of his foot. Now, that might not seem like much of a blow to the untrained, but trust me, the little bones in the top of your foot are actually pretty delicate. It doesn't take much to break them.

There was no mere groan from the wizard that time. He howled out in pain.

That's when he cheated. I don't know what else to call it.

He didn't let go of the Horn, he didn't punch or kick me, but somehow he managed to send me flying. It felt like an invisible three-hundred-and-thirty-pound offensive tackle slammed into me out of nowhere. I skidded along the concrete floor of the warehouse, and slammed into a crate ten feet away.

I'd lost my grip on the Horn, but not my rifle.

I took a shot, hyped-up on adrenaline. That's not an ideal state for marksmanship, but I wasn't trying for points on a target. It was purely instinct shooting. Sometime back, I heard the term 'subconscious competence'. It allows us to walk around without having to consciously think about lifting our legs up and placing them back down again for every step. We've been walking for so long, we just look where we want to go, decide we want to go there, and automatically end up there.

Well, I have been going to the shooting range for so long now, I think that's what happened. I didn't look down my sights and aim, I didn't have time. I just looked at the wizard, decided I needed to shoot him, and the next thing I know, bang! The rifle went off, and there was a spray of blood.

The wizard dropped the Horn and staggered backwards.

I'd learned the hard way, those assholes didn't die easily, so I quickly worked the lever action of the rifle. I ejected the spent shell and chambered a new round without the stock of the rifle ever leaving my shoulder.

The wizard did something I didn't expect. He spun around, one hundred and eighty degrees, and took off like a bat out of hell. I wasn't about to look a gift horse in the mouth. I sprang to my feet, dashed in, and scooped up the Horn!

There no time to celebrate, though. The monks may have had the upper hand at first, but in the brief amount of time I'd spent with the wizard over the Horn, the Kuari Senshi had turned the tables on them.

Chapter 46

Dispute Down in Dogpatch

I wore one of those new 'fanny packs' that are all the rage now, under my trench coat.

I quickly stashed the Horn in it, just as one of the monks thrust a spear at a Kuari Senshi. In a swim-like motion, the ninja brought his arms up in front of him. It looked like he was doing the breaststroke. He pressed his palms together, and then, just as the tip of the spear passed his hands, ready to strike home, he deflected the spear to the side while rotating his arm, so that his palms were facing outward. The action allowed him to grab hold of the shaft of the spear, and pull the monk in towards him. In an instant, he had disarmed the monk, and lifted him up over his head. He then threw him, crashing down onto Brother Lin.

The remaining two monks on Brother Lin's team rushed in. One monk thrusted high, while the other stabbed low. The ninja managed to bat aside the thrust that was aimed at his face, but the monk who came in low scored a hit to the his thigh. It was a solid blow that buried the spearhead into his quadriceps a good five or six inches deep. I couldn't tell for sure from where I was standing, but the spear tip probably stuck clear out of the other side of the ninja's leg. It was a crippling blow, or at least it should have been.

It may as well have been a surface scratch. Ignoring the wound to his leg, the ninja closed the distance between him and the monk who had thrust at his face. He quickly disarmed him, and grabbed hold of his head with two hands; one over the crown of the head, and the other under the jaw. With a quick twist, he rotated the poor monk's head 180 degrees with a horrible crack. His neck was broken.

Now I know they show that sort of thing in action movies all the time, minus the 180 degree turn part. I'm pretty sure the actors wouldn't appreciate that very much. Let me tell you though, it's pure fantasy. The muscles and ligaments in your neck provide a great deal of support. In order to fatally break someone's neck by twisting it like that would be extremely difficult, and take a ridiculous amount of force. The Kuari Senshi did it as easily as you or I could snap a pencil.

The monk's friend tried to intervene, and thrust his spear into the ninja's side deep enough that it should have punctured a lung. Again, the enhanced warrior ignored the wound. Once he'd dispatched the first monk, he charged the second. The second monk bravely stood his ground, angling his spear towards the Kuari Senshi in such a way that the ninja would have to break off the attack, or impale himself upon the spear.

The Kuari Senshi didn't turn aside. He charged straight in, heedless of the monk's weapon.

The spear entered the Kuari Senshi's abdomen, and emerged out his back. Yet, the terrible wound didn't prove fatal. Without even a flinch, the assassin worked his way up the shaft of the spear, to attack the monk.

When he was within arm's reach, the Kuari Senshi grabbed hold of the monk's throat with his right hand, and placed the palm of his left hand on the monk's forehead. The monk slammed both of his arms down in an attempt to break the ninja's grip on his throat, but he was held in a vice grip.

In a panic, the monk hammered the ninja with a flurry of punches to his face. Again, the Kuari Senshi was unfazed by the monk's attacks.

While he held the monk fast with his right hand, he shoved forward with his left. He forced the man's head all the way back. When it was over, the back of the monk's head was buried between his own shoulder blades, the bones in his neck crushed, and his spinal cord severed. I've never seen an injury so gruesome.

Before the ninja could drop the poor monk, I had the Marlin firmly against my shoulder, aimed at his upper torso.

I squeezed off a shot.

I could tell from the resulting gush of blood, the bullet hit the ninja just under his left arm, right in the armpit.

Father Dominic's demon killers packed one hell of a wallop.

The ninja didn't ignore *that* wound. He staggered sideways from the force of impact.

Instead of going down, he regained his balance, and charged straight at me.

I worked the lever action on my rifle, ejecting the spent shell casing. I put my sights on the ninja's sternum, and squeezed the trigger. The instant before the shot rang out, the ninja leapt straight up, flipping once in the air as he sailed clear over me.

The ninja's speed was incredible. Technically he wasn't fast enough to dodge bullets, but he moved fast enough to dodge me, and I was the one doing the aiming.

As rapidly as I could, I ejected another shell casing and spun around to face him. I quickly acquired my target, and squeezed off another shot. The ninja, faster than a striking serpent, bounded forward at an angle, agile as an acrobat. He planted a foot against the wall of the warehouse, a good six and a half feet off the ground, narrowly avoiding my shot. Then, using only a single leg, he kicked off into a back flip that carried him back, past the end of shelves, and out of my line of fire.

Rifle snug in my shoulder, and cheek against the upper receiver, I panned back and forth like my head was on a swivel, trying to re-acquire my target. The rifle moved with me, so I could take the shot the instant I saw him. My eyes quickly scanned back and forth, searching in the dim light. I saw boxes, more boxes, crates, loading gear, and some barrels, but no ninja. I couldn't find him. There were just too many places to hide.

As I crept slowly through the warehouse, I heard one of monks cry out in agony. The hairs on the back of my neck stood up.

I wasn't the only one doing some stalking.

Chapter 47

Bird's Eye View

Then I saw it.

At the end of the shelving unit there was a rolling ladder that ran all the way up and down the length of the shelves, to provide easy access.

The warehouse was darker up near the ceiling, than at floor level.

It was exactly what I needed.

I raced up the ladder to the top of the shelving unit. It would be like a deer stand for a hunter, giving me a good, clear view of the enemy.

I went up the ladder to the top of the shelving unit, and hit the jackpot. I found a crate nestled in shadows. It provided both cover and concealment. It was the perfect height to provide a nice standing supported firing position.

From my new vantage point I had a clear view of the warehouse.

Master Onosai and Brother Lin were the only two monks left alive. They were near the center of the building.

There were two Kuari Senshi left as well. One made a beeline straight towards them, while the other one worked his way around them to the left, along the outer edge of the warehouse, in an attempt to flank them.

I sighted in on the Kuari Senshi that was making a beeline, as he moved faster than the other ninja, and looked like he would reach the pair of monks first.

Just as I was about to squeeze off a shot, the ninja stopped in his tracks. I had to take my eye off the rear sight in order to avoid tunnel vision and get a clearer idea of what was happening.

The wizard had reappeared, and directed the super ninja to back off the monks, and come back to him.

I wasn't sure what they had planned, but I didn't have time to mull it over. The other Kuari Senshi was almost on top of Master Onosai and Brother Lin. I put the rifle up to my eye, and sighted in on the Kuari Senshi's head. That seemed to be the only way to bring the bastards down.

Then, taking his forward momentum into account, I squeezed off a shot.

It was text book perfect. Father Dom's demon killer hit him right in the side of the head, and the powerful round blew his skull apart like an overripe watermelon.

Back on the ladder, I grabbed hold of the rails on either side, and slid down, instead of using the steps. I wanted to be long gone before that wizard and the other super ninja came back. I ran towards Master Onosai and Brother Lin. "Over here! This way!"

We quickly regrouped, and I relayed the good news. "I have the Horn! Now let's get the hell out of here before the wizard or those super ninja come back!"

They nodded vigorously, and we raced towards the exit.

Chapter 48

There is Power in the Blood

The preparations had been made the previous night, after he had used his mantra to block out the pain. It had taken several hours, because he had been forced to employ ritual magic, which was more time consuming, but had its advantages. Mainly, it did not tap into his own mana. He hadn't dared deplete his magical reserves any further. It was a good thing too, for the blow he struck against the American while fighting for the Horn, had cost him dearly.

Daraku stumbled, and barely caught himself on the wall, using it for support so he didn't fall. His vision narrowed, and his knees began to buckle. Very soon, he would lose consciousness. The gunshot wound would prove fatal if he didn't act quickly. Damn American! He would kill the dog slowly. He beckoned for his Kuari Senshi to come closer. The Hikari and the American had proved themselves quite skillful, and had managed to wound his retainer terribly.

Daraku smiled. Luckily for him, he had always excelled at blood magic.

He stripped off his clothing so that he was naked from the waist up, exposing his wound. He then ordered the Kuari Senshi to do the same.

Both men were covered in tattoos, and bled profusely. The Kuari Senshi was branded with the dark symbols that granted him power, and Daraku had a magnificent tattoo of a dragon.

Because of the positioning of the gunshot, the lifelike tattoo looked as if the dragon itself was mortally wounded. It was a detail that was not lost on Daraku, to whom the tattoo held special significance.

As a small child, Daraku's grandmother told him stories of how he descended from the line of the great emperor Di Ku Gao Xin Shi, who was said to have ridden upon dragons. His grandmother informed him it was only possible because Di Ku was half dragon himself, his mother having received a nocturnal visit from one of the shape shifting creatures. Daraku's grandmother told him the blood of dragons flowed through his veins, and that it made him powerful.

Daraku placed his fingers into the wounds of his Kuari Senshi servant, gathering as much of the warrior's spell enhanced blood as he could. He slathered it across his own wound, and he smeared the gruesome serum into a macabre symbol as he chanted a spell. There was great pain, but he could actually feel some small portion of his strength return. His wound started to mend.

Daraku then took a jade goblet and his sacrificial dagger from a small table near the symbols he had made upon the warehouse floor in his preparations the night before. He took the Kuari Senshi's arm, slashed his wrist open with the dagger, and poured the blood into the jade goblet.

His servant, as docile as a lamb, made no complaint.

Returning to the small table, Daraku took a small pinch of a mysterious black powder from a gold bowl. He sprinkled the powder into the goblet while chanting. After a few seconds, he abruptly stopped. He immediately guzzled the blood from the goblet, as if he were a parched and weary soul in the desert, who had stumbled upon cool, refreshing water from an oasis.

Daraku felt the effects of the spell course through him as his strength and powers began to return.

More! He needed *more!*

Daraku turned to his servant, eyes wide and frenzied. Blood dripped from the corners of his mouth. "Come closer, Shinobi."

Chapter 49

Pride Cometh Before the...

Brother Lin, Master Onosai, and I stumbled into Father Dominic as we weaved through the maze of boxes, headed towards the exit.

"Good to see ya boyos."

"Father Dominic, I thought you couldn't lend a hand on account of only being allowed to kill monsters, and not people."

Father Dominic nodded. "Ordinarily, yes. I got the sudden feeling you could use my help. I have found those feelings are better heeded than ignored."

"Well, I wouldn't call those Koala Shi Shi guys human anyway."

"Kuari Senshi," Master Onosai corrected.

"Yeah, them."

Father Dominic looked mortified. "Kuari Senshi! Master Onosai please forgive me. Had I known, I wouldn't have waited."

"You know about them," I asked.

"I'm afraid so. They are the demonic possessed minions of a powerful dark sorcerer named Daraku, who's been the cause of much suffering since the late 1500's."

"Even longer," Master Onosai corrected. "Daraku was a scourge in Japan hundreds of years before the Catholic Church became aware of his existence due to his persecution of Christians in 1587. He was a disciple of the half-human, half-demon sorcerer, Abe No Seimei, in the late 10th century. His master was the first wizard to use the seal of Seiman in Japan, to conjure forth demons. It is known in the West as the pentagram."

"Well, he seemed pretty spry for a guy who's nearly a thousand years old! I would have guessed closer to forty. He took some good shots without going down as we fought over the Horn. I still kicked his ass though. He cheated and used magic."

Onosai smiled. "The Chosen One does indeed seem to be a thorn in Daraku's side."

I sighed as I spoke. "Even though 'thorn in the side', sounds like a promotion from my more often used moniker of 'pain in the ass', I think the struggle between my arch nemesis and me is at an end. I shot him with one of Father Dom's demon killers. Those have even been game enders for the koala shi shis."

"Kuari Senshi," Brother Lin corrected.

"Yeah, them."

Father Dominic let out a low whistle in appreciation.

"He doesn't die easily that one, but if you did manage to kill him boyo, you've done the world a great service."

"And the Chosen One has recovered the Horn," Master Onosai added.

I began to feel my chest puff-up with manly pride, as the realization of what an epic butt-kicking I'd just dealt out, dawned on me.

"So, we appreciate the sentiment Father Dom, but it looks like your services won't be needed. We've taken care of business, and got it all under control."

That's when the demon crashed through the wall of shelves.

Chapter 50

Struggle with Powers and Principalities

It was my *flight*, and *not* my *fight* instinct, that kicked in. I was sprinting down the aisle, before I even knew what was happening. And it's a good thing too! If I'd been half a second slower, I think it would have been 'game-over' for me.

There was a great crash, and the demon smashed through the lower level of the shelving unit. It tossed aside a couple of fifty gallon steel drums and a wooden crate larger than a coffin as if they were made of Styrofoam.

The Demon's claws missed slicing me open by mere inches.

If it had been a track meet, I'm sure I was fast enough to win a gold medal.

I could hear the demon's massive footfalls hammer the ground just a few feet back. It gained on me, despite its mass. I felt like a squirrel run down by a ravenous wolf. If the demon caught me, I was sure it would end up pretty much the same way. So I played squirrel. Instead of running in the open, I turned a hard ninety degrees to my right, and dove in between two stacks of pallets on the lowest shelf.

I could hear the demon's claws, high pitched, squealing on the concrete floor like finger nails on a chalkboard, as it applied the brakes. Having gained too much momentum, the demon slid past me.

Moments later though, it blasted through the shelf wall like it was made out of Legos. In the second and a half it took the beast to tear its way through, I managed to get off a shot with the guide gun.

The bullet struck the demon in the upper torso, and I could tell the modified round did indeed penetrate the demon's tough hide as it was designed to do. Thick, black ichor sprayed out as the demon roared in surprise and rage.

Working the lever action, I honed in on the demon's head, and pulled the trigger. Instead of the usual mighty report of the rifle, there was an ominous *click* instead. I was out of bullets! So I did the only thing I could do. I ran like a blind rabbit into the dark, and the demon tore after me like a rabid bulldozer.

As I raced on, I saw a stack of crates piled precariously high at the end of one of the rows of shelves.

The words of Father Dominic echoed in my head. *Demons loathe mankind with a great and terrible fury. All that hatred? It blinds them! You can use it against them in a fight.*

I skidded to a halt in front of the stack of crates.

Then, I spun around to face the demon, like I'd done back at my office with Rhino Man. I didn't make a mad dash for an exit. I just stood directly in its path, oozing belligerence, and dared it to come at me.

Man, did it ever come at me!

It roared out a nightmarish challenge, and with its multiple eyes all burning with hate, the thing picked up even more speed.

The demon's fury was terrible to behold, but fury alone doesn't win fights. In fact, it can be a deadly weakness.

In the second it took the thing to reach me, I tapped into the reservoir of calm in myself, calm that was earned through endless hours of practice and discipline.

I judged the distance and timing as the demon closed in on me. As it reached out with its massive claws to tear me to shreds, I ducked under its huge tree trunk arms. Twisting, I swept my left leg into its right foot with every bit of force I could muster, just before it hit the floor.

The demon may have been preternaturally strong, but the laws of physics still applied, and gravity pulled just as hard on it as it had Rhino Man.

The demon slammed into the ground, face first. Its forward momentum kept it sliding forward, directly into the stack of crates, which cascaded down, burying it underneath.

The demon exploded out from under the pile, sending crates flying out like deadly shrapnel. I dove for cover, narrowly avoiding being struck by one of the massive containers.

As the monster regained its feet, I dug franticly in the pockets of my trench coat for rounds to load into my rifle.

I came out with a vial of holy water instead.

I lobbed the vial like a hand grenade, and it shattered on the hard concrete floor at the demon's feet. The consecrated fluid sprayed across its lower extremities.

The reaction was much like a snail that had come into contact with table salt. The demon's skin bubbled as it was eaten away. It howled in agony, and collapsed onto the floor, its feet and ankles being reduced to goo. The holy water barely slowed the thing down.

It still scuttled towards me like a monstrous spider, and pulled itself forward with its arms at an alarming rate of speed.

I desperately searched my other pocket and fished out a handful of rounds. I managed to clumsily feed one into the rifle as I pushed with my feet, scooting backwards on my rear. I just needed to gain a bit of distance between me and the monster. Too late! I'd just brought the rifle up to bear, when the demon slapped it out of my hands. Its hideous mouth, full of razor sharp teeth, opened impossibly wide, ready to tear into me.

Chapter 51

Warring with Wizards

When you hear a BAR being fired, there is something about the power of it. It doesn't quite have the rate of fire of the smaller sub machine guns, like the MAC10 or the UZI, which can spit out more than ten rounds a second with no more than a BRRRAATTT!!! When the BAR fires, you can hear each individual BOOM, BOOM, BOOM, in rapid succession. The distinctive sound struck fear into the hearts of German and Japanese soldiers during World War II, but to me, it will always be a thing of beauty. BOOM, BOOM, BOOM, BOOM, BOOM! Five, 30.06 caliber armor piercing rounds from Father Dominic's rifle, tore into the demon's face, and exploded out of the back of its skull. The monster collapsed on the floor, dead.

I quickly regained my feet. "Ha! Take ***THAT***!" I whooped as if I was the one who'd delivered the killing blow.

My celebration ended as quickly as it began, when someone grabbed me roughly by the shoulders and pulled me backwards into their knee. Pain exploded in my kidneys, and I involuntarily arched my back. My assailant took advantage of my ruined balance, and flung me into the wall. I didn't go down, but I leaned on the wall for support. Before I could even turn around, my attacker slammed my head into the wall.

I saw stars, and suddenly I was out on my feet. In boxing, that's when a fighter hasn't collapsed to the canvas, but is too stunned to fight effectively, and is essentially helpless.

My feet were suddenly swept out from under me. I barely even felt it when I hit the floor. As I tried to regain my footing, I was kicked in the ribs. I did feel *that*, and I instinctively curled up into the fetal position.

He began raining blows down onto my back. I tried to scramble away, but my opponent tackled me. Then, leaning his weight into me, he pinned me in place. The blows stopped, and I felt him lift up my trench coat. He was going for the Horn!

With a surge of adrenaline, I tried to explode out from under my attacker, but was only partially successful. Instead of laying directly on top of me, my move left him perpendicular to me, which was still a dominant grappling position. He took advantage of his new position and launched a knee into my side. Gritting my teeth, I took the blow, and tried to spin out from under him again. That time, I managed to turn around enough so that we were face to face. I realized I was fighting the dark wizard, Daraku.

We both came up to our knees.

Snarling like a rabid dog, Daraku leaned in with his hands open, to re-engage in our grappling contest.

I leaned in as well, to throw a left uppercut, which landed right under his jaw.

Daraku wasn't expecting that, and he leaned back, so as not to get hit again. Not far enough to avoid my follow-up right-cross! He tumbled backwards, and I dove after him, but the wizard was slippery as an eel, and managed to squirm out from under me before I could get a hold of him. Suddenly, he had my back again. He pulled my trench coat up over my head, like it was a jersey and we were a couple of hockey players.

I mentally prepared for the cheap shots but none came.

Not being one to look a gift horse in the mouth, I took advantage of the brief respite, and escaped from his grasp. I heard maniacal laughter, but couldn't see why, as my view was still obstructed by my trench coat. I flicked it aside, and saw why he was celebrating.

In one hand he held a dagger, and in the other, my fanny pack. Instead of hitting me, he used the time to cut the strap, and consequently, he had the Horn. He quickly tucked my fanny pack into the folds of his robes and crouched down a bit into a fighting stance. There was a maniacal gleam in his eyes as he gestured menacingly with his dagger.

I didn't rush in. The fact that he had a knife made it a completely different ball game. Watching like a hawk, I let him come to me.

Daraku made a couple of quick slashes, but I kept just out of range, waiting for him to commit with a stabbing attack. The wizard may have been armed, but I was still in my element. I had prepared for that exact scenario, and practiced hundreds of times over the course of my fourteen years of martial arts training. I knew the techniques worked too. They were field tested. Over the course of my seven-year career as a P.I, I'd had to defend myself, and disarm assailants armed with knives, on three separate occasions.

Daraku feinted. Then, changing levels, he came in with a stabbing attack.

I grabbed his wrist and stopped him short. The dark wizard delivered a quick punch to my cheek with his free hand, while simultaneously yanking backwards with his knife hand, freeing himself. He then shot back in and threw another punch at my face with his free hand, in an effort to bring my guard up, while he fired off a rapid succession of stabbing attacks down low with his knife hand. It nearly worked, and I was barely able to parry his attacks. Damn, he was good! Better than any opponent I'd faced before.

Daraku then disengaged. With a wicked grin, he changed the hold on his knife from a forward grip, where the blade extended out from the thumb side of his closed hand, to a reverse grip, so the blade extended out from the pinky side of the hand like you would grip an ice pick. Instead of coming at me with a downward stabbing motion, like you see in the horror movies, he kept the blade tucked in close to his forearm, and waded in with a flurry of strikes. His attacks resembled punches, but as he thrust, he turned his wrist in a figure-eight pattern at the last instant, changing the angle of attack, and making it extremely difficult to track.

I managed to avoid being stabbed, but because of the deceptive manner in which he held the blade, I suffered a few defensive wounds on my forearms.

Finally, I managed to step offline of one of his attacks at a forty-five-degree angle, so I stood on the outside of his forearm. I managed to grab his knife arm with both of my hands, pulling him forward and off balance. As he attempted to straighten, I twisted my hips and leveraged him into a wrist-lock throw, called kotogaeshi. The technique could easily break a man's wrist.

Daraku expertly went with the throw, however, and rolled smoothly out of it.

The silver lining was that he had to drop the knife in order to pull it off. At least I'd managed to disarm him.

Without the advantage of his dagger, Daraku decided that discretion was the better part of valor and bolted.

I took off like a shot after him, not about to let him escape with the Horn.

We darted through the maze of shelves and boxes until we emerged on the other side, the back door clearly in sight.

We both sprinted for all we were worth, but once in the open, I gained on him, and caught him in a flying tackle.

Instead of going straight to the ground though, we both went flying backwards. Tangled up, we crashed through a big plate-glass window that was next to the door.

Chapter 52

Round 2

We landed on a large pier directly behind the warehouse.

I got disoriented for a second, but quickly scrambled to my feet.

Luckily, the glass hadn't cut me. I think my trench coat may have protected me. I noticed with some satisfaction, that Daraku hadn't fared as well. He had a nasty looking gash on his cheek.

He came at me with a flurry of punches, which I took on the forearms like a boxer. I instantly regretted the action, as the defensive wounds I'd suffered from his dagger were pummeled. Searing pain shot up my arms.

I countered with a series of kicks, which Daraku managed to block, but at least I'd bought myself some relief for my poor forearms.

I wasn't content with just creating some space for myself, I wanted to kick that asshole into next week!

I fired off several more kicks in rapid succession: some high, some low, but Daraku managed to block them all.

What the hell? Wizards are supposed to be nerdy bookworms, not bad-ass kick boxers, I thought to myself. *Well at least he isn't throwing lightning at me! I guess what Father Dominic said was right. Magic users only had so much mojo. Apparently Daraku had finally run out.* My train of thought was interrupted when, instead of blocking one of my kicks, he managed to catch one, sweeping the leg I was standing on.

I used a judo break fall, so I didn't get the wind knocked out of me, or worse, sustain an injury. Daraku didn't stop there. He was on top of me in an instant, trying to rain down more punches. I brought my knees up, put my feet against his chest, and pushed back with everything I had. My legs are a good bit longer than his arms, so he couldn't quite connect with any of his blows. He finally became frustrated, and stood back up.

I took the opportunity to regain my own footing as well, and we circled one another, each seeking an opening.

I noticed that with each pass, Daraku was subtly changing the distance. He inched closer. Before long, he would be too close for an effective kick, and force our little showdown to become a striking contest.

I let him know what I thought of his ploy, by firing off a quick kick at his groin.

By shifting his stance, he narrowly avoided the blow. He came at me, screaming a martial arts *"kiai"*, and launched a barrage of punches.

I sidestepped, and landed a good, solid crescent kick to his leg. It wasn't a fight ender, but I knew that a few more of those would have ruined his mobility.

He answered my low kick to his leg, with a high kick to my head, which I barely had time to block. It was a set up though. He used the kick to close the distance, and while my guard was up high, he landed a punch to my ribs.

I brought my elbows in close to my sides, protecting my ribcage like a boxer. As soon as I did, Daraku got me in a clinch. He wrapped his hands behind my neck, and pulled down and in towards a series of knees, which he launched at my body like a Muay Tai fighter.

Let me tell you, that is *not* a pleasant sensation.

After the first knee landed, I quickly adjusted the angle of my elbows, so he brought his knees up into them, instead of my gut.

The blows stopped, and I changed tactics. Instead of fighting against the clinch, I went with it, and dove in for a wrestling style, double-leg, take-down tackle. It worked perfectly, and we went to the ground hard. Once there, I quickly went for the Horn. As I dug inside his robes, I felt my hands close around the material of my fanny pack.

Daraku continued to resist, expertly pulling me into a triangle choke, a type of figure-four, judo chokehold, which strangles the opponent by encircling his neck and one arm with the attacker's legs, in a configuration that resembles a triangle.

As he applied the choke, I felt tremendous pressure, like my head was caught in a vice. The edges of my vision began to blur. I'd been caught in that choke before, in my judo classes. I knew I didn't have much time before I blacked out. I had to act fast. I stood up with Daraku still wrapped around me like a boa constrictor. I grabbed hold of his legs, and crashed down. The move slammed his back onto the ground. I'm sure it must have hurt like hell. Although he didn't release his hold on me, his vice grip had loosened considerably.

I stood up once more, ready to slam him down to the ground again. Daraku obviously didn't want to repeat that. I could feel him try to untangle his legs in an attempt to get free, but I wouldn't have it. I held on to him, preventing his escape, and slammed him down to deliver another devastating blow.

Daraku seemed stunned. I seized the opportunity and retrieved my fanny pack.

I realized an instant too late that it was a trap!

He held me fast with his left hand, and with his right, went to stab me in the gut with his dagger.

I batted his knife arm down, so he couldn't gut me. Instead, the blade of his dagger sunk deep into my thigh. The pain was horrific, but galvanized me into action. I clamped down on his wrist with my left hand, so he couldn't pull the dagger free and stab me again. I then let go of the Horn, and placed my right hand behind his elbow. Savagely, I yanked against the direction the joint is intended to bend, simultaneously hyper-extending the elbow and breaking his arm.

Howling in pain, he disengaged, and raced down the pier with the Horn. I noticed a sleek black yacht, moored at the end of the pier. With a dagger in my thigh, there was no way to catch him before he reached it.

Chapter 53

The Best Laid Plans

There was a reason I asked Jimmy Chen to contact Tommy Wang and Johnny Tao when we learned of the ninja's base of operations down in Dogpatch. I wanted to lay a little trap for them. I wasn't too happy with Daraku and the ninja for the way they trashed the Tin Hau Temple, and blew up their Buddha. I felt a little pay back was in order.

You see, Johnny Tao was a demolitions expert.

Before we made our attack on the warehouse, we did a little reconnaissance. When we saw the yacht, it seemed pretty clear that was their getaway vehicle. We couldn't have them absconding with the Horn now, could we? So, we had Johnny rig the pier with explosives.

I took the detonator out of trench coat, and depressed the button. Unfortunately, I'm no expert when it comes to explosives, and I didn't realize how far back I should have been. I should have known better, or asked Johnny. Things never seem to go my way.

I knew it was time to leave town when the Buddha exploded. That is very rarely a good sign. I thought, as I went sailing through the air. It's odd, the things that go through your mind when the concussive force of a massive explosion knocks you off your feet, and sends you flying. I noticed the peculiar flapping sound my trench coat made, and I enjoyed the sensation of weightlessness. I wondered if that was what it felt like for Superman, when he took to the skies.

Then my training took over.

By sheer instinct, I tucked my chin to my chest. Exhaling, I slapped down with my arms to absorb the impact, and rolled into a judo break fall. The dagger in my thigh made that a less-than-pleasant experience.

Cursing, I took the blade out, and used the belt of my trench coat as an improvised tourniquet, to stop the bleeding.

There was still some small justice left in the world though. Daraku, who had been running towards the explosion, was now lying flat on his back, moaning.

I limped over to the wizard, and kicked him savagely in ribs a few times, before I stooped down to retrieve the Horn.

Forgiveness was never a strong suit of mine.

As I limped away, he started laughing. *An odd reaction to being kicked in the ribs*, I thought. I'd had enough though, and I was too damned tired to give a shit.

"Well played, gaijin, well played. The monks were wise to have secured your services. You have been a worthy adversary."

I wasn't sure what he was playing at, but I had a bad feeling, and I didn't want to stick around to find out why.

Quickly as I could on my injured leg, I moved on.

"That's far enough, gaijin. You will give back the Horn now."

I turned around to face the wizard. He slowly staggered back to his feet, but didn't look too steady. Apparently, being so close to the explosion, had taken its toll. I bet his broken arm, and probably a few ribs, hadn't helped matters any.

"I don't think so. If you want it so bad, come and get it, tough guy," I taunted.

He stared laughing again.

"What's so damn funny, asshole?"

"Oh, I don't have to take it from you, gaijin. You are going to hand it over of your own free will."

"You're high on crack!"

"Am I? Takeru, show the gaijin why he has lost."

A ninja emerged from the shadows. He had Doctor Nia Lockhart. One hand was cupped over her mouth, to prevent her from screaming, and the other held a knife to her throat.

"You will hand over the Horn, gaijin. If you do not, the woman dies."

"You dirty, rotten, son of a bitch!"

Daraku tilted his head back and laughed even harder. He had me by the short and curlies, and he knew it. "As I said, gaijin, you have been a worthy adversary, but you are beaten. Now, hand over the Horn, before I lose my patience."

One look at Nia, and I knew there wasn't a choice. I threw the Horn at Daraku's feet. He quickly bent down, and took the gem-encrusted conch shell from my fanny pack. Cackling maniacally, he lifted it high over his head in triumph.

"You have what you want Daraku! Now let the girl go."

The wizard stopped laughing, and fixed his gaze upon me. His eyes burned with a hatred that rivaled that of the demon's. "You know my name, gaijin, but I do not know yours."

My stomach tied itself in knots. I didn't like where the conversation was going. "Gideon. Gideon Jones. You've won man. Now *please,* just let the girl go." I said 'please', hoping to somehow placate him, but I could tell it was in vain.

"Know this Gideon, I am no mere man. I have walked this earth for centuries. I am a wizard of the first order. I am descended from the bloodline of the great Di Ku Gao Xin Shi, and I do not suffer insults lightly!"

"Okay! Okay, I get it! I've pissed you off. If you're looking for payback, that's fine. Take it out on *me,* not the girl."

"Oh, rest assured Mr. Jones, you *will* answer for your deeds this day. The good Doctor will suffer for your actions as well. Her death will be a slow and painful one. All because of you!"

I can't even begin tell you just how much that situation sucked. The look on Daraku's face, as the bloody sword blade emerged from the forehead of the ninja holding Nia, nearly made up for it. At first I thought Master Onosai had come to the rescue, but as the assassin collapsed dead to the floor, I saw it was another ninja that had done the deed.

I was just as surprised as Daraku, and stood there for a second, wondering what the hell was happening.

Nia didn't care at all who had done what. As soon as the knife point fell away from her throat, she sprinted into my arms. That was not the time for tear filled reunions however. I cut the embrace short and positioned myself between her and the others. I made myself a human shield, and slowly started to back away, watching for sudden moves on anybody's part.

My precautions may have been unnecessary, as the two seemed completely unaware of our existence. They were too busy shouting at each other in Japanese.

Chapter 54

Honor Among Thieves

"Takeshi, you treacherous dog! What on earth do you think you are doing!?!"

"What should have been done long ago, vile one."

"You fool! We have the Horn!"

"Yes, and now the Kagé no longer need taint ourselves with your foul presence!"

"What on earth are you talking about!?!" But Daraku knew full well what was happening. Takeshi may have been a skilled assassin, but he also operated by a strict code of honor, never killing or harming in any way, those whom he considered non-combatants, especially children. Daraku looked upon the practice with disdain, but tolerated it because the man's skills were needed. He thought it might pose a problem one day, and had planned to deal with the fool eventually, but had not considered him an immediate threat. Too late, he realized his mistake.

Takeshi's timing was perfect.

Daraku knew if he attempted a lethal spell with his mana reserves so low, he might very well kill himself! It was the very reason he was forced to fight the American hand to hand. But he would have to risk it, for to face a shinobi as skilled as Takeshi, unarmed, would be suicide. Daraku began to draw upon his power.

"No longer will you prey upon women and children, coward," Takeshi shouted as he leapt forward, his attack as deadly as a pouncing lion's. As he did so, green lightning shot out from Daraku's fingers, and struck the ninja. Electricity coursed through his body, causing excruciating pain. Tt was over in an instant. As the Takeshi's sword pierced the dark wizard's heart, Lord Daraku, wizard of the first order, descendant of the great Di Ku Gao Xin Shi, fell to the ground dead.

Takeshi paused a moment. The wizard's attack, although brief, had taken its toll. He barely held onto to consciousness. Focusing his Qi, he steadied himself. Then, the ninja bent down slowly, and reverently picked up the mighty Horn of Ryujin, his quest nearly at an end. As he stood back up, he saw the eyes of the American upon him, watching like a wary predator.

Chapter 55

Worthy Opponent

The ninja was literally smoking.

I knew just how much pain he was in because Daraku had zapped me with that funky green lightning, too.

The fact that he was still standing, meant that guy was a grade-A badass! There was something in the way he moved. He still had his mask on, so there was no way to tell for certain, but I was sure he was the same ninja I'd faced at the underground poker game. We locked gazes, and something passed between us. It's hard for me to put it into words, but let's just call it 'a deep, mutual respect'.

I don't know why I did it, but it seemed like the right thing to do at the time. I bowed, just like I did at the dojo, or the many martial arts tournaments I'd been to. This time it was a bit slower, a bit deeper, and with a bit more meaning behind it.

The ninja sheathed his sword, and returned my bow. Then, much to my surprise, he took off his mask.

"Gideon Jones, my name is Takeshi Hanzo. You, sir, have fought bravely, and with honor. You have my respect, and if you walk away, our paths never need cross again. If you try to take the Horn from me, I will kill you."

I glanced at Nia.

"Don't do it Gideon. It's not worth it," she whispered.

I turned back towards Takeshi. "Keep it. I don't feel much like dying today, anyway."

I turned around and, arm and arm with Nia, I limped away.

Chapter 56

Off the Record

Mac switched off the tape recorder. "That was one hell of a story, Gideon."

"Don't I know it! I get that certain parts will have to be omitted, Mac. You having a reputation to maintain and all. Sorry, I mean Mark."

"Oh, what the hell. You can go ahead and call me Mac."

"Good. Mac suits you, and like I said, I know too many Marks that are assholes. Todds too for that matter."

Mac smiled good naturedly. "Whatever floats your boat, man." He stood up and shook my hand. "You certainly were telling the truth when you said I would want to print this for the paper. Just like I promised, you sir, will be compensated accordingly." Mac grabbed his tape recorder and headed for the door, but stopped short. "You know that I *do* have to cut some parts out for the San Francisco Chronicle, but maybe we could still tell the rest of the story in book form. Most people will assume it's a work of fiction, but who knows? Maybe some will believe. We just might make a pretty penny doing it, too. If that's something you'd want of course."

"That's a great idea Mac! A great idea!"

Mac beamed. "I've always wanted to write a novel, and your story will make a great one. I don't want to make light of your ordeal, but it's almost a pity that this is a once in a lifetime thing. Just think of the possibilities if we had a series!"

"You know it's funny you should say that. A client called me about a strange sounding case, just before I came over here to meet you."

<h1 style="text-align:center">Epilogue</h1>

Father Dominic and Master Onosai waited in the corner booth for me at the Mighty Mug. The good padre waived me over with a smile. "So how did your meeting with the reporter go, boyo?"

"Pretty much like you thought. When I showed them the pictures of the Hikari and Kagé fighting it out on the college campus, the San Francisco Chronicle wasn't just willing to pay me. They were very eager to talk to me, but they aren't about to print anything about wizards and demons."

"Mankind's capacity for denial can be frustrating," Master Onosai replied, nodding sagely.

Father Dominic, ever the optimist, chimed in cheerfully. "Don't look so glum Onosai, we did win after all."

Master Onosai smiled at Father Dominic's words. "Yes. The Chosen One saved the Horn as foretold."

"Speaking of which, boyo. You promised to tell us how you managed to pull the wool over that ninja's eyes."

"It's all thanks to my local contacts. When Johnny Toa blew the pier, it didn't just cut off an avenue of escape. It also served as a diversion."

"What do mean, boyo?"

"It allowed me to make the switch. You see, I didn't wear that trench coat because it looked cool. It helped conceal everything. I had Tommy Wang, the knockoff artist, make me a copy of the Horn,

325

and then we modified my shoulder rig to carry it. I had the real Horn in the small of my back in the fanny pack, and the knockoff under my arm in a near identical bag. When Daraku forced me to trade the Horn for Nia, I gave him the fake. So now the real Horn is the hands of the Hikari to keep secret and safe once more."

"You have done well Gideon, and you have the Hikari's undying gratitude. Please tell me, what are your plans now?"

"I think I'll take a page from the good padre's book."

"Oh? What page is that, boyo?'

"I shall continue to fight the good fight."

The two warriors smiled at my words and Father Dominic raised his glass. "To the good fight."

Master Onosai and I raised our glasses in salutation as well, and the three of us repeated the toast in unison.

"To the good fight!"

The Gideon Jones Saga

Continues With

DEADLY DIVINATIONS

Winter 2018

Chapter 1

La Llorona

Somewhere along the way, most adults forget essential components to living a worthwhile life. Chief among them is that having fun is *crucial.* It was a shame his parents were among those who had forgotten this important fact or else there would be no need for him to sneak around like this, Blake thought to himself. He sighed dramatically and continued with his covert preparations. He put the bag of cookies next to the comic books in his backpack and zipped it shut. Grabbing his flashlight, he crept silently from his bedroom. That evening, he would meet Dave at the fort; a little tree-house the two of them had built near the river. Mom had forbidden it, saying there was no reason to play with Dave in the middle of the night. The two could meet tomorrow after breakfast. Where was the fun in that? There was no sense of adventure, no element of danger! What was Mom so worried about? He was ten now after all, not some baby. Besides, it was said La Llorona stalked the banks of the Rio Grande at night. If he and Dave were lucky, they might catch a glimpse of her!

The story of La Llorona dated back to the early 1800's. La Llorona is Spanish for the weeping or wailing woman. She was the ghost of a young mother whose children had drowned in the mighty Rio Grande. The legend said the woman's two small children had been playing near the banks of the river. Despite their mother's warnings not to do so, they wandered out into the water while she was distracted and got swept away by the strong currents. The mother tried to save them but was too late. Devastated by the loss of her children, the poor woman walked the banks of the river day and night. Weeping and wailing, she called out to her lost children until one day she snapped and committed suicide, drowning herself in the murky waters.

Now the woman's ghost haunts the banks of the Rio Grande, searching for her lost children. Some nights you can hear her eerie tormented weeping and wailing. For generations now, the locals have warned their children not to play near the banks of the Rio Grande alone, especially at night, or La Llorona would snatch them up.

Blake didn't think they would actually see any ghosts but grabbed his aluminum baseball bat just in case. Despite his best efforts to make no sound, the door to his room squeaked loudly on its hinges and Blake froze in place; sure his mother would emerge from the shadows, slipper in hand, ready to smack him with it mercilessly and double his chores. He'd get grounded for a month! When she didn't appear, he decided not to look a gift horse in the mouth and moved quickly but more silently. He left his little adobe house and ventured out into the night to rendezvous with Dave.

Soon he had walked the two blocks to the stucco wall that surrounded his little neighborhood and scaled it, agile as a monkey. He scrambled over into the trees and shrubs on the other side to make his way down towards the river. It was late September, but summer had not yet fully given way to autumn. The evenings were still fairly mild and not too cold. Blake wore a denim jacket anyway, mainly to protect himself from getting scratched by the dense tangle of brambles that grew along the banks of the river. Pretending he was a famous explorer, Blake held the flashlight in his left hand. With his right, he swung the baseball bat back and forth, like a machete. He hacked his way through the jungles of South America looking for Aztec gold.

As he noisily made his way closer to the river bank he abruptly stopped and listened. He didn't know why but something didn't seem quite right. He could hear the babble of the rushing river as the water rolled over rocks, but nothing else. That was it! The *lack* of noise was odd. Usually, there was a cacophony of night sounds: the constant chirping of crickets, the buzzing of other insects, the croaking of frogs, the occasional hoot of an owl, or the distant cry of a coyote. Now there was nothing, not even the faint sound of the wind rustling leaves.

Blake stopped swinging the bat and started to shiver, not because he was afraid but because it was suddenly cold. The temperature had dropped several degrees. Low enough he could now see his breath. Now *that* was odd. He wasn't sure why, but he turned off the flashlight. Using the bat, Blake slowly parted the branches in front of him, taking care not to make a sound and break the eerie silence. He carefully peeked out into the now ominously quiet night. The scene the parting branches revealed was truly terrifying. Crouched by the banks of the river was a grotesque and horrific thing. It must have been at least seven and a half feet tall, quite possibly eight. It had elongated arms that hung past its knees, ending in wicked looking claws. The thing was lanky almost to the point of being skeletal. Its skin was unnaturally white like an insect that crawled out from under a rock. Also, it was stretched tight like a shirt several sizes too small. In places the skin was cracked and peeling or hung off its frame in long bloody ribbons. Its jaw was almost unhinged from its face and its cheeks were gaunt and corpse-like. The eye sockets were dark and sunken in like they were hollow. It was mostly bald but had patches of long stringy black hair that clung to its scalp in clumps. The smell, Jesus, the stench of rotting meat was overpowering and made Blake nauseous.

Although Blake had been careful not to make a sound, the thing immediately looked up from whatever it was inspecting and stared right at Blake with those dark sunken eyes. It opened its mouth wide to reveal sharp needle-like teeth and cried out. It was a shrill earsplitting shriek impossibly long, high-pitched, and piercing. It froze Blake in place as if the terrible wail had managed to physically hold him in its clutches. He was unable to break free.

The ghastly creature shambled towards Blake at an alarming rate of speed, its arms outstretched and its nightmarish claws flexing, ready to seize him in their awful grasp. Snapping out of his fear-induced trance, Blake took off like a shot; bounding over fallen logs and ducking under low hanging tree branches. Zigging and zagging, he tore through the dense underbrush. Sheer terror drove him to run faster than he would have at a track meet, despite the many obstacles.

It was too dark to see, and he was unable to avoid some of the branches and brambles. He paid for it with several scratches on his unprotected face. Heedless of the nasty scrapes, he sprinted blindly into the night desperate to escape the horror that pursued him. In his blind panic, Blake didn't see the arroyo. Head over heels he tumbled down the steep bank of the dry gulch. There was an audible crunch as his ankle snapped and Blake cried out in pain.

Blake's wail was answered by the terrible piercing shriek of the creature. Without thinking, Blake tried to run but collapsed in agony when he put weight on his injured ankle. In alarm, he scanned for his baseball bat. He'd lost both it and the flashlight in the fall. The long terrible wail of the creature sounded once more, only this time much closer. Then the creature, with its ghostly pale skin and patches of stringy black hair, peeked its head over the bank. Its lips curled back in an evil predatory smile revealing hungry, razor-sharp teeth. Gazing down at the helpless boy with those eerie sunken eyes, it let out another terrible high-pitched screech.

Blake scrambled away on his hands and knees as fast as he could to the opposite side of the gorge. Desperately, he tried to climb up the steep bank, but the soft dirt gave him no purchase. For every two feet he clawed up, he slid a foot and a half back down. The nauseating smell of decaying flesh wafted over him and the dreadful piercing cry of the creature sounded once more, much louder and dangerously close. Sobbing hysterically, Blake redoubled his efforts and desperately clawed his way up the steep bank of the arroyo. He reached the top in elation and used a nearby tree branch to help pull him to more solid ground.

A ghastly white hand clamped down around his injured ankle and dragged him screaming, back down into the arroyo.

"Mommy!!" Blake screamed in terror. But the young boy's cries for help were drowned out by one last, awful shriek from the creature.

www.ingramcontent.com/pod-product-compliance
Lightning Source LLC
Chambersburg PA
CBHW070750190726
48292CB00002B/478